MW01502960

Virginia and the Kidd

A Story of Virginia Irwin and Kidd Hofer

by James "Catfish" Chapman

Inspired by true events

edited by Richard Schweitzer
cover design by Peter R.J. Deyell

PO BOX 1917, Burbank, CA 91507

THIS BOOK IS RESPECTFULLY
DEDICATED TO THE MEMORY OF
RALPH "KIDD" HOFER, VIRGINIA IRWIN,
THE MEN OF THE FOURTH FIGHTER GROUP
AND ALL THE KNOWN AND UNKNOWN
HEROES OF THE GREATEST GENERATION.

FOREWORD

By the author

By the time the United States entered World War II, in December 1941, many of the pilots of the 4th Fighter Group had extensive combat experience as members of the legendary "Eagle Squadrons" of the Royal Air Force. The performance of Squadrons 71, 121, and 133, Royal Air Force, is a proud chapter in American military legend.

The "Eagle Squadrons" were comprised of American citizens who defied U.S. neutrality laws by joining the military forces of England in 1940 to help stem the tide of tyranny perpetrated by the Nazis. This was not a casual decision. The law provided for prison, and loss of citizenship. By defying such draconian punishment for opposing Hitler, and by joining the Royal Air Force when England was "on the ropes" and in desperate need of pilots, by 1942, the crazy Americans (by staid English standards) eventually became much beloved by the English people despite the somewhat shaky start.

When they first arrived in 1940, with their impish sense of humor, their irreverent attitude towards military style and discipline, and their unerring ability to have fun when fun was not technically the object of the exercise, American pilots were much derided by the stiff-upper-lipped British. By and large the attitude of the British military, and the civilian population as well, was accurately summarized by those who felt the Americans were a pain in the arse, since they were "over paid, over sexed, and over here."

But in the summer of 1940, during the dark days of the Battle of Britain, when every plane and pilot lost was a critical blow to the English war effort, the "Eagles" never flinched when it came to giving their all for the "Mother Country." The Americans even jokingly boasted about being "from the colonies" and helping God and Country because it was the right thing to do. As noted in the Book of John, "greater love hath no man than to lay down his life for his friends." The Eagles loved England, and England learned to love the Eagles.

As a direct result of their stepping into the breach when it was do-or-die, every American aviator who was trained by either the Royal Air Force or the Royal Canadian Air Force, when transferred into the U.S. Army Air Corps, was entitled to wear the wings of either the RAF or RCAF, and the U. S. Army Air Corps. Any pilot who wore two sets of wings was automatically recognized and revered by other aviators, as an "Old Sport". The Eagles wore their "dual wings" with great pride. They claimed, expected and deserved special privileges and courtesies because of their noble service and sacrifice. They led the way for the 8th Air Force. They were special, and they knew it.

The 8th Air Force of the Army Air Corps, under Command of General Ira Eaker, a native of Eden, Texas, landed in England in February 1942, and gradually began the buildup designed to pound the German industrial might, and by extension its military forces, into submission. The first raid into German held

France was a mere dozen B-17's attacking the coast on August 17, 1942.

Barely six weeks later, on September 29, 1942, the RAF reluctantly transferred the Eagle Squadrons into the service of the United States of America as the 4th Fighter Group, 65th Fighter Wing, 8th Air Force, stationed at Debden, England, which was located about 30 miles northeast of London, the nearest train station being Saffron Waldron.

The base, a permanent RAF station before the war, had always been the home of the Eagles and was a genuinely luxurious accommodation by war standards. Instead of just Quonset huts it had brick buildings, apartment-like personnel accommodations, complete with "batmen" for the officers, relatively formal dining accommodations, and very good food, tarmac aprons, three huge hangars, and long asphalt and concrete runways, providing ample space for large squadron scrambles. The base had room for wounded war-birds to get down safely; safely being defined, rather bluntly, as a pilot who survived a crash.

A most unusual feature of Debden was a mounded rise in the center of the field, caused by repairs from German bombs. It caused limited vision, so that you couldn't see the other end of the runway from either end. This geographic anomaly would later play a significant role in one of the most infamous incidents of the war, involving a pilot who at the time was arguably the most famous pilot in the 8th Air Force. RAF 71 Squadron had been the high scorer of the Eagles, with 41 victories from September 1940 to September 1942. RAF 121 scored 18 victories, and RAF 133 scored 14½ kills, giving the group a respectable total of 63.5 victories. Initially assigned the obsolete Brewster Buffalo, they had transitioned into the solid Hawker Hurricane, and eventually the Spitfire. When they transferred to the U. S. Army Air Corps, 71 became the 334th Fighter Squadron, 4th Fighter Group, 8th Air Force, designated "QP" on squadron planes. RAF 121 became 335th Squadron, designated "WD" and RAF 133 was assigned 336th, designated "VF", together they were the 4th Fighter Group.

After the Eagles were reincarnated as the 4th Fighter Group of the 8th Air Force, their esprit de corps was royal and regal. Their rivals in the European Theatre of Operations destruction derby, (especially the 56th Fighter Group, known as "Zemke's Wolfpack" named for their Commanding Officer, Hub Zemke) deeply resented them for it; their admirers thought they were the best. The 4th agreed, as shown by their base signage. On the front gate was their Group Motto: "Fourth But First."

However, by October 1943, the 4th was an average fighter group, with average losses and average victories. Zemke's Wolfpack was the leading group in total victories.

But a new day was dawning. On January 1, 1944, Lt. Col. Donald Blakeslee, a steely-eyed ace from the Eagle Squadrons and a man of iron will, determination, and resolve, became Commanding Officer of the 4th, a date that coincided with the Group's birth as premier Luftwaffe killers of World War II. Blakeslee's goal, his motto, and his obsession was reflected in the motto of the 4th.

Until the end of 1943, Conventional Allied Air Doctrine was based on the assumption that daylight strategic heavy bombing with massed bombers in combat boxes, coupled with the massed defensive firepower of interlocking fire zones from the 10 .50 caliber machine guns on each aircraft, would adequately protect the bomber formations, and would result in control of the air and allow successful bombing raids on continental targets. The *brass hats* couldn't have been more wrong. The RAF had already learned that lesson, and limited their bombing missions to night raids, so that darkness could provide cover for the bombers. American air planners, supremely confident in America's heavy bombers (which at the time were the largest aircraft in the world), advocated bombing "around the clock". England at night, 8th Air Force during the day. The English accepted the proposal, but the bombers were unable to prevail. They had to have help to survive and accomplish the mission of strategic bombing of targets and crippling the vast German industrial war machine.

Hitler's Luftwaffe possessed truly magnificent fighter planes. The Messerschmidt 109s and Focke-Wolf 190's were as good as anything the Allies could put in the air in 1943, and in some performance characteristics superior. The P-38, the P-47, and the P-40, all developed in the interim between World War I and II, had various limitations and flaws in range, armament, and maneuverability that made the Bomber missions over the Continent virtual bloodbaths.

In 1943, the Allies were stuck in England after over two years of bitter fighting which had pushed them off the Continent of Europe. The miracle rescue of the British Army from Dunkirk, France, in May of 1940, saved England by making invasion too difficult and the outcome too risky for the Germans because of the huge military forces England had awaiting them. The initial air assault on England in the Summer of 1940, and known in history as the Battle of Britain, had been a near thing, but when the Luftwaffe failed to wipe out the Royal Air Force, Hitler unwisely turned his attention to Barbarossa, the invasion of Russia. 1943 evolved into a strategic stalemate on the western front.

Churchill and Hitler knew the Allies would have to invade. When and where was the question.

To win the war, Hitler's "Fortress Europe" had to be assaulted, but without control of the air, any invasion was doomed to fail. The massed German Armies waiting just across the English Channel were battle hardened and equipped with some of the best combat gear in the world. Hitler's roof was protected by the crack Aces of the Luftwaffe, which had been fighting in active combat since the Spanish Civil War in 1936. German aces only stopped flying combat if they were killed, captured or so severely wounded they couldn't fly any more. As a result, their scores mounted into the hundreds. They dominated the skies of the continent.

But by the summer of 1943, it was apparent bomber escort all the way to the target and back was critical and essential. In 1943, if you were a bomber crewman in the 8th Air Force, your chances of being killed or wounded before rotating home was 100%. Even being in the infantry on the front lines was safer than flying in a bomber.

On August 17, 1943 (the first anniversary of the feeble 1st raid), the 8th mounted a maximum effort raid that tried to knock out the German ball-bearing production at Schweinfurt and Regensburg. The raid was not decisive, as hoped, and the losses suffered required two months to build up for another assault.

Two months later, on October 14, 1943, the 8th Air Force finally mounted the follow up raid, a daring double strike designed to split the Luftwaffe response, and enhance the chances of success. The mission was an unqualified disaster. 291 B-17's and 60 B-24's were sent out. 60 B-17's were lost. 17 were so badly damaged they never flew again. Another 121 had battle damage, and crew losses. A 22% loss rate was completely unacceptable, and the morale of the 8th bomber crews was so eviscerated that bomber missions were suspended for the remainder of the year. The day would forever be known in Air Force lore as "Black Thursday."

Twenty-two-year-old Ralph "Kidd" Hofer, of Salem, Missouri, joined the 4th Fighter Group in September 1943. On October 8, 1943, the day of his first mission, the Luftwaffe controlled the skies over Europe. By June 6, 1944, D-day in Normandy, the tables had been turned, and the Allies controlled the skies. Bitter German infantry on D-day complained that they could identify the air force overhead by the color of the planes: if they were olive drab, they were British; if they were silver they were American; if they were invisible, it was the Luftwaffe.

The intervening nine months involved the most violent, bitter, and brutal air combat ever recorded in the annals of military history. The Luftwaffe was filled with extraordinary pilots, flying superb fighters. The Allies were taking on the cream of air warriors in the world. The 4th Fighter Group, and Kidd Hofer were at the "tip of the spear" during these critical months.

Coupled with the ascent of Blakeslee, the P-51 Mustang, the finest piston engine fighter ever built, was starting to come off production lines and would be pushed into combat in early 1944. The men of the 4th Fighter Group were competing most directly with the aces of the 56th Fighter Group for "ace" honors, and the fierce competition had even prompted members of the two groups to occasionally come to blows in London pubs arguing over who was the best.

Only the best the Allies could offer would survive the crucible of combat over France in between "Black Thursday" and "D-Day." The 4th FG proved it was the best, and Kidd Hofer proved he was the best the 4th had to offer. He was the highest scoring Ace of the European Theater of Operations, flying with the 334th Fighter Squadron, the highest scoring squadron of the 4th FG, in the highest scoring Fighter Group in Air Force history. They destroyed 1016.5 German planes in the war. He outscored every ace of the Eagles, and the 4th in only 276 hours of combat flying.

Virginia Irwin was an equally remarkable woman of her era. Before the war, she was a garden editor for the St. Louis Post Dispatch. As the war escalated, and news about the front became an obsession with virtually every news outlet, she asked to be assigned to duties as a war correspondent. She was politely told "women can't be war correspondents."

Rather than making an issue of it, she decided to use the age-old weapon of feminine guile. She changed her request to asking for a leave of absence, so she could join the Red Cross and hand out donuts to the troops. Since that was suitable for "women's work", it was approved. Once she got overseas, however, she began sending freelance articles back to her paper. They finally got the message and gave her credentials.

In covering the European war theater in late 1943 and early 1944, she naturally gravitated towards the air war in general, and the fighter war in particular, since there was not yet a ground war in England to cover, and the fighter boys were the "knights" of the air and made extremely exciting copy. In reporting on the exploits of the various fighter groups, she encountered Kidd Hofer, who was the first Enlisted Ace in the 8th AF. She became his Boswell and wrote what is probably the definitive newspaper story of his life and success which was published in St. Louis Post Dispatch the summer of 1944.

When the Allies allowed correspondents on the continent, she kept close to the front, and eventually made it into Berlin before it was officially opened to reporters. It was a feat for which she was scolded and disciplined, but she got her scoop. A genuine maverick in her own right, and a pioneer in women's rights and opportunities, Virginia Irwin was as unique in her world and profession as Kidd Hofer was in his. The pair made a dazzling impression on their contemporaries and on knowledgeable historians. Their story is fascinating. It's the inspiration for this historical fiction.

PROLOGUE

JULY 4, 1944

The striking woman in the little red MG sports car screamed off the M-11 at Weddington, about halfway between London and Cambridge, and careened down Water Lane towards Debden, England, weaving through light traffic, dangerously passing on curves, scaring locals, and scattering birds as she darted between the other cars, braking hard, tires screeching on the dry asphalt, and gears crunching as she clumsily worked the four-speed manual transmission. The driver, Virginia Irwin, a lovely, lithe brunette in her mid-30's was crying so hard she could barely see, adding to the craziness of her journey. Only divine intervention was keeping her on the road and preventing death or injury to her or anyone else before she could reach the base of the United States Army Air Corps 4th Fighter Group at Debden.

Making the last turn by Mr. Tetley's farmhouse, she swung into the entrance, which was flanked by a huge sign:

Debden
Home of the 4th Fighter Group
"Fourth but First"

She lurched up to the gate, where the guard quickly stepped back into his guardhouse to avoid being run over. He recognized Virginia from the plethora of previous visits, and although she really made no effort to come to a complete stop for inspection, he waved her through.

She sped down the wide main road of the base, which was festooned with American Flags in honor of America's Birthday, heading towards the hangars on the edge of the apron next to the runways. Pedestrians jumped up on the curb and made plenty of room, as virtually everyone recognized her, and knew from base "gen" (general information) why she was in the state she was in. Maniac civilian drivers at Debden were extremely rare, but Virginia had wormed her way into the hearts of the officers and men of the base with her unabashed admiration for the Fourth, her impish sense of humor, her great dancing, and sheer elegant personality. And they understood her actions this Fourth of July 1944.

Her dangerous driving did not abate as she approached the flight line and whipped onto the tarmac parking pad of the first cavernous hanger. She skidded to a stop and killed the engine by leaving the car in gear, leaped out, leaving the car door open, and burst into the ready room of the 334th Squadron.

The first person she encountered was Tech Sergeant Jim Scudday, a grizzled middle-aged cowboy from Texas, a retread from WWI. Scudday, who had obviously lied about his age to get into the war, was sitting at a battered desk reading a paperback western and drinking coffee with his cowboy-boot-shod-feet propped on the desk. When the door crashed open and Virginia barged in, he sat back and waited, knowing the question that was coming.

"Where is he?" she sobbed, wiping her red eyes and runny nose with a pink silk hankie embroidered with the initials VI.

Scudday simply nodded towards the hangar door.

Virginia rushed into the dark, cavernous hangar, which was empty except for a single P-51B Mustang, sitting in the far corner. The plane was bathed in a halo of sunlight from high dormer windows which only seemed to highlight the artwork beneath the canopy—a cartoon Missouri mule, with golden wings, wearing golden boxing gloves and army green boxing shorts with a large black "M" and a big golden championship Golden Gloves belt buckle At the tip of the tail was a golden horseshoe, hanging tangs down—which she noticed, but it only served to fuel her anguish.

As Virginia hurried towards the plane, across the concrete, only the ghostly, echoing click of her heels could be heard.

CHAPTER ONE

AUGUST 17, 1943

Sitting in the left seat of the lead bomber, preparing to lead the biggest raid by the 8th Air Force to date, Colonel Curtis LeMay clamped hard on his cigar as he waited in his B-17 for the signal to depart. It had been exactly one year since the first bomber mission of the 8th Air Force, a small token force of a dozen bombers slipping over the channel to bomb the Coast of France. 8th AF Mission 84 was different.

Part of "Operation Pointblank", the goal of the offensive was a simultaneous strike on the centers of German ball bearing production in Schweinfurt and Regensburg, Germany, with 376 B-17's to cripple the Luftwaffe and Germany's aircraft production capabilities in support of the main cross-channel invasion, "Operation Overlord." The reason for the "double strike" by two separate bomber streams simultaneously crossing the coastline, was to dilute Luftwaffe fighter strength by forcing them to divide the Luftflotten (air fleets) defending two raids, reducing their effectiveness on both.

Arcing into the soft, foggy, English summer morning, a green signal flare shot skyward and LeMay advanced the throttles on his bomber. Being first off, he circled a wide gentle turn to port, while the remainder of the force got into the air, and gradually joined up on him. Once all 146 bombers were up, they formed into their combat attack wings, and headed east for Regensburg, Germany.

The plan for the raid had been brutally simple: The first group would fight its way into Schweinfurt and fly out over the Alps to bases in French Algeria. The second group, coming in behind LeMay, would have lighter resistance in approaching and attacking Regensburg because the German fighters would be on the ground refueling, and rearming after their attacks on LeMay's planes.

As fate would have it—as fate tends to have its way—the departure of the second group, 230 bombers lead by General Robert Williams, was delayed so long by weather that the "dilution" aspect of the plan was lost. Due to the delays, the Germans would have time to attack LeMay, land, refuel, rearm, take off and climb to altitude, where they could then attack Williams's bombers as they passed through the crucible of fire towards their target. Williams wouldn't have any help coming back, either. And the Germans would have time to rearm and refuel again, so the ferocity of attacks on the returning bombers would be as overwhelming as the attacks when they approached.

LeMay would fight his way in, Williams would fight his way in and out, having lost the critical factor of simultaneous attacks. Despite the loss of the critical simultaneous aspect of the plan, when the weather cleared, Air Force command ordered Williams to depart. Eventually Williams' wing took off, heading for Schweinfurt.

American air planners still possessed the conceit of believing that massed American heavy bombers, with their ten defensive .50 caliber machine guns, woven into combat boxes to insure interlocking fields of fire, could defend themselves from the swarms of German fighters awaiting them over the Continent. The fact that the targets were an hour's flying time beyond the range of escorting Allied P-47 fighters was deemed of little or no consequence. They couldn't have been more wrong.

Returning eleven hours later, the remnants of William's force limped into their various bases. Reviewing air reconnaissance photographs that evening, General Ira Eaker, Commanding General of the 8th Air Force, realized that while Regensburg was heavily damaged, Schweinfurt was virtually untouched, and the cost of the mission was staggering. The Luftwaffe obviously controlled the skies over Europe.

Sixty bombers, carrying 600 men, were lost. Dozens of others, full of wounded airmen, were so badly damaged that it exceeded the ability of the 8th Air Force to economically make repairs within a reasonable time frame. There was just too much destruction. So, no follow up raid could be mounted. The 8th was severely bloodied, an exhausted pugilist staggering back into his corner after being thoroughly pummeled.

Both the 4th and the 56th fighter groups were assigned that day as escorts for the forces of General Williams, heading for Schweinfurt. The 4th scored no victories escorting the bombers en route, but the 56th, helping the bombers fight their way out, scored 16 victories.

The Fourth was frustrated; they weren't able to help the bombers much. But help was on the way in the form of the best piston engine fighter ever built, and a character to fly one of them who was straight out of central casting.

CHAPTER TWO

SEPTEMBER 23, 1943

Captain James Goodson, a respected, dapper 24-year-old Canadian with a pencil mustache, was lounging in his jeep with his driver, Sergeant Jim Scudday. The two watched lazily as a C-47 cargo plane entered the pattern and dropped in to land at Debden, the most luxurious fighter base in England.

When safely parked on the apron, the rear hatch opened, and two men stepped out. They seemed to match the descriptions Goodson had been given by Colonel Blakeslee when dispatched to pick up the latest fighter pilots assigned to the 4th Fighter Group.

The first man was a slender, athletic, Adonis, over six feet tall, with laughing blue eyes, a broad dazzling smile, and shaggy blond hair. He was wearing the uniform of a Flight Sergeant. Right behind him was a slightly taller, distinctly lanky, dark-haired native of Rhode Island, bearing the gold bars of a second lieutenant. He had the dark eyes of a hunter, and a jaunty pencil mustache similar to the one sported by Captain Goodson. As the two sauntered up to the jeep, which was obviously there to provide transportation for someone, they smiled at Goodson, a silent "are you waiting for us?"

Goodson smiled back, acknowledging they had guessed right. "Hofer and Godfrey?" Goodson asked, holding out his hand.

The dark-eyed hunter replied, "Lt. Johnny Godfrey, Captain"

The *Adonis* looked around, taking it all in like a kid arriving at summer camp. He smiled broadly, and his sharp blue eyes looked directly at Goodson as he shook the proffered hand with a strong and confident grip, "Flight Officer Ralph Hofer, sir."

Goodson felt an immediate connection with this enlisted pilot. His manner, his guileless smile, the direct eye contact, obvious athleticism, and youthful exuberance, projected an unmistakable charisma. He was self-assured, but not in an unpleasant way. Goodson recognized an Ace in the making, if he survived the crucible of combat. The other man, Godfrey, had a baby face, but a close look at his eyes revealed the hint of a malevolence that suggested a man with a purpose, a goal, a man on a mission. Revenge? Another Ace, if the Gods of War smiled on him.

In his Canadian drawl, full of aristocratic grandeur, Goodson crooned: "Capt. James Goodson, but pilots can call me "Goody."

He returned to the front passenger seat, Godfrey and Hofer threw their duffel bags in the back of the jeep and clambered in as Sgt. Scudday started the engine. With all aboard, and gears grinding in careless familiarity, off they roared, everyone but Scudday holding onto their hats with one hand and the jeep with the other. Scudday careened off the apron and down the main road of the base.

Goodson had to yell above the noise to the men in the backseats, "We'll drop your bags at your quarters and hit the officer's mess before you report in. You guys must be hungry."

Godfrey and Hofer grinned at each other, enjoying the madcap ride and trying to take in the sights as they zipped past base personnel dodging the jeep at every swerve, with knowing looks—*new pilots, fresh meat for the grinder. How long will these FNG's last? A week? Two?*

Scudday skidded to a stop and turned off the engine. The men exited the jeep, Godfrey and Hofer retrieving their bags as they climbed out and entered the quarters. A fine brick building, the Officer's quarters looked like an apartment complex. Goodson led them down the ground floor hall to two rooms that were across from each other. Nodding to Godfrey, he points to the room on the left. Then, opening the door on the right, he gestured to Hofer, who entered a nice little room with two beds, two closets, a window peeking out on the parade ground, and two small desks, one for each bed.

"Gentlemen," Goody said, "welcome to Casa Debden. The batmen will sort out your luggage if you're ready to eat."

Hofer and Godfrey dropped their bags, closed the door, and quickly filed out, following Goody back to the jeep for another wild, but short ride around the corner to the officer's mess. After the screeching halt by Scudday in front of the mess, the three pilots climbed out, and strolled up the concrete walk bifurcating the manicured lawn toward the Debden's officer's mess.

As they approached the door, Hofer glanced over his shoulder. Lounging in the grass with a look akin to a lion casually and regally surveying his domain, was a large German Alsatian dog, black, brown and tan, with erect, pointed ears, and bright, deep brown eyes that studied the pilots curiously, as if asking, *Who are you?*

Hofer noticed the dog was eyeing him intently, as if sizing him up, judging him. Their eyes met for a split second and Hofer felt a preternatural connection, almost electric in its intensity. He smiled. The dog broke into a brilliant, laughing smile, his tongue lolling over his teeth. He became more alert, as if suddenly spotting a rabbit in the brush, or smelling a piece of steak from the mess hall. The men entered the mess hall and the door shut behind them.

Taking a seat in the dining room, at a table worthy of the finest restaurant in London, the men were quickly attended by the batmen, civilians who worked for the USAAF in one of the plumb jobs available for Englishmen during the war—taking care of the Americans—who were "oversexed, overpaid, and over here." The table was set with fine china, crystal glasses, a crisp white linen tablecloth, and an elegant vase of flowers in the center. Any lady from the United States would be duly and properly impressed.

Spreading their napkins, the three men quickly perused the menu, ordered their dinner, and continued their conversation.

"Just so you know," Goody said, "you guys are lucky enough to be assigned to the best fighter group in the ETO. If you don't believe it, just ask any of the pilots. We all love flying for Colonel Blakeslee."

"Blakeslee?" Godfrey frowns. "I heard he's a major hard ass. Really difficult and picky."

"True," Goody smiled, "but if you want to survive, if you want to score, if you want to be the best, there's nobody like him. He flew with the Eagles, and he is an Ace."

Goody paused to let the frightening specter of Colonel Don Blakeslee sink into the neophyte pilots. The silence became thick.

"Say," Goody continued, changing the subject, "either of you guys play any football?"

Hofer smiled. "Yeah, a little. I was a tight-end on a semi-pro team in Chicago. Brought my 78 jersey with me. It's one of my lucky charms. Why?"

Goody noticeably brightened. "It so happens we have a football game coming up with the Brits. Seems there has been a lot of talk about which game is most challenging, Rugby or American football. So, Colonel Blakeslee worked out a game with the English where we play a 60-minute game. First 30 minutes American Football. 20-minute halftime. Last 30 minutes English Rugby. Whoever wins by the biggest margin is declared the winner of the game, and the losers play Camp Mary for the winners for a week."

Godfrey, "Camp Mary?"

"Oh, they have to do all the camp chores for a week. Mow the grass, cook the meals, clean up the rooms, maintain everything. You know, be the maids."

Godfrey and Hofer smiled in understanding. Silence again.

Finally, Hofer broke the heavy atmosphere. "What do you know about that dog that was outside, Goody?"

Goody laughed as he warmed to the subject. "That's Duke, the Wonder Dog. Everybody loves him. They pamper him, feed him, and try to make friends, but Duke's royalty, with his own set of priorities."

The dog was obviously a very special member of the compliment of men assigned to Debden. With the exception of perhaps Colonel Blakeslee himself—whose presence, personality, and skill as a fighter group commander made him a legend in his own time, and the subject of envious conversation by military and civilian alike—Duke held a status somewhere just above everybody.

Johnny spoke up, "Who takes care of him?"

"Well," said Goody, "everybody, and nobody. Duke used to room with Digger Williams, but Digger got shot down. He's a guest of the Reich. Duke's been batching it, although every pilot on the base spoils him and would love to adopt him. I'm not sure where he sleeps, but he eats when and where he wants. The cooks let him in the kitchen, and the officers and enlisted men are always bringing him leftovers from London. That dog lives better than most of the people on this island."

"When I was growing up in Missouri, I had a horse named Duke. Think they're related?" laughed Hofer.

"If your horse understood everything said to him, and was very picky about his friends, maybe so," grinned Goody.

The batman arrived with their meal, and the conversation lagged as they dug in. While Hofer ate, he felt a presence to his left. He glanced down and back. Sitting silently, eyeing him intently again, was Duke. Hofer met his gaze. Duke smiled broadly. Hofer's big grin lit up his cherubic face. Looking to Goody with a big smile, he asked, "What's he want?"

"Dunno. Mooching, I guess."

Hofer stopped eating and put down his knife and fork. He looked directly into the eyes of Duke, placed his hands on each side of his head, and began to pet him and coo at him while stroking his great head and coat. Duke returned the gaze. The seconds ticked by. Duke's eyes were half closed.

After a few moments, Goody said, "Are you going to eat anymore?"

"Oh, sure," Hofer answered, "but when a dog comes up to you and offers attention, I always let the dog choose how long we make contact. Most people will give a dog a few seconds, and then shoo them away. My philosophy is that a dog's worthy of your attention as long as they want it. Dogs give so much and ask so little. All they ask is to be with you, if you're their master. In return, they give unconditional love, and protection. No matter what you do, or what kind of day you've had, your dog is always overjoyed to see you. That's a bargain in anybody's world."

He turned his attention to Duke again, who stayed another 15 to 20 seconds, then turned and padded silently away. Hofer resumed eating.

A few minutes later, Duke sidled up next to Hofer, looked up at him, and placed his left front paw, protectively, on Hofer's right thigh. Hofer glanced around the table, and surreptitiously slipped Duke bites of his roast. Duke took the offerings like a gentleman, gently accepting each piece like a tribute to royalty.

Observing the bonding, Goody shook his head, and smiled. "I've never seen Duke behave like that. You got a female dog in your pocket?"

Finishing their meal, the three men exchanged looks, rose to leave, and made their way towards the door. Duke sat silently, eyes slightly squinted, and patiently watched them depart.

Hofer stopped, and looked back. "Hey!" he called to Duke.

As if tickled that *his choice* of Master had been accepted, Duke heeled at Hofer's right knee as if he were trained to do so and accompanied him out of the mess hall. Once outside, everybody clambered back into the same positions in the jeep. Without hesitation or prompting, and with an air of certainty and finality,

Duke jumped into the back of the jeep and again put his left paw on Hofer's right thigh.

Duke looked directly at Goody with a look that seemed to say, "What?"

Goody marveled softly, "I'll be damned."

CHAPTER THREE

A few days later, standing on the tarmac in front of the 334th Squadron hangar, Goody and Sgt. Scudday watched as, in the distance to the east, a lone P-47 was cavorting around in the sky; diving, looping, rolling, turning, twisting, and stalling among the fleecy white clouds. Its engine strained as the plane clawed for altitude, climbing into a stall spin, pulling out near the ground, and zooming back up into the crystal blue sky.

Leaning towards Scudday, Goody asked, "Is that the new guy from this morning?"

"Nope," said Scudday, shaking his head slightly.

Pointing, Goody asked, "Then who is that?"

Grinning, Scudday said, "Guess."

Noting the mischief in Scudday's eyes, Goody turned back to watching the plane, which continued to twist and turn, an agile silhouette against the azure backdrop. He chuckled in recognition, "Oh."

In a different corner of the Debden airspace, another P-47, with the white cowling markings of the 4th Fighter Group, was being piloted by an anxious FNG (F**king New Guy, as they were known to base personnel), who was peering out to his left, obviously disoriented as to his location and trying to get his bearings with the unfamiliar landmarks on the ground.

To make things even worse, his goggles were beginning to mist over with the heated sweat of anxiety.

Then, in his headphones, came the reassuring voice of Debden air control.

"Don't panic, son. The field should be about halfway between your nose, and your right wing. See it?"

Turning his head as instructed, the FNG was startled to see another plane flying formation on his right wing. It had the white cowling of the 4th FG, and the nose art said, "The Missouri Kid, Sho-Me". It's markings, unfamiliar yet to the new guy, were that of the 334th Fighter group designation of "QP, plane L," the Thunderbolt plane assigned to "Kidd" Hofer. But even more amazing was the pilot. Peering at the FNG from the cockpit, with a goofy grin, was Duke the wonder dog, there being no sign of a human being.

"Holy Shit!" he exclaimed in genuine shock.

The air controller, equally startled by the pilot's exclamation, responded immediately, readying to notify base rescue personnel to stand by for a life-threatening emergency.

"Holy Shit? What's happened? You OK?" he barked at the pilot.

Incredulous, the FNG stated the improbable, "There's a dog flying on my wing!" Then he listened as what was transpiring in the air quickly filtered round the invisible room of faceless personnel in the Debden tower, and each man in turn took up the chorus of laughter that filled the FNG's headset.

The air controller responded and in a reassuring tone that implied business as usual at Debden, he said, "That's just Hofer."

"Hofer!? Who's Hofer!?"

"The hottest screwball pilot in England. If you see the field, son, you're cleared to land." The laughter in the background continued through the pilot's headset.

Moments later, Scudday and Goody watched as the FNG carefully landed, taxied up, cut his engine, and climbed out of his plane. Just then, Hofer's P-47 roared by, almost on the deck doing victory rolls. The giant fighter pitched up into a perfect break, entered the pattern, dropped flaps and gear, and Hofer made a perfect main gear only two point landing, taxiing by their position at high speed, tail up, until his airspeed bled off, and the tail dropped gently to the tarmac.

Goody chuckled in amazement at Hofer's skill. "That dog is a helluva pilot," he said.

Hofer made a smooth and quick U-turn and headed for the hangar, taxiing into position next to the plane of the new guy. Once he cut his engine, and the prop wind milled to a stop, Hofer opened his canopy. Duke hopped out and jumped down, circling happily as he waited for Hofer to climb down. Wearing a blue wool football jersey with an orange 78, Hofer pulled off his RAF Type C leather flying helmet and jumped down off the wing gracefully, a natural athlete. Duke and Hofer—playing, laughing and barking—trotted by Goody, Sgt. Scudday, and the FNG. Hofer waved at them, "Hey, Duke's getting real good at flying!"

Goody bantered back, "Anybody can do a loop. How is he on instruments?"

Hofer said, "Good as me!"

Shaking his head and waving, Goody called out, "Duke, you've just been insulted."

Duke barked happily, reveling in spending time with his master, and continued to cavort with Hofer. But to all present, it sure seemed like he was responding to Goody.

Turning to Goodson, the FNG asked, "Sir, was that dog on his lap?"

Acknowledging the truth, Goody smiled somewhat ruefully, "Yeah. He leaves off his parachute to make room."

Marveling, the FNG was soaking it all in, "That's fantastic!"

"Don't get any ideas," Goody cautioned.

"Uh, no sir, not me," the FNG said, sheepishly.

Just then, a jeep came skidding around a corner, and jerked to a halt on the apron cutting off Hofer and Duke. "Mr. Hofer," the driver said, "Colonel Blakeslee wants to see you, right now. Mr. Goodson, can I give you a ride?"

Sgt. Scudday interrupted, "I'll take it from here, Airman."

The driver jumped out and gave the jeep over to the Sgt., who slid into the driver's seat, grinding the gears in anticipation of a quick departure.

Hofer, mocking fear, grinned puckishly at the other men with wide eyes and pursed lips. He motioned to Duke and hopped in behind Scudday. Duke jumped in right behind him, assuming his usual posture next to Hofer's right knee with his left paw protectively resting on Hofer's leg. Swinging into the front passenger seat, and grabbing on for dear life, Goody waved and saluted the Airman and the FNG, who return his salute as Scudday's legendary bad driving caused the jeep to lurch into motion, whipping them around them in a rough U-turn.

Once turned around, the gears grinding on carelessly timed manipulations of the clutch and gear shift, and again weaving around pedestrians forcing them to dodge out of the way to make room as the jeep sped by, they headed off towards the office of the Commanding Officer, Lt. Colonel Donald Blakeslee.

The office of the Commanding Officer at Debden was known in some circles as "The Throne Room." No one on the base liked to be summoned there. Few had seen it in any light but the wrath of Blakeslee. It's almost always serious.

Inside sat Colonel Don Blakeslee, 26, a tall, lean native of Fairport, Ohio. The Colonel was known for having the eyes of an eagle, no pun intended, an iron will, and a commanding presence, with the natural charisma that seems to radiate from fighter pilots. Many a friend, and all his enemies remarked to others on the riveting, steely eyed stare that was often generated by his piercing grey eyes when someone or something was the object of his attention.

And, he was an Ace, with a handful of victories, supremely confident in his abilities in the air and on the ground, who naturally received respect, admiration and deference due those few who have been given gifts ordinarily denied to mortal man.

Grudgingly recognized by even his detractors as a legend in his own time, he had little tolerance for nonsense, and was obsessed with the determination to build the best fighter group in the U. S. Army Air Corps.

He was sitting in his swivel chair, gazing impatiently out the window, drumming absent-mindedly with his fingers on the arms of his chair.

Waiting with him, somewhat nervous, standing in respectful silence in the back of the office, were two crack fighter pilots, Lt. Colonel Jim Clark, 25, a native of New York, the Executive Officer of the 4th Fighter Group. With him was Lt. Don Gentile, 23, a dark Italian from Piqua, Ohio, an ace, and a truly gifted fighter pilot with quiet strength based in a deep faith in God from his Catholic childhood. Colonel Blakeslee's orderly, Jack Minter, from Lubbock, Texas, a young staff sergeant of 20 years, was busy setting up a 16mm film projector loaded with a small reel of film, which was sitting next to a single wooden chair.

A knock.

Without turning, Blakeslee impatiently barked, "Enter."

The door swung open cautiously. Stepping in gingerly, aware of the potential for contention within, was Hofer; followed by Goody, insouciant as usual, and supremely confident in all situations. Hofer looked back for a second before pulling the door closed behind him. "Duke, stay."

Hofer's furry shadow laid in front of the door just outside the office. No man shall pass without the approval of Duke, whether coming or going.

Goody flipped a salute reserved for exchanges between peers, and aces. Hofer stopped, braced himself, and by giving his best salute, which to be honest, was truly a half-assed effort, tried his best to look and act military. Blakeslee waved it away. He motioned to the wooden chair by the projector. Hofer sat as Goody assumed a stance in the rear of the office with Clark and Gentile, nodding and shaking hands with his mates as they settled in to watch the inquisition of young Hofer.

Blakeslee looked at his orderly, "Sergeant." He then reached to pull the shade of the window as he turned to prepare for the viewing.

After turning off the lights, the sergeant flipped the switch to start the projector. The only sound that could be heard in the room was a soft whirring as the film passed over the projector's light, and everyone watched silently as the footage from a gun camera flickered on the office wall.

A German Messerschmidt 109 Fighter, twisting and turning violently, danced before the viewers, just 400 feet above the Zuider Zee, trying to evade the deadly fireflies streaking around him from either side of the screen. The gun camera on a P-47 was in the left wing root, so the tracers appeared from the two edges of the picture, and converged on the target.

Tracer rounds flashed passed and along the wings of the victim, then into the wing root, finally hitting the engine, inflicting obviously fatal damage. The outer one-third of the left wing tore off, and the plane began to tumble. Incredibly, the canopy flew off, and the dark form of a human being tumbled out. The film ended and the soft whir was replaced by the flapping sound of an empty reel.

Sergeant Minter switched off the projector and flipped on the lights. Blakeslee raised the shades.

He turned his steely eyes upon Hofer, who shifted nervously, but met the Colonel's gaze with a remarkably composed and direct look.

"So, you got a kill on your first mission. That's great." The Colonel said. Then looking at Goody, "Did you authorize him to break off?"

Goody, somewhat surprised at being included in the conversation, hemmed and hawed a bit before answering.

"Well, not exactly..." he started to say, not wanting to exacerbate Hofer's situation, but still seeking to deflect any blame from himself, but he could not finish his reply.

Blakeslee snorted, "Not exactly."

Turning his full attention back to Hofer, the inquisition continued, "How long have you been here, Hofer?"

"I got here three weeks ago with Lt. Godfrey, Sir," Hofer replied.

Shifting his gaze to Gentile, "Your new wingman?"

Gentile, not wishing to be further involved, was concise in his reply. "Yes, sir."

The Colonel gazed into Hofer's eyes, gauging his reaction. Getting little, he seemed to be warming to his subject. "What are you after, Hofer?", in a stern tone turning up the heat.

Hesitating to be honest, but compelled by the force of Blakeslee's personality, Hofer confessed his innermost secret. "To be the Ace of Aces, Sir".

Such a revelation voiced openly by a relatively inexperienced enlisted pilot among experienced, commissioned fighter pilots, at least three of which were already Aces, caused an exchange of glances around the room, some discreet coughs, and slightly perceptible shifting of positions. Even though the same goal was a secret wish of all those who gambled their lives four miles high, to make such a brash statement in the presence of these men and Blakeslee, even though prompted by a direct question, some would call hubris. But not Blakeslee. And eliciting such an answer was indicative of the force of the Colonel's personality. It was impossible not to bend to the man's will.

Blakeslee leaned forward dauntingly, scoffing at the impertinence of the young pilot.

"Crap. By order of the Commanding Officer of the Eighth Air Force, the bombers come first. You follow?" He ground the words at Hofer like coffee beans.

Squirming, but resisting the idea of totally giving up his position, Hofer offered a mild, but capricious retort, "With respect, Sir, I thought my job was to kill Germans."

Blakeslee's gaze hardened at the assertion of the newest, lowliest enlisted pilot in his elite Fighter Group even offering to do any thinking in combat. Standing up slowly, and seeming to get bigger, he leaned over the desk even more to emphasize his point. Hofer sat, iron willed, meeting the Colonel's gaze calmly. Externally, Blakeslee's countenance was his usual dominating self, but his thoughts were different, they reflected what he had suspected. Hofer was a warrior, a fighter, a man's man. Most pilots, when confronted with "the look" shrink, wide-eyed, visibly withering under Blakeslee's stare. Hofer did not shrink, wither, or get wide-eyed, but rather calmly and respectfully met his gaze. As Hofer's back was to the others, they couldn't see the silent confrontation of wills, but the connection between Hofer and Blakeslee was one of warriors bonding.

For the benefit of the others in the room, Blakeslee didn't flinch, "Enlisted pilots are not paid to think, son. You follow orders. You follow *my* orders. Are we clear?"

Hofer conceded, "Yes, Sir."

Blakeslee sat back down, swiveled in his chair, and gazed out, contemplating the exchange, and giving him a chance to secretly smile to himself, appreciating Hofer's backbone, and mulling over options. No one would ever know Blakeslee had a favorite, but he knew intuitively, this young man would make his mark.

After a single, long, excruciating minute, he turned back to Hofer. Everyone present breathing very quietly, awaiting verdict, judgment, and sentence.

"You're off combat flying until further orders," he growled. "I've got no use for a glory-hound. You may continue flying hack, and slow timing fighters coming out of maintenance, but you are not to be assigned to any combat missions without my specific permission."

Looking at the other pilots present for confirmation that there was no doubt as to his wishes, Blakeslee inquired mildly, "Does anyone have any questions?"

All the pilots present shook their heads. Verbal answers were neither necessary nor wanted. And everyone knew it.

"Dismissed."

Hofer stood, flipped a half-assed salute, turned and bolted for the door, exiting first, without even a cursory attempt at military courtesy in letting senior officers precede him.

After a brief, resolute silence, and an implied acknowledgment between Hofer's uppers that justice, such as it was, had been meted out, they exited anxiously. No one spoke as they all worked their way out the door.

At the sound of the door shutting, Blakeslee, still staring out his window, smiled broadly. *This kid*, Hofer, he thought, *is something special*. And he laughed out loud.

Duke was waiting patiently just outside Blakeslee's door, and was, as always, overjoyed to see Hofer appear. Hofer, needing the affection himself, petted the dog warmly as he rapidly slid by, and summoned his canine Huckleberry to follow with his usual terse command. "Hey." As always, Duke promptly obeyed without any hesitation.

Together, Hofer and Duke exited the building in tandem and found a significant crowd of "loungers" who, hearing of Hofer's summons to Blakeslee's office, just happened to be around for any scuttlebutt that might leak out. After all, most fighter pilots don't even see an enemy fighter on their first mission, so Hofer's legend was already born and growing with the fact that he not only *saw* an enemy plane but shot it down.

Johnny Godfrey, one of the curious, casually sidled up to Hofer, "Alleswell"?

"I guess," Hofer replied, "any of my ass left?" Hofer peered over his own shoulder. They laughed together.

"Catch up, later, OK?" Godfrey melted away.

Duke began nosing Hofer while he and Godfrey exchanged comments, so Hofer began roughhousing with his furry wingman and constant companion, who was a willing and joyous participant for any play. Duke barked and ran in circles, as Hofer swiped at him with his hands, and tackled the big dog. Master and dog rolled happily on the ground, being watched enviously but with admiration by all those nearby. Duke's tail whipped back and forth almost invisibly, the dog quivering with joy and contentment at the attention, and play. Hofer's own sense of contentment was already ascending, the roughhousing with Duke making Blakeslee's scolding a distant memory.

As man and dog frolicked in the grass in front of Headquarters, the remaining eye witnesses to Hofer's ass-chewing filed out, and with incredulous disbelief took in the spectacle of Hofer and Duke playing. It seemed that the dog and pilot were behaving like nothing had happened just moments after Blakeslee had grounded Hofer from combat. This man just got his butt handed to him by the most capable aerial combat leader in the European Theatre of Operations, and he's playing with his dog?

Colonel Clark couldn't resist speaking up, "Hofer, what the hell are you doing?"

Hofer, rolling around on the ground, the dog trying to chew on his collar, almost laughed his answer.

"Well, sir," he said between licks from his devoted guardian, "I figured that if I was going to be in the doghouse, I may as well play the part."

Clark, dismayed, looked at Goody, "What the hell can you do?"

Goody suppressed a big grin and trying to maintain his composure and status as a leader of men, responded quickly, "Not a damn thing."

CHAPTER FOUR

Mail call at Debden. Hofer and Duke clambered up the steps of the Officer's Club and headed into the designated mail room. Hearing the piano being played in the Officer's Mess, Hofer and Duke peeked in to see what was happening. Seated at the piano was one of his favorite buddies, Pierce McKennon, 23, a lanky farm boy from Arkansas with a mischievous grin, banging out swing tunes. Although trained as a classical pianist at the insistence of his Mother, McKennon had found his forte in playing honky-tonk piano for his fellow fighter pilots.

Never one to pass up the fun of watching and listening to Pierce play around, Hofer and Duke slipped in the door. Hofer sidled up to the bar, ordered a pint of bitters, and turned around to watch. The barman, after filling up Hofer's glass, reached over to the accumulated personalized steins of the Officers, and selected the ceramic bowl embellished with "Duke", reached into the fridge for a bottle of milk, and filled Duke's bowl with a couple of ounces of fresh milk. He slid it to Hofer, who set it on the floor next to Duke.

Duke, ever the Dog who was half human, laid down, crossed his front paws, lapped a couple of sips in a gentlemanly manner, and turned his attention to the piano. Only an enlisted dog would lap up all the milk in a couple of gulps.

The appearance of McKennon at the piano quickly attracted a crowd of pilots, as always. After a quick boogie-woogie version of "Rock of Ages", the crowd chanted for *their star* to perform his unique signature trick, and feat of skill.

"Tiger Rag, Tiger Rag, Tiger Rag" they loudly and laughingly cheered him on. From the bar, a pint of bitters was passed to McKennon. Taking it between his teeth, he began to play the song as he drained the stein, without missing a note, or spilling a drop. When the stein was empty, he put it on the piano, and finished the tune with a flourish, to the cheers and laughter of his appreciative audience.

Encouraged by the general conviviality, Hofer approached the group and tried to join in the fun, but as he was still in Blakeslee's doghouse, he was politely but pointedly ignored. Rejected, a pariah to a degree, Hofer drifted over to the victory board, and studied the totals. Beeson, Clark, Goody, Evans and Blakeslee all had 5. Other pilots had victory credits, and many were on the board. Hofer gazed momentarily at his own name, at the bottom of the list with his only victory. He studied the situation, and then turned to leave, calling to Duke, who paused to finish his bowl of milk.

"Hey." Hofer picked up Duke's bowl, handed it to the barman with a 50-cent tip, and thanked him for the special attention to Duke, "Thanks, Michael."

Michael smiled, "No problem, Mr. Hofer. Duke's the best mannered visitor we have at this club."

Man, and dog, exited and headed towards the Day Room, where mail was distributed. They arrived just as the mail carrier was beginning to call out names and hand out mail and packages.

"Fiedler. Baker. Cox. Scott. Netting. Carpenter. Harris."

As each name was called, the pilots stepped forward to claim his prize. As the mailbag emptied, the room gradually emptied too, as the men whose mail had been delivered departed to their rooms or the squadron ready rooms to share stories, pictures, and "goodies," like cookies, from home. Finally, there was no one left but Hofer, Duke, and the mailman. He searched his bag to insure it was empty.

"Sorry, Mr. Hofer, nothing again today," said the mailman in an apologetic tone.

In the time Hofer had been at Debden, no mail had ever been received for him, and he had never mailed anything to anyone. Hofer, pretending to be very busy with Duke, waved it off, and left, he and Duke playing as they exit, headed down the hall, and out to the door. As usual, Hofer gravitated towards the flight line and his beloved fighter, walking alone, hands in his pockets, with Duke faithfully trotting by his side.

On the apron of the 334th hangar, in the cool of the English early winter evening, Hofer climbed into his P-47, and sat quietly, contemplating the setting sun, while Duke laid on the left wing, watching intently in case Hofer needed him.

After a few moments, Hofer reached over the side of his cockpit, and placed his hand on the dog's nape, rubbing him softly, and purring his name. "Duke. Duke".

Only Duke could see the faintest hint of moisture in Hofer's eyes.

After sunset, Hofer climbed out, and started back to his barracks. Duke gave him a "special look," and the two confirmed their understanding about the mess hall. It's just about time to close, and there would be leftovers.

"Ok, buddy, get your treats, but remember, don't hassle anybody, and don't bring anything back to the barracks. And if there's nobody there, don't go in. I'm not bailing you out of jail tonight."

Duke seemed to smile, and wagged his tail appreciatively, and agreeably. Anyone looking on would swear the two understood each other perfectly. As they reached the intersection where Hofer turned towards his barracks, Duke turned the other direction, and trotted off purposefully for his nightly visit to the back door of the mess hall.

Upon arrival at the mess hall, Duke scratched on the door, which was quickly opened by one of the cooks. They were expecting him.

Several of the cooks brought out scraps of meat, smiling, chattering, and cooing at him, and petting the great dog, while he took each offered bite in a gentle, respectful way; never lunging, or grabbing, but waiting for the tribute that was his natural due. Everyone considered it a privilege to dole out Duke's nightly ration of scraps. Life was good. God was in his heaven, scraps were tasty, Duke was on duty, and Hofer was close by.

Half the world away, copper-haired Mac McKenzie, the Editor of the St. Louis Post-Dispatch, with his shaggy long hair, reminiscent of Wild Bill Hickok, was sitting at his desk, peering intently at the mock-up of the next edition first page. He had a raggedly trimmed mustache and goatee; he was rumpled, frazzled, chewing on an unlighted cigar, and was, as all editors of all big city newspapers, impatient with interruptions.

A knock at the door.

Looking through the glass, Mac saw the lovely garden editor, Miss Virginia Irwin; 36, tall, slim, brunette, a newly minted divorcee with no children. She had worked her way up from gopher to a position of great responsibility, at least in the world of gardeners who read his paper. Of all the people on his staff, Virginia (Ginny to her friends) was probably the only person Mac was actually happy to see. She was always a breath of fresh air. If only he were 40 years younger...

Mac laid down his work, and motioned for her to enter, a small smile playing irresistibly on his lips. With the dazzling and talented Miss Irwin, it was hard to be the tough big city newspaperman mentoring the cub.

Virginia entered, shut the door softly, and with perfect aplomb, and the confidence borne of knowing you're special to someone, sat on the corner of Mac's desk.

"Mac, can I go over to England and be a war correspondent for the paper?"

Without missing a beat, Mac answered.

"No, you absolutely cannot. Women can't be war correspondents. That's a man's job. Soldiers, sailors, airmen, and officers and gentlemen have neither the time nor inclination to pamper women in a combat zone."

It was the response she expected. She astutely gauged that there was more than one way to skin the proverbial cat. Without missing a beat in return, she purred softly and seductively, making sure to bend over a little so that her ample cleavage was emphasized, (and of course unaware of the open top button), and changed the subject slightly to accomplish the mission of "getting across the pond."

"Well, then, can I take a leave of absence to join the USO, and hand out donuts and coffee. They have openings in England, and maybe I can find someone to rent me a room cheap."

Mac was not stupid, despite that suspicion among others whom he had chastised. And he was as appreciative as any older man at the molded smoothness of a well-turned bosom. He glanced quickly at the scenic view, sat back and contemplated his answer. Being born at night, but not last night, he rightly suspected an ulterior motive to the lovely Miss Irwin's offer for patriotic service. He looked at her with unabashed suspicion. She smiled back, certain of the righteousness of her cause, and of the ultimate outcome.

"Virginia."

"Yes, Mac."

"Do you consider me to be a stupid, old dodger who is dazzled by a view of your bosom?"

"No, Mac."

Squinting over his glasses, Mac inquired, "Well, then, do you think I'm not aware of the fact that you're just using the USO to get to England, and then you will send me combat interviews, and articles of interest on the war, and then you expect me to pay you as a war correspondent?"

"Mac, whatever gave you that idea. I'm a woman, and a garden editor. What do I know about being a war correspondent? And besides, no soldier, sailor, airman, or officer is going to pamper me in a war zone. How silly of you to even suspect me."

Sighing slightly, Mac continued. "What's the difference between a war correspondent's pay, and your salary as Garden Editor?"

Feigning ignorance, Virginia said, "Well, I'm not sure. I think it's about $10 a week, plus lodging, and a meal allowance if you're not allowed to eat at a military mess. But I'm not sure."

"What's a flat in London cost?"

"I have no idea", she shrugged, "shall I find out?"

"No, Virginia, it's not necessary. My maternal grandmother lives in London and has a room she will let me have for nothing. But you better be the best donut/lemonade wrangler in London."

He laughed at the look on Virginia's face as his meaning registered.

Virginia jumped off the corner of the desk, came around, and smothered Mac in a big hug, his face comfortably smushed between her breasts. She laughed and skipped out of his office, while Mac, face red with embarrassment at the open display of affection, resumed the mantle of crusty editor.

CHAPTER FIVE

A mere week later, back in England, Brigadier General Jesse Auton, a lean, debonair 39-year-old native of Piner, Kentucky, with a dashing pencil mustache, was sitting in his office at the Headquarters of the 65th Fighter Wing of the Eighth Air Force, Eighth Fighter Command, located in Bushey Hall, near Watford, Hampshire. The office was elegant, complete with fireplace, couches, and a desk large enough for a deck landing. He was contemplating his glass of single malt Maker's Mark Kentucky Bourbon as the flickers of the flames twinkled in the crystal of his glass.

Silent and pensive, each with their own glass of bourbon and awaiting the lead for the direction of the conversation, were Colonel Hub Zemke, 27, the Commanding Officer of the 56th Fighter Group, the 4th's closest and most intense rival, and Colonel Blakeslee.

Finally, Auton spoke.

"Gentlemen, we're desperate for fighter escort. The P-47 doesn't have the range to protect the bombers on the deeper penetration raids. The Germans simply wait for you to run out of fuel, turn back, and then they attack. The bomber crews are being decimated. Morale is shot to hell. Right now, if you're a bomber crewman in the 8th, your chances of being killed or wounded before rotating home is 100%. They've got to have help."

Zemke, a dedicated Thunderbolt jockey, spoke up, "General, the P-47 is the finest high-altitude escort fighter in the air. All we need is under-wing fuel tanks to increase our range, and the new paddle-blade props to increase the rate of climb, and it will do everything we need from ground to ceiling. Those eight .50 cals are devastating to any target they hit."

"All those modifications are in the pipeline, Hub, but we need some help right now. The new Mustang seems to be the answer to a maiden's prayer," mused Auton.

Blakeslee interjected, "General, you give the Mustang to the 4th, and we'll sweep the Luftwaffe from the sky."

Shaking his head, Auton answered, "Sorry, Don, but we can't spare the 4th while you transition into a new fighter. We need every available plane and pilot on every mission."

Leaning in to emphasize his point, Blakeslee pleaded with urgency, "General, you give the 4th the new Mustang, and we'll not miss any missions. I promise".

Brushing off the plea, Auton stared into the fire. "Well, that's an issue that has to be deferred until we get more data on the respective strengths and weaknesses of the two planes. Tomorrow is the fly-off at Debden. Who's flying what?"

Zemke responded first, "Our top ace, Gabreski, is flying the P-47, sir."

Blakeslee said, "We opened it up to every pilot in the group with a fly-off, sir, and an Enlisted Pilot Officer named Ralph Hofer won the honor. He's flying the P-51, even though he's only got about five hours in the plane."

Auton turned to face him directly, "Are you serious?"

Blakeslee was confused, "sir?"

"You're having a pilot with 5 hours in the Mustang compete with one of the most experienced, accomplished Thunderbolt pilots in Europe?"

"Yes, sir. It was a competition, and Hofer won by a vote of all the pilots of the group. He's already mastered the aircraft."

Auton sipped his bourbon while he digested the information. "Remember," he said, "this is a demonstration for Ike and the other brass. Stay low."

Zemke protested, "That's not fair, sir, the P-47 is heavy and less maneuverable at low level and low speeds."

"Or high altitude and high speed," snorted Blakeslee.

Auton shushed them like two quarreling schoolboys. "Stop it. Work it out. But remember, don't let anyone get too eager. This is a demonstration only. You both follow?"

Speaking simultaneously, Zemke and Blakeslee nodded in agreement, "Yes, sir."

Standing and walking to the bar, Auton changed the subject. "What's the status on the Football/Rugby game at Debden?"

Both Zemke and Blakeslee relaxed a little.

Blakeslee responded, "Well, General, we're hoping to put it together at the next *stand down*. The Brits have assembled a group from among the batmen, the anti-aircraft crews, the MP's, and other base personnel. The Group football team is comprised of both enlisted, and officers who volunteered, and then voted on the final 22 members after tryouts."

Zemke was listening with interest. This was the first he'd heard of the matter. "Is the team limited to members of the Fourth?" he asked.

Blakeslee wondered aloud, "I hadn't thought about it. It's just to settle an ongoing controversy between American and English base personnel about the relative merits of football and Rugby. I hadn't thought of it as any kind of organized competition."

"Lemme know how it goes," said Zemke. "It might be something I'd like to import to Halesworth".

Smiling, Blakeslee patted Zemke on the back, "Sure, buddy."

Auton piped up, "I want to see the game, Don. Lemme know when it's set."

"Of course, General. We'd be honored to have you attend."

"Well men, it's late, and you've got to put on a good show for the brass, so good evening."

There's an expectant pause. Neither Zemke nor Blakeslee move.

"Uh," the General continued, "dismissed."

Taking their cue, both men set their unfinished drinks down, shook hands, and exited into the early evening.

The next morning dawned mild, bright and clear, a blessing to all concerned. The sun was just beginning to make its appearance over the horizon. Sitting on the tarmac in front of the 334th Squadron hangar was a "Razorback" P-47B with the markings of the 56th Fighter Group, "Zemke's Wolfpack." Next to it was a "Birdcage" P-51B/C Mustang, in the livery of the 357th Fighter Squadron, since the 4th had nothing but Thunderbolts to fly.

Both were surrounded by ground personnel and were idling to warm up. It takes a few minutes for the big engines to warm to operating temperatures, so the ground crews had been working with them since before sun up.

Since the group wasn't flying on this day, everyone not on duty somewhere else was lined along the tarmac, and the runway. All were eager to see what the new Mustang could do, and equally curious about how Hofer would fare against one of the best fighter pilots in the ETO.

Francis Gabreski was an ace, headed for multiple ace status, and known for his skill at low altitude and low speed with the heavy P-47. Hofer is already known as a legend in his own time, a terrific pilot who won the right to fly the P-51 in a contest with every other pilot of the 4th. Not only his ability, but the prestige of the 4th was on the line.

Affectionately nicknamed "Juggernaut" from its massive size (the biggest and heaviest single engine fighter of World War II), shortened to "Jug" by admirers and detractors alike (whether "Jug" was short for Juggernaut, or milk jug depended on your point of view), The P-47 Thunderbolt was a massive engine of destruction. With a 40-foot wingspan, a fuselage 36 feet long, and a tail 7 feet tall when sitting on the apron, it was huge by fighter standards. It weighed 10,000 pounds empty, almost twice as much as the Spitfire and Mustang, and was three feet wider, and four feet longer than the Mustang

Based on the design of the P-35—which won the Bendix Trophy in 1937 with an average speed of 258 MPH between Burbank, CA, and Cleveland, OH—the Jug utilized the superb Pratt & Whitney R2800 "Double Wasp" radial engine (the same engine used in the B-26 Marauder, the Corsair, Hellcat, A-26 Invader and others) powering a massive prop just under 14 feet in diameter. The engine, first developed in 1937, was made up of twin rows of 9 cylinders, producing a displacement of 2800 cubic inches, and maximum takeoff thrust of just over 2000 horsepower, a power rating the engine maintained all the way up to 25,000 feet. It had a unique single-speed two-stage turbocharger mounted in the fuselage. And it had water injection for short bursts of added power in combat, giving the Jug a top speed of around 440 mph, compared to the top speeds of the Focke-Wolf 190 of 408, and the Messerschmidt 109 of 350 mph.

The engine was close to perfect from its inception. It was the first radial engine so good, a fighter plane was developed specifically to utilize it. From the greatest radial engine ever designed was born the Navy's iconic F-4U Corsair.

The strong point of the Jug was its rugged durability, and its truly awesome firepower. It was essentially a flying tank. With eight of the marvelous M2 Browning .50 caliber machine guns in the wings, carrying 3,400 rounds, the Jug could unleash a full 30 second burst of fire. It was also capable of carrying up to 3,000 lbs. of external ordinance, including bombs and rockets. When loaded with its maximum bomb load, it could carry about half what a B-17 could carry, and when it's external ordinance was limited to eight 4.5inch M8 rockets, it had firepower equal to a salvo from a battery of 105 mm Army field Howitzer artillery.

But the Achilles heel of the Thunderbolt was its range. Although its massive wing area could get the plane to 40,000 feet at a time when other fighters, and all bombers could barely achieve 35,000 feet, it had a range of around 800 miles, half that of the Mustang.

The issue of range, and the massive losses of bombers in daylight raids was the genesis of the marvelous Mustang. When the war started in 1939, both the British and the French were looking for a fighter to match the German 190, and the 109, generally considered at the time to be the best in the world. James H. "Dutch" Kindleberger, head of North American aviation, in a conversation with Sir Henry Self, Chairman of the British Purchasing Commission, represented that North American Aviation, (a holding company for various interests in such diverse aviation companies as TWA, Eastern Airlines, Curtiss Aviation, Sperry Gyroscope, Douglas Aircraft and Ford Instrument), could design a single-seat fighter around the same Allison engine used by the P-38 Lightning, and the P-40 Warhawk. It would, however, have superior performance through low-drag airframes, and advanced developments in weight reducing techniques.

Sir Henry was intrigued. On April 24, 1940, Kindleberger telegraphed his Bavarian engineer, Edgar Schmued, at the home factory in Englewood, California, to draw up a single-engine fighter design for presentation to the British. The plans and data were airmailed the next day to New York, where Kindleberger and Self were meeting. On May 29, 1940, the British ordered 320 of the new planes. North American had 120 days to produce a prototype, a combination of clock and calendar that was extraordinary but understandable under the circumstances.

The resulting design of the prototype P-51 was an inspired exercise in weight savings, and aerodynamic streamlining. The nose featured a close-fitting engine cowling and propeller cowl, with only a small opening for the carburetor air, a tiny fuselage cross-section that barely exceeded the width of the engine. And the aerodynamic problem of the radiator "brick" for the liquid-cooled engine was solved by placing the radiator far back in the lower fuselage, with coolant lines carrying hot glycol fluid back from the engine and pumping cooler glycol liquid forward.

Though it was an ingenious solution to the problem of streamlining the frontal mass of a radiator, the exposed radiator hanging beneath the fuselage was also the Achilles heel of the Mustang. Puncture the cooling system, in the radiator, the cooling lines, or the engine block, you were down in minutes with an overheated engine. An air-cooled engine, on the other hand, could keep running, albeit roughly, if part of the motor was damaged, (at least up to a point).

Although not part of the original proposal, the laminar flow wing was proving so promising it was incorporated into the final prototype. The laminar flow wing moved the "thick" part of the wing-chord back into the middle of the wing, which delayed leading edge turbulence, and improved the speed of the air flowing over the wings (and hence the speed of the plane). It also delayed the onset of leading edge turbulence, which resulted in improved stall characteristics. That is, it delayed the onset of stall, when the wing lost it's lift, and the plane would fall out of the sky.

On April 16, 1941, the first P-51 took to the air. The British named the new plane the "Mustang," but the Allison engine proved woefully inadequate for the high-altitude bomber escort job for which the plane was commissioned and designed. The Allison's power fell off rapidly above 12,000 feet, and was so poor at 25,000 feet, the usual operating altitude for bomber operations, the plane was deemed unsuitable for bomber escort. The English had the best description of the plane, "It's a bloody good aero plane, laddie; it just needs a bit more poke."

The "more poke" came in October 1942, in the form of the British Rolls-Royce Merlin, the engine that powered the Spitfire. The inspired mating of the Spitfire engine with a four-blade prop (as opposed to the three blade Allison arrangement) to the Mustang airframe, was first proposed by Rolls Royce test pilot Ronald Harker, and championed by Air Corps Major Tommy Hancock, the Assistant Air Attaché in London. This pairing produced the long-range escort fighter of a general's dreams. Top speed increased to around 440 mph, at an altitude of 25,000 feet, and its range was an astounding 1600 miles. It could climb to 20,000 feet in 6.3 minutes as opposed to 9.1 minutes for the Allison version. The ceiling of the Mustang exceeded 36,000 feet.

The P-51B/C only had four .50 caliber machine guns in the wings, and could carry only two 250 lbs. bombs, but that was beside the point. Accompanying the bombers, and fighting the German fighters was the goal, and it had been achieved, at least on paper.

Now, Hofer and Gabreski were going to see if reality met theory, and which plane was going to get the job of protecting the bombers over Berlin.

In the makeshift grandstand constructed for the occasion were all the brass hats and heavyweights of the Allied Command in Europe: Four Star General Dwight D. "Ike" Eisenhower, Commanding SHAEF, the Supreme Headquarters, Allied Expeditionary Force. Seated next to him was Lt. General Carl "Tooey" Spaatz, Commanding General, Strategic Air Forces, Europe.

Next, Major General Jimmy Doolittle, of Doolittle Raid fame, a holder of the Medal of Honor, and Commanding General of the Eighth Air Force. On the other side of Ike was Major General William Kepner, Commanding Officer of the Eighth Fighter Command, and Brigadier General Jesse Auton, commanding the 65th Fighter Wing. Behind Eisenhower, whispering in his ear was Air Vice Marshal Sir Arthur Tedder, RAF, Second in Command of SHAEF.

Sprinkled all around were various ranks and branches of every staff of every officer, and many visitors who were aware of the test flights, including members of the press invited to the occasion.

Standing unobtrusively to one side, trying to gain a vantage point without attracting any attention, was Virginia Irwin. It was her first day at Debden, and she hadn't officially even reported into her "command." Notebook in hand, and dressed in army fatigues, with her hair up under a fatigue cap, she barely registered as a female, except to those close enough to see her luminous blue eyes.

As she maneuvered around the crowd trying to find a good vantage point, she was surprised to encounter a lovely redheaded woman in the uniform of an American Lieutenant. The two ladies smiled at one another.

"Hello," said Virginia, sticking out her hand. "I'm Virginia Irwin."

The redhead smiled an equally luminous but Irish smile and returned the handshake warmly. "Kay Summersby. How are you?"

"Very well. Are you a correspondent?"

"No, I'm General Eisenhower's driver. You?"

"I'm a correspondent for the St. Louis Post-Dispatch. Do you get up here much?"

"No, only when General Eisenhower comes. He loves the 4th, and loves Debden, so he's always looking for an excuse. He's supposed to get to fire the guns on a P-51 today, so I think the opportunity to play with a fighter plane is more attractive than the fly-off, but I'm not sure."

The thought of General Eisenhower "playing" with the 50 caliber machine guns on a P-51 Fighter brought a mischievous smile to Kay's face.

Before moving away in the crowd, Kay smiled at Virginia. "You must call me when you get to London. I'm sure Colonel Blakeslee has the General's office number, and I can be reached through the switchboard. Maybe we could have lunch?"

Virginia nodded her head, "That would be lovely. I look forward to it."

Their attention turned towards the field as both Gabreski and Hofer exited the 334th hangar ready room. The contrast in their appearance was utterly striking. Gabreski was in a full flight suit, with combat boots polished to a brilliant shine, a fresh military haircut, and regulation USAAC gear all around.

Hofer, accompanied by his furry alter ego, Duke, wasn't. He was dressed in regular fatigue trousers and his ubiquitous number "78" jersey; and was wearing an RAF type "C" leather flying helmet, resembling something a football player would wear, with his mop of shaggy hair finding every opportunity to stick out from underneath it. "Sharp" and "sloppy" would only suggestively summarize the contrast.

Hofer motioned to Duke, who obediently turned to the jeep in the shadow of the tower and hopped into the front seat next to Scudday. Scudday and Duke had the best seats in the house.

The two pilots clambered into their respective aircraft, and settled in, while the ground crew helped secure their belts and harness. As the sunrise cleared the east horizon, a single flare rose from the observation deck of the tower. Time to go.

The planes began to taxi to the main east-west runway, both slowly weaving with an enlisted "guide" perched on the left wingtip, so that the pilots could see over the huge engines and long noses of the planes. In moments they were poised at the end of the runway, oriented west, away from the rising sun, and ready for takeoff. To the spectators in the grandstands their engines were barely a rumble in the distance as they idled at the end of the runway, awaiting the signal to takeoff.

Another single flare from the tower. The song of the powerful engines began to rise as they powered up, drawing everyone's attention. The contrasting engine sounds reminded more than one spectator of the basic differences in the planes. The engine of the P-47 put forth a throaty deep growl, like a truck. The engine of the P-51 was a sharp razor like sound of a race car.

As they accelerated down the runway, the two black dots in the distance grew into recognizable aircraft, both beautiful, powerful, and menacing in their approach to flight. The Mustang and the Thunderbolt accelerated together, according to the instructions of their respective commanding officers.

As soon as they rotated, left the ground, and raised their landing gear, the Mustang began to accelerate away, climbing at a steeper angle than the Thunderbolt. A not unexpected circumstance given the difference in their weight, even with equal fuel loads. The Mustang, empty was about 8400 lbs. The Thunderbolt weighed 9800 lbs.

The Mustang reefed port, making a hard-horizontal turn, obviously trying to get behind the Thunderbolt. But Gabreski saw the maneuver, pulled flaps, and quickly turned the Thunderbolt in the same direction, setting up a sharp turn to duck in behind the Mustang. But the Mustang was quicker, and the P-47 turn expands. Even with someone skilled in dancing on the rudders, and nursing the flaps and ailerons, the Mustang had a smaller turn radius.

Gabreski, a pilot as skilled as anyone in the air, slammed the throttle all the way forward into max military power with water injection, and pulled up, using the tremendous power of the P-47 to climb out before the Mustang could complete its turn. But the Mustang came around and dropped in behind the Thunderbolt.

Gabreski tried to evade, as they turned and circled, climbed, twisted, and dove above Debden, but the Mustang easily maintained its trail position, the chosen and preferred point of attack. The point of the demonstration was well made. The Thunderbolt was a draft horse, a flying tank compared to the nimble Mustang, which had the quickness and agility of the fabulous Spitfire. Murmurs and quiet conversation among the brass, and along the field, in the various groups of spectators, all attested to the unalterable fact: the Mustang was it. The P-51 was the best air combat superiority fighter the Allies have.

After a few minutes, the Thunderbolt flared, dropped flaps and gear, and came in for a landing. Instead of following in the landing, Hofer streaked above the Thunderbolt, his engine singing a high-pitched powerful song, gunning his Mustang in a low level high speed pass doing Victory rolls, and then pulling up sharply, and climbing out of sight at a breathtaking rate. The crowd was very appreciative of what they've observed, exchanging looks and discussing the results excitedly.

Gabreski taxied up to the hangar, cut his engine, and climbed out. Standing on the wing, he watched as Hofer did one more high-speed low-level pass, and then pulled up sharply, turning into the pattern, dropping flaps, and gear almost simultaneously, and lined up on the runway for a landing. Instead of dropping into his normal three-point touchdown, Hofer just couldn't resist a last opportunity for grandstanding, so he came in hot, made a perfect main gear, tail-high landing, and taxied high speed past the reviewing stand with his tail in the air. His tail did not drop until the airplane was almost stopped, a rather impressive feat of airmanship, to those who understood the dynamics of flight, and what the hot shot pilot from Missouri had done.

The brass remained somber and dignified, but this last bit of airman-ship, showmanship, and one-upmanship, designed to proclaim "Blakesleewaffe" as "fourth but first" was more than the gathering of 4th personnel could stand. They spontaneously erupted into cheering and catcalls, emphasizing what was apparent to nearly all who just witnessed the contest. Not only was the P-51 a superb plane, "Kidd" Hofer was a superb pilot.

In the jeep, Duke turned to Scudday, and gave him a look of smug satisfaction, and then broke into one of his patented big, goofy grins. Scudday laughed out loud, realizing the dog had just said, "I told you so."

As the crowd was disbursing at a leisurely pace, Virginia again encountered Kay Summersby.

"Oh, hello again," she said. What did you think of the demonstration?"

Kay turned to the unfamiliar voice, but when she saw it was Virginia, her face broke into a warm smile, obviously glad to see her again.

"Marvelous, just marvelous. I overheard the General talking with Air Marshal Tedder. He intends to pull out all the stops to get the Mustang into the theatre in as large a number as he can get. He was obviously very impressed."

Virginia looked appreciatively at Kay's uniform. "I don't know what branch of service you're in. Are you in the U.S. Army Air Corps?"

Smiling, Kay explained. "No, I'm a lieutenant in the British Motor Transport Corps."

Virginia was formulating another question, when Kay, looking over her shoulder, interrupted. "The General is motioning for me, I must go. Please do contact me if you get to London. I'd love to have lunch."

Virginia nodded, they shook hands and parted. Virginia wondered if the story of the highest ranking General in England and his driver would make good copy.

CHAPTER SIX

The next morning, Blakeslee was sitting pensively at his desk, staring at the paperwork, but not really seeing it.

A knock.

"Enter"

The door opened, and James Goodson stepped in, smiling, and reaching out to shake hands. Since it was just the two of them and they'd been flying together since the days of the Eagle Squadrons of the RAF, they shared an easy camaraderie, and didn't adhere to formalities when they were alone.

"What's up, Colonel?" asked Goody.

"Goody, the bombers are getting clobbered," answered Blakeslee. "They have to have escort all the way to target. The P-47 can't do it."

Settling into a soft chair, Goody took off his cap, and scratched his head. "What's the gen on the Mustang?"

Frowning slightly, Blakeslee sighed, "That ship can win the war. It's just what we need. But we can't get it. Zemke and the 56th are tearing up the sky with the Thunderbolt. Auton doesn't understand why we don't do as well. He thinks it would take us too long to transition, and he wants us up every day for every mission."

"Well, Colonel, we're used to the Spitfire, a thoroughbred, not the milk jug P-47," laughed Goody. "Anybody ought to be able to tell that the Mustang is a thoroughbred, too."

Blakeslee smiled ruefully, acknowledging the truth of that statement, and turned back to stare out the window.

After a respectful moment, Goody inquired, "Have you considered my request on Kidd?"

Turning back, Blakeslee grimaced a little, flavored with a rueful smile, "Speak of the devil. I'm thinking of booting him out of the Group. Zemke's pissed about getting embarrassed at the fly-off. Rumor has it we'll have a little party with the 56th at the Cracker's Club next time the Fourth shows up. Auton thinks I did it deliberately to show up the 56th. I specifically told Hofer to keep it military, and he deliberately defied me. I can't have that kind of disrespect in the group. Discipline saves lives."

Leaning forward, Goody said, "Don't, Colonel. Hofer's not defying you. He's like Duke. Throw him a stick, or let him smell the mess hall, and he just reacts. Hofer's the same way. Put him in a hot ship like the Mustang, and he can't help but play with it. Same thing when he sees a Hun. He's young, dumb, and full of cum. He'll learn. Discipline saves lives, sure, but not without good pilots. And the Kidd is not just a good pilot, he's one of the great ones."

Blakeslee nodded his head a bit, "But the 4th is a team. Hofer's a prima donna. A truly gifted fighter pilot, but nevertheless a prima donna. As crazy as he is, someday he won't come back."

Sitting back, and putting his hands behind his head, Goody looked up at the ceiling, contemplating the truth of that statement. He looked back at

Blakeslee. "Well, the war's changed from our Eagle days. We used to defend, now we attack."

A small smile played across Blakeslee's lips, "The Mustang's the ship for that. Give me three reasons to keep him." He sat back, waiting.

Goodson smiled, the Colonel was weakening. As he ticked off the reasons, he raised a finger for each.

"How about four? A fighter pilot is either the hunter or the hunted. If he's the hunted, he's in trouble. One; Hofer is a hunter. Two; he's a helluva pilot. Know anyone else that got a kill on their first mission? Look at the way he handled the Mustang at the fly-off with only about five hours in it. Three; he's good for morale. He's a great dancer, and funny as hell, and the other guys have warmed up to him after getting to know him. Everybody wants to go on pass with him. He's always in the middle of the fun, and the English ladies seem to take to him like bees to honey.

"And how can you not like a guy that Duke specifically picked out? Obviously, that dog is something special. So's Hofer. And anybody that pampers a dog the way Hofer does Duke is a good guy in my book. Four; I'd fly with him."

Protesting mildly, Blakeslee retorted, "But he's so wild."

Closing the deal, Goody cajoled, "C'mon Colonel, I can't believe the 4th doesn't have a place for a guy like Hofer. Can't you find a way to keep the Kidd with us?"

Capitulating, Blakeslee mused, "The 56th is clobbering us in victories. We need all the help we can get. They're close to 200, and we've got less than 50."

"Kidd's not just help, he's Jack the Ripper in a P-47," Goody said, smiling at the thought.

"I'm trying to get him a Mustang to do his ripping," the Colonel said, caving, "but meanwhile we all have to make do with the Jug."

A knock interrupted their conversation.

Blakeslee spoke up, "Enter."

Hofer stepped inside, nodded at Goody, and stood at attention for the Colonel. "You sent for me, sir?"

Blakeslee's expression was inscrutable as Hofer coolly waited.

"Mr. Hofer," the Colonel began, "we were just discussing your future. It appears you have single-handedly opened another front between the 4th and the 56th fighter groups."

Interjecting to relieve the tension, Goody spoke up, "Kidd, we've got a tough show tomorrow. We need you with us over Germany to protect the bombers."

Glancing at Blakeslee to insure it's okay to answer, Hofer responded, "I'm still in hack, I think?"

Blakeslee answered the question. "Want out?"

Shifting a little at the sliver of hope, Hofer looked back to the Colonel. "Yes, sir. How?"

Blakeslee was direct, "Be Goody's wingman."

Looking at Goody, then back to Blakeslee, Hofer asked, "Does that mean I can't chase a Hun when I see one?"

Goody answered, "It means you stick with me."

Hofer smiled, "What if I see a Hun and you don't?"

Scoffing at the absurdity of that question, Goody's response was concise, "Bullshit."

Standing up with a look of mild aggravation, Blakeslee put his hands on his hips, "Do you want to fight or not?"

Flashing his dazzling smile, and not wanting to ruin his opportunity, Hofer answered, "Oh, yes, sir, of course, sir."

Sitting back down and tossing his pencil on the stack of papers, Blakeslee gave Hofer the good news.

"Ok. You're in, Flynn. Ramrod tomorrow. We press at 0900. It's going to be a very tough show, Hofer. We're bombing the ball bearing plants at Schweinfurt, and Regensburg for the second time. We hit them in August but didn't get the job done. The 4th is at the tip of the spear."

OCTOBER 14, 1943
"BLACK THURSDAY"

All over England, men at various bomber bases were huddled in somber groups around various makeshift chapels and altars, saying prayers, receiving absolution, and preparing for the crucible of fire and death they were about to endure five miles in the sky. As the prayer services disbursed, bomber crews were ferried in jeeps, and on bomb carts to waiting bombers, which were already gassed up. The ground crews had been up virtually all night, cleaning and checking defensive armament, making sure all systems and circuits were in perfect working order. They were exhausted from cleaning and repairing machine guns, patching bullet holes, and previous battle damage, cleaning the planes, filling oxygen and petrol tanks, loading the 500 lb. bombs, and storing thousands of rounds of .50 cal machine gun ammunition in the ready racks for each gun.

The tested and proven B-17 Flying Fortress and the B-24 Liberators were marvelous instruments of destruction, the largest airplanes in the world. Each four-engine bomber carried a crew of 10 men: Pilot and

Co-Pilot, Navigator, Bombardier, all four of whom were officers, and 6 enlisted sergeants: the radio operator/gunner; the chief engineer/top turret gunner, two waist gunners, a ball turret gunner, and a tail gunner. The teamwork necessary for the machines to accomplish their mission of precision daylight bombing was remarkable, and the result of hundreds of hours of training, and practice.

The Pilot and Co-pilot, the senior officers on board (usually a Captain and a Lieutenant) were in charge of operating and flying the bomber. They started the engines, flew the directed course, and maintained formation for mutual protection. They take off and land the aircraft, in all kinds of weather, and regardless of damage. Not a job for the faint of heart, or easily excitable.

The Navigator would maintain the course and direction to and from the target, and keep the Pilot and Co-Pilot informed of their exact location. He was also cross-trained on other jobs, including turrets, guns, and radio.

The Bombardier's job was the point of the entire mission. Everyone else on the crew was designed to get the bombardier to the target and back, so he could accurately aim the bombs, and deliver the designated ordinance onto the target.

Bombs dropped from an airplane were essentially darts, and forward speed over the ground (as opposed to indicated air speed, which didn't necessarily coincide), altitude of the drop, the position of the target relative to the bomber, the rate of ordinance fall, wind drift, and curve of the drop all have to be calculated from 5 miles in the air so that the bombs will fall where needed and wanted. The top secret device that calculated all of that was the Norden bombsight, which was always in the exclusive care, custody and control of the Bombardier.

The Norden was a remarkably accurate sight in the hands of a skilled Bombardier. The sight, which was a marvel of technological achievement in its day, consisted of an electromechanical computer which received information fed into it by the Bombardier concerning altitude, drift, atmospheric conditions, ground speed, air speed, and data about the bomb load, since different ordinance had different "flight" characteristics.

The Bombardier, who was also cross trained as a gunner, was controlling the aircraft and directing its altitude, direction, and speed during the bomb run by slaving the Norden bombsight to the automatic pilot. During this 6-8-minute portion of the flight, the bomber had to fly a steady predictable course, the riskiest part of the flight because it allowed anti-aircraft guns to accurately forecast the point at which their projectiles and the blast from them, and the Bomber would coincide.

The radio operator was the man who made sure there was communication between the planes, ground/air control, other aircraft, and the crew. He also assisted in navigation by using homing beacons on various radio frequencies to known locations on the ground. He was also cross-trained as a gunner and had a gun to man during part of the flight.

The Chief Engineer/Top Turret Gunner's job was to know everything about every system, and to be able to assist, troubleshoot, and repair systems damaged in combat. He was the chief enlisted member of the crew responsible for the safety of everyone else.

The four main stations for the gunners were left and right waist, tail, and ball. Of the four, the ball turret position was by far the most technologically advanced, the most specialized, and also the most dangerous.

The ball turret gunner was specially picked because he had to be small enough, and agile enough to fit into the Sperry turret, where he would lay in a semi-reclined position with the breeches of the twin 50 caliber machine guns just inches away from his head.

The ball turret guns paralleled the fuselage during takeoff and landing. After reaching altitude the guns were rotated straight down, so the gunner's hatch was presented. The gunner climbed down into his little world, the hatch was shut, his controls were activated, and he brought the guns up to horizontal firing positions. From that time on, he was effectively isolated from the rest of the crew until the end of the mission.

Ball turret gunners always carried a .45 caliber pistol into the turret, to give them a way out if the turret was damaged, and they couldn't get out if the bomber was shot down, or the landing gear wouldn't deploy.

The tail gunner sat on a bicycle seat, and used handlebar-like devices to aim and fire his twin 50's. Because the closing speed of a fighter on the rear of a bomber allowed slower targets, both for the attacking fighter, and the defending gunner, tail gunners got a lot of action.

The waist gunners were firing single 50's. Their firing solutions were the most difficult to assess, and they spent many hours practicing on drones, and stationary targets. The sight picture of an attacking fighter, and the trajectory of the bullets fired at it is deceptive because of the relative motion of the target, and the firing platform, making hitting a fighter a cause for major celebration, as it almost called for defying the laws of physics.

Nicknamed the "Flying Fortress," not because of its defensive armament but because it was first flown in 1935, a time when two engine bombers were the norm, and in the days when the coastlines and harbors of the United States were protected by Forts like Sumpter, in South Carolina; Fort Morgan at Mobile, Alabama; and Fort Point in San Francisco, California. At the beginning of the war, it was America's best bomber.

Powered by four 1200hp turbo-charged radial engines, the framework and skeleton of the plane made it difficult to shoot down, but its thin skin of aluminum was no protection for the crew inside. When loaded with bombs, ammunition, oxygen tanks and fuel, it was an explosion looking for a place to happen.

A B-17G (the one with the chin turret) fully loaded with its 4,000lb bomb load, and the 5,700 rounds of .50 caliber ammunition used in her 13 machine guns, climbed at 900 feet per minute to her combat altitude of 25,000 feet. Here she cruised at 200mph (155 indicated because of the thin air), with a range of about 1500 miles, meaning she could travel 750 miles out and 750 miles back. This indicated air speed didn't always coincide with ground speed, as the direction of the wind at altitude would affect it. A bomber flying at 155 indicated air speed, with zero wind would cover the ground at 200 mph. If you had a 25-mph head wind, your ground speed was 175. If you had a 25-mph tailwind, your ground speed was 225. All of this had to be constantly monitored, calculated, and conveyed to the flight deck by the navigator. All the while dealing with subzero temperatures, flak, enemy fighter planes, and the gnawing fear of death which accompanied every minute aloft over the Continent.

The temperature at 25,000 feet could, and did, drop as low as 50 degrees below zero. B-17's were unheated. The crew wore steel helmets, heavy flak jackets, heavy woolen clothes, and had electrically heated flight suits, in an effort to survive.

The B-24, designed several years after the B-17, flew faster, farther, and longer with a 3-ton heavier bomb load, mainly due to the then innovative "Davis" wing, which was narrower, with a steeper wing chord, giving it a higher lift capacity. But it had a service ceiling of only 28,000 feet; 7,000 feet lower than a B-17, which had a wider, fatter wing that increased wing loading, so it was more exposed to flak.

One of the more interesting design features of the B-24 was the doors on the bomb bay. On the B-17, the bomb bay doors swung down into the slipstream, slowing the bomber, but more importantly, signaling to enemy fighters that the bomber was on its steady bomb run, and unable to take any evasive action. Enemy fighters would wait for the tell-tale sign of the open doors to attack. This problem was alleviated to a significant extent by the roller doors on the B-24, which slid up inside the fuselage. They didn't cause drag or signal when the plane was on its bomb run. A not insignificant development.

The B-24 Liberator also was easier to shoot down than a B-17, because of the flammability of the hydraulic fluid in the flight controls and continuing problems with leaks in the self-sealing fuel cells. The inside joke among fighter pilots in 1943 was that the best defense for a B-17 group was a nearby group of B-24's because the Germans would concentrate on the Liberator as the softer target and leave the Flying Fortresses alone.

Because of the combat performance perimeters and flight characteristic differences between the aircraft, they seldom flew in the same formations, but frequently were assigned to the same targets with different arrivals and bombing schedules.

The British had tried daylight bombing, but the losses were so high, they opted for night missions. When the Americans arrived, it was decided that the Americans could have the daylight missions, and alternately, the English would dominate the night. It was characterized by the brass as "round the clock bombing," designed to reduce the German war machine to rubble and inflict major psychological damage on civilian, workforce, and military morale.

8th Air Force Mission 115, on October 14, 1943, was the Army Air Corps Bomber Command's second visit to the German industry ball bearing plants of Schweinfurt, and Regensberg, following up on the disastrous raid of August 17, 1943. The theory was that destroying Schweinfurt, where 40% of the ball bearings of the Third Reich were produced, would reduce the Germans' capability of producing ball bearings. This would cripple the Wehrmacht by interfering with the production of all vehicles, as every vehicle in an industrial age army, from jeep to tank, to airplane, needs ball bearings.

But Schweinfurt was also one of the most savagely defended targets in Germany, because they knew its value as much as the Allies. It would be a titanic struggle. The first raid against the same target in August 1943, had produced over 20% casualties, wounded, missing, captured. So, morale was very low that foggy October morning. Every man on every bomber climbed into his combat position with his heart in his throat.

The engines of the bombers were turning over slowly, warming for the long dangerous mission ahead. Gradually, each bomber was manned, and ready. Planes with names and pinup nose art such as "Yankee Doodle," "Miss Behavin'," "Memphis Belle," "Nine O'

Nine," "Bit O' Lace," and "Gambler's Choice" prepared to assault one of the most heavily defended targets in Germany.

Every man knew the danger and had a taste like dirty copper in his mouth. Almost every man's breakfast sat in a pool of acid in his stomach. The sweat was not from heat but from fear. A bomber falling out of the sky from 25,000 feet takes a long time to impact the ground, giving every trapped crewman plenty of time to contemplate one's instant death in a fiery explosion. Also, every crewman had heard about what happens to a man hit by a bullet from a fighter plane. They use water hoses and small bags to clean up what's left. But they go. They can only hope in divine providence to come back.

Two hours later, the bombers were nearing their target. The 4th was one of the groups that had picked up the bomber stream as they neared the end of the fighter planes' range. The mission objective was farther on, but the 4th escorting P-47's must turn back shortly.

In his P-47, Colonel Blakeslee was rapidly and thoroughly scanning the sky above and ahead of the lead bombers. He keyed his mike.

"This is Horseback. Bandits twelve o'clock high. Keep an eye on' em, boys."

All through the squadron, pilots shifted their gaze up and out, leaning forward to flip on gun switches, and waited for the next order. Hofer realized his heartbeat was beating faster as he anticipated the coming combat. He glanced at Goody off his left wing.

Goody, going through the same procedures, glanced at Hofer, and gave him the thumbs up, since radio silence was dictated for everyone, except Blakeslee, the quarterback.

On the flight deck, in the lead B-17, a 92nd BG B-17, piloted by Captain James McLaughlin and co-piloted by Mission Commander Colonel Budd Peaslee, everyone who could see above and ahead eyed the black dots in the distance, circling like vultures. They nervously monitored their instruments continually. Flying in a "combat box," the bomber's crew hoped that the shape of their formation, the number of planes defending against attack, and the crisscrossing and interlocking fields of fire of the 10.50 caliber machine guns on each B-17, would combine to make a wall of lead that couldn't be penetrated by any German fighters who got past the escorting fighters. But those fighters were an important cog in the defensive wheel.

Seeking reassurance, McLaughlin called to Blakeslee, "Horseback, this is Pointblank One. Little Friend, this is Big Friend. You with us?"

Silence.

Then the response that chilled the hearts of every man on the bombers who heard it.

"Pointblank One, Horseback. Sorry, Big Friend, fuel bingo. Little Friend, return to base."

As the fighters broke off and began their slow turn back west, another transmission came from Blakeslee, "Good luck, and God speed."

In the static of the increasing distance came McLaughlin's answer.

"Luck ain't enough, Little Friend. Pray for us."

Aboard his P-47, Hofer muttered to himself as he turned off his gun switches. He looked back at the bombers and saw the distant black dots of the Luftwaffe forming up for an attack of the vulnerable Big Friends.

He cursed loudly into his mic, "SHIT!"

Noting the departure of the escort, the German fighters were forming up into lines abreast of 8 to 15 fighters and streaking down into the bomber formation from twelve o'clock high, guns winking as they headed directly at the nose and cockpit positions, knowing the difficulty of destroying a bomber, but the relative ease of killing a bombardier or a pilot. Aboard the bombers, the nose guns and top turrets started firing back. In a matter of seconds, the sky was full of tracers arcing back and forth. Every tracer signaled five rounds down range, as the usual sequence of ammunition was four founds of ball (solid) rounds, and 1 round of incendiary.

As the fighters found their marks, and incendiary bullets struck their target, fires and smoke billowed from wounded bombers. As the attacking fighters flashed through the formation, they were met with a hail of fire from the waist, ball turret, and tail guns of the bombers.

Aboard the stricken bombers, a steady barrage of bullets shattered glass, instruments, Plexiglas, and tore into human flesh, killing pilots, gunners, navigators, bombardiers. The smell of gunpower, the acrid, sweet smell of cordite, along with burning flesh, metal, kerosene, gas, and clothing punctuated the chaos of mortality gripping the formation in its icy clutches. Bombers started to fall out of formation, like leaves in the autumn breeze, their wings on fire, smoke trails marking their fall, tail sections shot away.

One bomber, its nose blown away to just forward of the upper turret, lazily maintained formation for fifteen seconds of so, before it began to slowly turn on its back, and head down to its fatal rendezvous with terra firma. Two parachutes were observed, but assuming all four of the crew in the nose were already dead, that only accounted for six, meaning four men were trapped inside for the long fall towards certain death.

Terrified airmen leaped from dying bombers, putting their life in the hands of parachutes and luck, fighting gravity and wreckage in an effort to escape the doomed planes before they impacted. Some made it, some didn't. The air was full of spent cartridges, lead bullets falling to earth after losing impetus, wreckage, bodies, pieces of bodies, debris of every imaginable size, shape and description. An airman with a flaming parachute began the slow fall to his death. A rain of destruction, debris, and death.

For three long hours the bombers fought their way to the target. Dropping their ordinance, they turned for home, aware that they will have to fight their way out. The Germans, almost directly over their own bases, landed, rearmed, and rejoined the battle, attacking the survivors on the way out.

Adding to the bomber's misery, the fighter planes intended to provide their return escort were grounded for bad weather, leaving the Fortresses and Liberators all alone in the skies above Germany fighting for their lives. England seemed an eternity away.

CHAPTER SEVEN

In the early English evening, with the setting sun behind him, Sgt. Scudday stood, with increasing frustration, on the apron in front of the 334th hangars supervising ground crews. His crews were trying to fit the squadron P-47's with paper under-wing auxiliary fuel tanks, and the tired, dirty, cursing ground crewmen were struggling. The tanks didn't fit. They would fall off and split open. Having been mass produced under wartime conditions, it was hard to tell if a tank would fit without actually trying to mount it on a fighter. If it didn't fit, the crewmen simply had to discard it and get another one. It was back-breaking, repetitive work, taxing everyone's patience, and causing rising tempers all around.

Blakeslee pulled up in a jeep and walked up to the Sgt., who gave him an exhausted salute.

"Good evening, Colonel. What's the report on Schweinfurt?"

With a genuinely pained expression, Blakeslee shook his head and gave him the news.

"A total fuck-up, Sergeant," he said. The Germans waited for the escort to turn back, and then attacked. They wiped out 40% of the bombers. 65 Bombers shot down, another dozen and a half so badly shot up, they'll never fly again. We lost over 600 men. Unescorted, deep penetration raids to the German interior have been suspended for the rest of the year. Those poor bastards were sitting ducks."

"They'll stay sitting ducks until you can stay with 'em to the target," Scudday said.

Changing the subject slightly, Blakeslee asked, "Help me out, Sgt. Tell me something good. How's it going with the new paper fuel tanks?"

"I wish I could, sir, but SNAFU is quickly becoming FUBAR."

Smiling sarcastically, Blakeslee delivers the bad news, "Well Sgt., bend over, here it comes again."

Giving Blakeslee a faux-pained look, Scudday responded, "Sir, with all due respect, the preferred response to FUBAR is not BOHICA. Now what?"

"Sorry, Sgt, but no rest for the weary. We have a rodeo in the morning. We press at 0900 hours. So, what's the gen on the fuel tanks?"

Shuffling his feet just a bit, Scudday smiled back. "Well, this entire situation is a total nightmare. This plane wasn't designed for under wing drop tanks. They won't feed right. They won't release right. They fall off. We're having to jury rig everything. It's a wonder no one's been killed."

"Yeah, I know. We really need the Mustang."

"Are we getting it?"

"Dunno. I'm going to the 357th next week to lead a mission in 'em. So, do what you can with this mess."

"Sir, it's just a matter of burning the midnight oil," Scudday gestured towards the ground crews. "We'll do our part."

Smiling, Blakeslee patted the sergeant on the shoulder, "I know that Sgt. Every pilot on the base owes his life to your men, and they know it."

Appreciatively, Scudday smiled back, "Thank you, sir, I'll pass that on to the men."

Shaking the Sergeant's hand, and turning to leave, Blakeslee asked a final question. "How many we got for tomorrow?"

Calling after the Colonel as he climbed into his jeep, Scudday gave him the final verdict. "All of em."

Yawning sleepily at the unholy hour of 0305, Hofer and Duke entered the Group Briefing Shack, already filled with pilots awaiting the morning's briefing. Right behind him was Colonel Blakeslee. Hofer jumped when Blakeslee spoke.

"Well, Hofer, glad you could join us. Sleep well?"

"Ah, sir, yes, sir, sorry I'm late sir." He quickly took a seat as Blakeslee strode up the aisle and assumed the center stage. After briefing them on the Rodeo (fighter sweep) to Emden, he let them in on the good news.

"Oh, yeah, new orders from Doolittle. You no longer have to stay with the bombers at all times. You may engage the enemy anywhere, and anyway you can find him. Just remember to protect the bombers, and don't leave them without any help at all."

Raising his hand, Goodson asked the question that was undoubtedly on the mind of every pilot in the room, "You mean we can attack them instead of waiting for them to attack?"

Blakeslee smiled, knowing what it meant to his men, "Absolutely. Find the Germans. Kill them. Anywhere. Everywhere. All the time."

Slapping Goody on the back, Gentile smiled, "Watch out strafing, Goody. Down on the deck, there's no room for error. Take a hit, you're clobbered."

Continuing with the good news, Blakeslee added, "Doolittle changed victory credits, too. Ground kill, air kill, it's all the same. Enemy aircraft destroyed is the goal. But remember to stay with your wingman, no matter what."

The pilots murmured loudly at this news. It means they were being encouraged to go down and get the Germans on the ground, and the carrot of victory credits was designed to lure them from the relative safety of high altitude to the extremely dangerous environment of being shot at going 400 miles an hour, 50 feet off the ground. A mission not for the faint of heart. The pilots began filing out of the briefing shack and loaded into jeeps headed to the revetments and flight line, where their fighters were already warmed up by the sleep deprived ground crews.

~~~

Cruising over the Continent at 22,000 feet, with the bombers below and slightly behind them, Goody and Hofer had a ringside seat for the German attack forming ahead of them. Maintaining radio silence, and signaling to his section of four fighters, Goody signaled "guns on, follow me," and accelerated up into the fight. The Germans, seeing the rising Thunderbolts, accepted the challenge, and headed down. Goody dropped his wing tanks, and the others followed suit. Hofer's concentration immediately focused on the oncoming swarm of black dots. Combat, at last. Kill or be killed.

In seconds, the ascending P-47's, and the descending Focke-Wolfe 190's had flashed past at a combined speed faster than the speed of sound, and the fight dissolved into a whirling chaos of planes chasing and being chased. Hofer, the wingman, stuck close as Goody dove away chasing four FW-190's. All six planes went screaming into a dive at high speed, the ground rushing up at them at 100 feet a second.

Hofer concentrates on the two fighters immediately in front of him.

Concentrating on his prey, Hofer lined up on the plane to the left and gave him a squirt. The rounds hit home, black smoke immediately poured out in a death rattle and the fighter began to roll, out of control, and probably piloted by a dead man.

Hofer quickly shifted to the fighter on the right, which was pulling up and out to the right and then down in the familiar German split "s" in an effort to evade. Hofer concentrated, ready to fire, and didn't see what happened next.

Simultaneously, Goody broke up and to the left, following his two targets who were attempting to do an Immelman, wherein they would pull up sharply, do a half loop, roll out at the top, and zip away in the opposite direction, towards home, and hopefully, safety. In a millisecond, he was gone, and Hofer's alone with the single target growing larger in his sights.

The ground continued to rush up, and Hofer fired a long burst, catching the fleeing Focke-Wolfe just as the pilot tried to pull up. The plane exploded, and Hofer pulled out of his dive, just inches above the trees. He pulled up about 300 feet and looked around for Goody.

The sky was silent, and empty. He couldn't even find the battle above him.

Hofer looked around frantically to see where he was and quickly scanned his instruments to get a bearing home. Suddenly, he heard gunfire behind. His plane staggered, shuddering under the impact of the bullets, rounds pinging off the armor plate behind his head, tracers flashing past. A round crashed through his canopy just a few inches above his head, shattering the Plexiglas and filling the cockpit with dust, and particles, which danced like diamonds in the sunlight.

Glancing over his right shoulder as he pulled up and out, Hofer jammed the throttle to the firewall, activating the water injection for maximum power, and spotted his tormentor. Behind him, wings and nose winking with fire, were two more Focke-Wolfe 190's.

The hunter had now become the hunted. Hofer was trapped near the ground, disoriented as to his location, alone, and at a distinct disadvantage in the lumbering P-47. His only chance was to evade enough hits to survive until the enemy ran out of ammunition. If any plane could survive hits, it was the Jug, built like an aerial tank.

Hofer began to evade. Violently jerking the control stick, skidding left, then right, hanging on the prop until on the edge of a stall, twisting and turning, pulling up, diving down perilously close to the trees and ground, sometimes even below the tree line when there's an opening in the forest. Tracer rounds flew past his plane, a few hitting, but the vast majority missing.

Hofer pulled up, flipped over, and pulled an inverted dive to just above the ground. The two Germans, unable to follow that crazy maneuver just above the ground, lost him for a second or two.

Hofer yells for help over the R/T, "Help, help, I'm being clobbered!"

20,000 feet above, Goody answered, "Where are you, Kidd?"

Looking around, Hofer spotted the only landmark that might help. "I'm down here, down here, right by the railroad track!"

By then, the FW-190's had spotted him again and were coming around to continue their attack.

Goody, remaining calm in the midst of the strife, tried to sooth Hofer a bit, "Calm down, buddy.

Railroad tracks run for miles. Tell us your position, and we'll come help. Does anybody see anything?"

From an accompanying P-47, Pierce McKennon responds, "Sorry, Cap'n, nothing."

Hofer continued to bob, weave, twist, skid, turn, climb, and dive frantically. Bullets began to shred his wings and pepper the armor plate. The Jug was losing the battle against the onslaught. Time was running out.

"I'm on the deck! By the railroad tracks! I'm damn near on the ground!" he yells.

Goody pleads for useful information, "Kidd, give me something I can find."

Hofer, resignation beginning to creep into his voice, said dejectedly, "Shit, I don't know where I am. Tell 'em I got two if I don't make it back."

In one desperate maneuver, Hofer pulled up, throttle maxed, and managed to pull a loop, getting behind one of the German fighters. He fired, getting strikes. Suddenly, his guns quit. Out of ammunition.

"Fuck, I'm out of ammo," he moaned into the R/T.

The damaged German, deciding to live for another day, broke off east, heading for home. He'd had enough of the crazy American who was probably going to kill himself anyway by crashing his plane into the ground with his insane maneuvers.

The remaining FW continued the assault, getting random hits as Hofer, by now becoming totally exhausted, continued to fight, amazing even himself with some of the stunts he was able to coax out of the lumbering Jug. He thought to himself that he needed to write a letter to someone complimenting them on the incredible toughness of the Thunderbolt, if he lived through this fight.

Hofer pitched up, rolled over, and suddenly, the shooting stopped. Hofer looked back over his left shoulder. The German was flying straight and level. He was out of ammunition, too. The two planes warily dance around each other in a Lufbery circle. Hofer saw the German grinning at him, smiling broadly, he saluted. Hofer returned the salute weakly, utterly amazed at the prospect of surviving. The German turned east. Hofer turned north west.

A short time later, in the early English winter evening, Hofer taxied up to the 334th apron, cut his engine, slid back his canopy, and sat droopily in the cockpit, in his sweat drenched flying gear, completely spent. He sat silently, shaking and breathing deeply, staring vacantly ahead. The initial adrenaline rush had been replaced by an overwhelming fatigue that was completely dominating every fiber of his being. Duke jumped on the wing, stuck his nose into the cockpit, and nudged Hofer, who hugged the great dog, and nosed him back. Hofer smiled weakly. Unconditional love is a great energizer.

Sgt. Scudday jumped on the wing, and seeing Kidd's exhausted state, wordlessly helped him unstrap, and struggle to his feet. Leaning heavily on the Sgt, Kidd stood on the leading edge of the wing, and peed onto the tarmac. He'd been in the air over 8 hours. As soon as he finished, Duke added to the puddle. No one was going to be top dog around this hangar but the Dukester.

CHAPTER EIGHT

A little later, after the debriefing, and a medicinal shot of whiskey, Hofer got a ride to the Officer's Club. The last to return from the mission and still in his flight suit, he entered, his faithful canine guardian beside him.

He walked slowly to the bar where Goody awaited him. At the piano, Pierce McKennon was noodling around, and perked up when he saw Hofer enter. He began to play "Tramp, Tramp, Tramp, the Boys are Marching" while he fiddled around with inventing new lyrics. He mumbled indistinctly, so that only those close around him could hear as he started and stopped, building a song. The men at the piano begin to giggle, and grin at whatever Pierce was singing.

"By you a drink, Kidd?" asked Goody, motioning to the bartender.

The bartender grabbed Kidd's personal mug, and Duke's personal bowl, and filled one with bitters, and the other with milk, and slid them across the bar. Hofer sat the bowl down for Duke, who again, was the epitome of pure canine class. Lying close to Hofer's feet, he sipped his milk periodically while listening to the music, protectively curled between Hofer and Goody. By now, everyone on base had gotten used to the idea that Duke's personal space was right next to Hofer, and then there's room for the rest of the world.

"Thanks, Goody. Cheers." They clinked steins and drained them. The bartender refilled them. Don Gentile slid up and ordered a pint. "Rough mission, today, huh, Kidd?"

Hofer looked down at his glass, still shaken by the close call, and the feeling of being brought back from the brink by divine providence.

"Yeah, Gentle," he said, "I thought I'd had it."

Goody chortled, "Well, buddy, clean living triumphs every time. I don't know how you lost me."

Hofer looked perplexed, "One second we're chasing six Huns, the next second two Huns are chasing me. I never saw you."

Gentile observed wryly, "Well, the Colonel was browned off. He thought you cut out on your own."

Hofer finished his drink and motioned to the barkeep, who refilled his glass. "Nope, but I got two. Four down, one to go."

Goody eyed Hofer, hoping to make a point. "Make sure you're not the one to go."

Glancing back, recovering his natural sense of unshakable confidence, Hofer smiled tightly, "Goody, the German pilot doesn't exist that can shoot me down."

Goody smiled back, "Well, you proved it today. Cheers."

Gentile broke in, "What's your plan, Kidd? Being a lone wolf might run up your score but being alone can get you killed."

"I repeat, the German pilot doesn't exist that can shoot me down. I'd take 'em all on if I could." He drained his second drink.

"This is a team sport, buddy," cautioned Gentile, "Wingmen are pretty handy when you're getting your ass shot off."

Warming to the thought of being invincible, Hofer smiled at Gentile, only half kidding. "Well, wingmen couldn't help today. I did it by myself."

Gentile, the most religious, faithful, and spiritually sensitive pilot in the group, put down his drink and looked intently at Hofer. "No, you didn't. Don't forget the grace of God."

"God helps those that help themselves," Hofer replied flippantly.

Gentile smiled, "God helps those that ask for help, and you were asking fervently, believe me."

Hofer was taken aback. Genuinely surprised. He shot a stricken look at his fellow fighter pilots. "Ya'll could hear that?"

Goody began chuckling, "Your mike stuck open several times. Between the cussing and the praying, it was pretty impressive, believe me. I think the entire group was completely entertained. Even learned a few new prayers and curses in the same sermon. You've really got a gift for eloquence, buddy."

Before Hofer could answer, McKennon, through with his songwriting efforts, increased the volume on the piano, and began to sing, in a beautiful Arkansas twang, like an Irish tenor from Little Rock. To the tune of "Tramp, Tramp, Tramp, the Boys Are Marching," he lit up the room with his voice, to the delight of all concerned. Unable to carry on a conversation, Hofer, Goody, and Gentile turn to listen.

"IT WAS DOWN UPON THE DECK,
I BECAME A NERVOUS WRECK,
AS I DODGED THE TREES JUST EAST
OF OLD BEAUVAI.

JERRY'S NEARLY DROVE ME
FRANTIC,

AND I SOON BEGAN TO PANIC,
EVERYONE ON CHANNEL C THEN
HEARD ME SAY,

HELP, HELP, HELP, I'M BEING
CLOBBERED DOWN HERE
BY THE RAILROAD TRACK,
TWO 190'S CHASED ME ROUND,
AND WE'RE DAMN NEAR
TO THE GROUND,
TELL THEM I GOT TWO
IF I DON'T MAKE IT BACK.

I WENT DOWN AS NUMBER TWO,
JUST TO SEE WHAT I COULD DO,
AND I SOON FOUND OUT THAT
I WAS ALL ALONE.

HOW I SHUDDERED AS I TURNED,
ALL MY AMMUNITION BURNED,
AND I CRIED OUT
IN A VERY ANGUISHED TONE

Gentile, Goody, and all the assembled pilots join in a lusty version of the chorus, lifting their mugs, and slapping each other on the back; including Hofer. He grinned back appreciatively, as McKennon caught his eye, as if to say *Ok, buddy?*

Hofer smiled back, raised his mug in approval and nodded his head, to the beat.

HELP, HELP, HELP, I'M BEING
CLOBBERED,
DOWN HERE BY THE
RAILROAD TRACK,
TWO 190'S CHASED ME ROUND,

AND WE'RE DAMN NEAR
TO THE GROUND,
TELL' EM I GOT TWO
IF I DON'T MAKE IT BACK."

After finishing the tune, McKennon segued into a boogie-woogie version of "Rock of Ages," and the party accelerated.

A voice came over the intercom:

*THERE WILL BE A SMALL CRAPS GAME
IN THE GAME ROOM.*

A dozen pilots headed out the door. Soon, as much as $1,500 dollars would be at stake on a single roll of the dice. After gambling your life at 30,000 feet, betting money on ivory squares was child's play. The party would continue deep into the night, as the next day, the group would be standing down, and there's a party the next night as well.

CHAPTER NINE

At Eighth Fighter Command, the winter weather was firmly in command on this day, wet snowflakes covered the ground with a heavy blanket. Driving up in a steady fall of snow, Don Blakeslee parked, climbed out, and quickly made his way to General Auton's office. The General had granted Blakeslee's request for a talk, off the record, just the two of them.

As he entered the office a huge crackling fire was waiting for him, along with a freshly poured double-shot of Kentucky bourbon offered by a batman who took his overcoat and hat. The batman then motioned towards the General, who rose and greeted Blakeslee warmly. Auton was a big fan of the 4th, and everyone knew it.

The General stretched out his hand across his desk, and simultaneously gestured to one of the chairs closest to the fire. Blakeslee shook the proffered hand, then sidled over to the chair. He sat down and waited to be addressed.

The General sat back down. "Don, good to see you. Any problems driving in this weather?"

"No, General," Blakeslee said, "not bad if you're careful."

"I haven't heard anything about the great Rugby/Football game. Is it still on?"

Smiling at the General's interest in their sporting nonsense, Blakeslee said, enthusiastically, "Yes, sir, we're mainly waiting for a break in the weather to correspond with a break in operations. We even managed to cobble together 22 football uniforms. Enough for starters on both sides, but we'll have to trade gear during the game, since each side only has 11 uniforms. We're trying to figure out how to accomplish it without embarrassing the ladies at the field."

"Well, I'm glad we have some time together. I presume you want to whine about the Mustang?" Auton grinned.

"Let me get straight to the matter, thank you, sir." Blakeslee appreciated that and smiled, though in a somewhat grim manner, acknowledging the General's crack about whining. "General, the P-51 is the ship. It's the best fighter in the sky. Give it to us, and we'll slaughter the Hun."

"Zemke is equally passionate about the P-47. They're tearing up the sky. Why can't you?" Auton challenged.

"General, a good pilot is like a good jockey. He has to have confidence in his mount. We flew the Spitfire with the RAF. We found it a very nimble, fast, maneuverable fighter. The P-47 is just like its nickname. A milk jug. My pilots are used to a thoroughbred, and they're being asked to fight with a draft horse."

"I will remind you that the nickname 'Jug' is short for 'Juggernaut,' not milk jug. Zemke thinks you're a bunch of overrated prima donnas, whining about your equipment as an excuse for mediocre pilots." Auton verbally thrust then watched for the parry.

Blakeslee turned beet red, but suppressing his anger, replied evenly. "General, Zemke and the Wolfpack are as fine a fighter group as you have, next to us, of course. But they use different tactics, and their *Bull of the Woods* approach is ideal for the Thunderbolt. We prefer a more rapier-like attack. The Mustang will give us the equipment we need to not just win but excel."

It was a good argument and the General knew it. He strolled to the window and, shaking his head in regret, stared out at the wet, heavy snow blanketing Blakeslee's car. He hated disappointing his men, but he had a bigger picture to consider.

He turned back, "Can't do it, Don. As of now, the Luftwaffe has control of the skies over Europe. We can't invade without air superiority. The bombers are being decimated. We need every fighter pilot in the theatre on every possible mission. I can't spare the 4th while you learn a new fighter."

"General, the Mustang is a different type, but it's not that different in handling than the Spitfire. It's a very fast, agile plane, but very predictable, and very stable. A forgiving airplane if you have a capable pilot at the controls. Every pilot in the 4th can handle a Mustang with virtually no down time. May I remind the General of the skill exhibited by Hofer at the flyoff? He won the right to fly the P-51, but every pilot in the group is capable of adapting very quickly. They can learn to fly the plane on the way to Berlin."

"I know you've been flying with the 357th," Auton could feel the Colonel's desperation, "is this your honest opinion based on actual operations? Or a sales pitch to the General?"

Blakeslee smiled, "It's not *just* a sales pitch. But it is a plea for the tool we need to do the job." His heart leaped in his chest, he could sense the General softening.

"Making no promises," Auton said, "assuming we had a group we wanted to supply next, how long would you need for training? Are you sure you can get operational quickly? With all the losses in Bomber Command, I believe it will be February before we try another major bombing raid."

"No sweat, General," Blakeslee was beaming inside. "Give us the Mustangs, and I guarantee we'll have them in combat in 24 hours."

Auton looked up, surprised, "24 hours? You are exaggerating for comic effect, I suppose?"

"I'm not known for my sense of humor, General. 24 hours. I guarantee it."

Blakeslee downed the demon at the bottom of his glass, hoping it would help him contain his excitement and stay warm for the drive back, and set the empty glass down.

"I have to hold you to it. That guarantee could cost you your command if you fail, Don. Doolittle and Tedder want pilots in combat. The Eagle Squadrons have to be in the fight. You understand, don't you?" He rose to end the conversation.

Nodding, Blakeslee retrieved his coat and hat and headed for the door. Turning, he addressed the General's concern.

"The 4th never fails, General. I never fail."

Silently he donned his coat, and hat, and saluted. With a serious look, the General released his salute and Blakeslee slipped out the door into the darkening evening for the drive back to Debden.

~~~

FEBRUARY 23, 1944

A quiet mid-morning. In the 334th Squadron Ready Room, Hofer was napping in his big over-sized, overstuffed chair. Duke was curled up beside him, half laying in his lap with his big head tucked under Hofer's chin. The weather outside was amazingly mild for February. It was a cold day, about 45°, but the sun was shining brightly, and the 4th was enjoying a rare stand-down. Everyone was relaxed, conversing casually about every conceivable subject, playing cards, reading, or catching up on correspondence.

There was a muffled roar in the distance, background noise, but it was growing louder quickly.

Suddenly, Sgt. Scudday burst through the door, bringing all the pilots in the ready room to alertness. This kind of interruption was rarely good news.

"Hey, guys," he said, excitedly, "wait till you see this!" Without waiting for a response, he ducked back outside.

A throng of curious pilots bolted for the door, half expecting another raid by the Luftwaffe. Hofer and Duke joined them. Though not unheard of, an air raid would be rare. Hofer was mentally planning his run for the trenches, knowing Duke would stay right with him.

But there were no bombers. Instead, streaking by, was the first of 48 brand new P-51B/C Mustangs, engines at full roar, 50 feet off the deck, followed by 47 more. They had already been painted with the Squadron Letters, "QP" "VF" or "WD". There was no question, these planes were meant for the 4th.

As the new fighters broke, dropped flaps and gear, and started landing one by one, the men of the 4th celebrated deliriously. At last, a thoroughbred mount for the jockeys of the 4th! No one gave much thought to the pressure now on the group to perform miracles. That would come soon enough.

In the midst of the celebration, Scudday heard a phone ringing and stepped back into the ready shack to answer it. Back outside a moment later, he yelled over the din at Hofer.

"Mr. Hofer, Colonel wants to see you, right now."

Hofer motioned to Duke and he and the dog piled into the jeep.

A little confused, he said only half out loud, mostly to Duke, "I could not possibly be in trouble about the Mustangs. We just got' em."

Then Sgt. Scudday drove off with a lurch at his usual breakneck pace.

Minutes later, Hofer was on the tail end of his weekly ass-chewing as the Colonel finally started to wind down after reeling off a litany of Hofer's crimes against military discipline, of which the Kidd, and Duke, were accused. Then, he threw Hofer a curve.

"Furthermore, Hofer," he said, "I've got the press on my ass. The St. Louis Post-Dispatch, your hometown newspaper, has sent some old biddy reporter over here to keep the folks back home entertained with dazzling tales of combat with the 4th. I think it's mainly because they asked about interviewing a Missouri fighter pilot, and your name came up."

This didn't bode well. Daring to reply, Hofer did some whining of his own. "Some old biddy? Why me? Millikan is from Missouri, too."

Blakeslee smiled diabolically, "She's from the biggest newspaper in Missouri. You're from Missouri. You're our junior pilot. Shit rolls downhill."

"Colonel..." Hofer began, but Blakeslee cut him off.

"Hofer, it's settled. You're it. Done. She's due sometime this week. I'll let you know."

He paused. Hofer didn't move. Blakeslee eyed him with a visual warning flashing in his steel grey eyes. "Dismissed, Mister." The meeting was conclusively over. Hofer waved one of his patented half-assed salutes and left.

He hotfooted over to the Officer's Club, Duke in tow, went straight to the bar and called for a beer. After giving Duke his customary bowl of milk, Hofer sat silently, working himself into a first-rate pity party, enhanced by a slow burn.

Goody showed up and joined him. "You know this afternoon is the big rugby/football game. You in? Then a big party tonight to celebrate the change over to the Mustang. You coming?"

Hofer nodded moodily, still pouting about the *assignment* he had inherited without really doing anything to deserve it.

"I just got handed a first-class shit-detail. I'm supposed to babysit some old biddy newspaper lady from Missouri."

"Who? When? Does that mean you can't play this afternoon?" Goody was genuinely concerned; he had big money on the game, and Hofer was the star quarterback.

"Oh, yeah, I'll be there, I think she doesn't arrive for a few days. I don't know anything about the lady, but I guess I'll find out soon enough."

CHAPTER TEN

Promptly at 2, everyone had gathered on the athletic field. A staff car pulled up, and out stepped General Auton, beaming at the thought of watching some good athletic competition. With him, surprisingly, was Hub Zemke.

Blakeslee, outfitted in his football duds, walked over and greeted them. Then, waving, he trotted onto the field, where Hofer and the others were already gathered.

The teams met at the 50-yard line, while all the onlookers sat and lounged around the edge of the field, good-naturedly poking fun at the other side, and making bets on the outcome. A truly rare and festive atmosphere. P-51's in the morning, football in the afternoon, and a celebration in the evening. Debden was truly party central.

Eleven men from each side were in American football uniforms, but the jerseys, helmets, pads, and shoes were an eclectic mix of mismatched colors, so the Americans had an American flag on their white helmets, and the British had the Union Jack on red helmets. It was the best anyone can do, under the circumstances, to create different looks. The two teams were introduced to each other, and the Referee explained the hybrid rules.

"Based on the coin flip from yesterday, the first 20 minutes is American football. The clock doesn't stop for anything. We play for 20 minutes, and keep score using the American system. Then we break for 20 minutes so the teams can change into rugby uniforms. Then 20 minutes of Rugby, English rules. The biggest margin in terms of scores, not points, is the winner. Of course, if the same team wins both halves, they win the game and the losers have Camp Mary duties for the next week. Agreed?"

Everyone nodded, and the players gave each other good natured jibes and catcalls as they lined up for the kickoff.

Even using soccer-style kicking, the English team delivered a long kick to start the game, causing a touchback. So, the Americans ran their first play from the 20-yard line.

Gathering in the huddle, Hofer called the play. "Sweep right, Gentle on three."

As the players lined up, the size of the American linemen versus their British defenders was striking. The American offensive line, to a man, seemed at least three inches taller, and 50lbs heavier than the defenders.

A standard "T" formation. Hofer called the signal. "Hut, hut, hut."

The offensive line surged forward and Blakeslee, playing right halfback, and Goody as fullback, joined Hofer in running interference for Gentile, who took the pitch as left halfback, and followed the blocking in "everybody right."

It was no contest.

The beefier Americans bulldozed through the slight, but agile British, knocking them down or out of the way. Don Gentile cruised in for a quick 80-yard touchdown.

When the play was over, two of the British men remained on the ground. Unable to continue, they limped from the field, and were replaced by reserves.

The Americans lined up, and used American style kicking, the ball sailing to only around the 15-yard line. The British back caught it and weaved back down the field, their lightning fast runner making it almost to the 50-yard line before being brought down from behind.

But that's all they got. The Americans rushed seven, and dropped back only four, and the British, not used to passing plays, were smothered for losses of 3, 9, and 4 yards. On every play, the British lost at least one man, limping, or prostrate, and unable to continue. The attrition caused by the brutality of the game, and the unfamiliarity with how to deflect or avoid a blow was punishing the British more than expected.

A punt.

The Americans caught it and made a nice return, winding up at the British 29. Hofer called the next play.

"Fake sweep right, reverse left. On one."

The Americans lined up. "Hut," the line moved right, as if doing the sweep again, and the British were effectively "faked," as Gentle swept past Duane Beeson, the right end, who had started right, and then reversed left, Gentile tucked the ball solidly into Bee's gut, who rushed around the left side for 29 yards and a touchdown.

The Americans kicked off again, but the British fumbled deep in their own territory and the Americans recovered, getting a first down on the 11-yard line.

Hofer decided to try a rush up the middle. "Fake hand-off to Goody, me up the middle on a quarterback draw. Everybody blocks. On one"

"Hut!"

The line surged forward, Hofer dropped back as if to pass, then followed as all three backs hit the same hole, knocking down every defender. Hofer raced up the middle for another touchdown.

21-0, and the 20 minutes were up.

Halftime went by quickly and when the time came for the second period, the British team captain walked over to the Referee.

Hofer and Blakeslee, as team captains, went out to join the conversation.

The British team captain saw them coming and waited for them. When they arrived he said, "Sorry mates, our lads are more than a bit used up. We don't have 15 healthy players to play Rugby. We've only got 8 men who can walk."

Turning to Blakeslee and Hofer, the referee asked, "What do you want to do? Declare a win, or forfeit, or what?"

The British captain, assuming the worst, and dreading telling his players that they were going to be stuck with "Camp Mary" duties for a week, prepared himself for the gloating American attitude the British had come to loathe.

Hofer smiled, looked around at his team, and then directly at Blakeslee, silently asking permission to speak.

Blakeslee looked at the team, all of whom were grinning broadly, and looked back at Hofer. With a nod, permission granted.

Hofer said, "It seems to me the only fair thing to do is suspend the game until we can find time to finish it. Wouldn't be fair to penalize a team until they've had a chance to show their stuff in their native game, now would it?"

The Brits, who had all moved closer to the conversation, look a bit surprised as the significance of what Hofer had just said sank in.

Their captain said, "It might take a while for us to find the right combination of weather, and free time, mate. You sure you want to do that?"

Hofer grinned broadly, winked at Blakeslee, who winked back, and they both stuck out their hands. Blakeslee sealed the deal.

"Sure, mate. We'll be seeing each other around the base, and we can always find time to finish the game if we really want to."

Now, the referee smiled, understanding what Blakeslee and Hofer were offering. Peace with honor.

"All right," he said, "then, game is suspended until you two tell me you're ready to resume. Right?"

The Brits and the Americans both grinned at each other across the field, and the referee, gestured for a more vocal agreement.

In unison they all replied, "Right!"

The two teams came together and shook hands, and then returned to their own sidelines to inform the spectators and the team members who weren't privy to the decision.

Everyone was satisfied with the choice, especially General Auton, understanding that the camaraderie between the two had been boosted maybe even more than if they had finished the contest. They were really becoming a team against the Luftwaffe.

Hofer hollered across the field, "Don't forget the party tonight!"

The Brits waved back in acknowledgment, both at the reminder of the party, and of the bond of brotherhood that was forming among all the personnel on the base. They were becoming a real team in every sense of the word.

Party days at Debden were already legendary. In the early afternoon, the landing pattern began to fill with myriad squadron hacks, and planes from all over the ETO. Thunderbolts, Lightnings, Tiger Moths, Mustangs, Marauders, Fortresses, Liberators, Lancasters and Typhoons, even a Navy PBY Catalina. Every livery of every member air force of the allied command filled every available space on the tarmac.

A festive atmosphere prevailed. Out of every plane jumped officers of various rank. They were picked up in jeeps, and ferried to the Officer's Mess, where the group swing band, the Flying Eagles were setting up. Enlisted men have their choice, the Red Cross Aero Club, the enlisted men's club, or the 334th Squadron Hanger, where the enlisted men's dance band was warming up for the crowd. The 4th Fighter Group was made up of around 1,500 men, and only a small percentage were pilots. But the effort, goal, and mission of every man on the base was synergetic—putting those few men on the tip of the spear over enemy territory in the 48 planes assigned to the group.

At the front gate, it was nothing short of a traffic jam. Once word got out via phone calls from beaus, and with the "Debden telegraph" rumor mill at full tilt, ladies from all over England were showing up, some invited, others just knowing where a rollicking good party could be found. Elegant ladies in private cars, girls and Wrens (WRNS; Women's Royal Navy Service) on bicycles, and other girls of all ages arrived in 6x6 trucks, IDs at the ready to sign in.

An older Red Cross chaperone, shouting to be heard, tried to hand out written copies of the rules. Girls absent-mindedly took them, but most were just stuffed into purses.

She shouted, "If you are an invited guest of an Officer, please queue here so you may be escorted to the Officer's Mess. If you are a guest of the Group, please board a truck for transportation to the hangar."

The girls queued up accordingly and were eventually shuttled to the correct party.

Officer's dates, for the most part, were *café society*. Enlisted dates were mostly Wrens, WASPs (Women Airforce Service Pilots), WAVES (Women Accepted for Volunteer Emergency Service), and other girls of the wartime workforce.

Virginia Irwin drove up to the main gate in a snazzy red MG. She stopped to present her credentials. Instead of the usual paperwork, Virginia presented a letter signed by General Eisenhower, courtesy of Virginia's new best friend, Kay Summersby. The letter made clear that Ms. Irwin was a highly regarded war correspondent, not only a Red Cross volunteer. As the Guard read the crisp letter, Virginia chuckled at the thought of the lunch she and Kay had had when Virginia revealed her plan to turn her volunteer position into a correspondent's job. But Kay had a better idea. She thought she would be able to get credentials from General Eisenhower that would circumvent and short cut the subterfuge and get Virginia off to a running start. And from the look on the face of the gate guard, Kay was right.

The guard at the Gate realized he was dealing with a genuine VIP and promptly waved her through, stopping her only long enough to give her careful directions to the reserved parking in front of the Officer's Mess. He was careful to give her a first-class military salute, and he cleared her for entry onto the base.

As Virginia entered Debden Airfield and rolled past the throng, she could hear the chaperon as she continued to shout, unmindful of the hubbub, and trying to ignore being ignored.

"No girls outside. No walks. No private talks. All guests must return here by 2300 hours for return transportation back to your stations by midnight. AIR RAID SHELTERS ARE STRICTLY OFF LIMITS!!!"

Virginia chuckled to herself and thought, *Well, if that's not taking the fun out of the fun...?* But she accepted the offered sheet and filed the instructions away and promptly forgot them as easily as the girls who had stuffed them in their purses.

When he strolled nonchalantly into the party an hour after it began, Hofer noticed the new girl immediately. She was handing out lemonade and donuts at the USO table. It seemed the crowd at the donut table was a little thicker than usual, and it appeared it had something to do with the new donut wrangler.

In the Officer's Mess, the Flying Eagles were playing "One O'clock Jump." Goodson, Hofer, Gentile, and the crowd were watching the dancers, and sipping their pints and shots.

From across the crowded room, an intrigued Hofer pointed her out and asked if anyone knew her. They all shook their heads...

"New girl..."

"No idea, never seen her."

"Isn't that your mother, Kidd?"

"Ask Duke, maybe he knows her."

The music ended. Hofer winked at his mates and, *mother?*, with no interest in lemonade or donuts, sauntered over to the USO table, Duke trailed along in his accustomed place at Hofer's right knee.

As Hofer arrived at the table, the band struck up what everyone recognized was an introduction to the hit, "In the Mood." Hofer wasted no time.

"Excuse me, Miss," he said, with a small bow, "If you have the time, I wonder if I could have this dance."

As she shrewdly sized up Hofer, Duke was doing the same to her, watching her carefully, as if deciding if she could be allowed into Duke's personal space. Setting down the offered glass of lemonade, she stepped from behind the table and joined Hofer on the dance floor.

She was dressed somewhat mannishly, in a loose Eisenhower jacket, and slacks, her hair pinned up like Rosie the Riveter, her figure mostly obscured. Duke took up a sentry position on the perimeter of the dance floor, watching over Hofer and this new lady.

They began to dance, starting out with the Lindy Hop, then they began to explore each other's skills, and found they both were superb dancers, capable of almost any combination of moves. In sync right off, their extraordinary talent was quickly noticed, and in a few seconds, the other dancers had stopped to watch, or moved away to give them more room. Shortly, they were essentially alone on the dance floor, with the rest of the crowd yelling encouragement, whistling and clapping along with the song.

Encouraged, they began to strut their stuff, testing each other with a subtle unspoken *can you top this?*. The Lindy Hop, the Carolina Shag, the East Coast Swing, Hand Dancing, Boogie Woogie, the Charleston, and Lindy Charleston, Big Apple, and the Little Apple. They were marvelous to watch, and the crowd's encouragement spurred them on from dance to dance. Around Debden, Kidd Hofer was a legend already, and now he had found a girl that could match him step for step.

Several bars later, and the song was building to its climactic horn solo conclusion, Hofer timed his move to the last brass note of the song, he dipped Virginia, who laughed, and playfully kissed him on the cheek; when he lifted her up she impulsively threw her arms around him, leaving them both laughing merrily. As he walked her back to the USO table, the crowd applauded and parted to make way for them. They bowed their thanks, basking in the reflected glory of their teamwork, and their new-found celebrity.

Gentile and Goody exchanged a glance. Another facet added to the legend of multi-talented Mr. Hofer, of which they were previously unaware. They clink their pints in tribute to their mate.

"Bravo, Kidd!"

Hofer looked over at them and gave a nod.

Back at the table, Virginia slipped into her role of USO girl, and offered Hofer a cup of lemonade. Politely taking it this time, he gave her what he thought was his most beguiling smile.

"Hey. I'm Ralph Hofer. My friends call me Kidd. You're quite a rug cutter for a girl."

He held out his hand for a friendly shake. But she was put off by the comment and took his hand reluctantly and coldly. He detected the ice in the handshake but misinterpreted it as decorum.

"Hey, yourself, Mr. Hofer. You've obviously cut a few rugs in your few years." Her reply was sort of formal. She was already regretting the impulsive kiss.

"You're new." Hofer observed, as if it were a revelation, or a character trait.

Raising her eyebrows, she responded, even more icily, "So?"

He was starting to feel the chill and realized she had chosen to not give her name. Maybe this was salvageable. In a more conciliatory tone, he said, "I make new girls feel at home."

Crap! He knew that was wrong before it left his lips.

If possible, her iciness increased. "Then go find yourself a girl," Virginia was glaring at him now, not happy about being referred to as a "*girl.*"

Beating a verbal retreat, Hofer changed the subject. Trying to gloss over his faux pas, he said, "How long have you been here?"

She had enjoyed the dancing but was disappointed in the banter, so she welcomed the change. Continuing to smile at others and hand out lemonade as they dropped by, she said, "Just arrived a few days ago. This is my first dance at Debden."

Hofer, trying to mind his Ps and Qs, inquired politely, "Is Debden your permanent assignment?"

Squinting at Hofer and weighing whether it was any of his business, she hesitated a moment, but finally decided on something non-committal. "Don't know. First day on the job."

Continuing his impulsively devised strategy of carefully and clearly saying exactly the wrong thing, Hofer said, "Well, handing out lemonade and donuts doesn't take a lot of training."

This comment stopped her in her tracks. Her casually cool manner instantly escalated into genuine ice, as she fixed her big brown eyes on him in a stare worth of Johnny Godfrey. She bristled at the suggestion that she was only capable of menial assignments; the look reminded Hofer eerily of Colonel Blakeslee. Now, her dander up and on the edge of genuine aggression, she said stiffly, "I'm not here just to hand out donuts and lemonade. I'm going to be a war correspondent."

Confused, a still a little dense, Hofer asked, "Going to be?"

She looked at him like she was wondering which local village was missing their idiot and, condescendingly, offered an explanation. "Donuts just got me over here. I'm a writer for the St. Louis Post-Dispatch."

As the implication of what she had just said slowly sank in, Ralph's complexion had turned slightly pale, and his demeanor quickly went from over-confident to overwhelmed.

She noticed the change but didn't have time to react to it as she was about to offer another officer a donut and lemonade.

"Oh, no." He looked at her a moment, said, "Nice meeting you," and beat a hasty retreat. Duke, with a satisfied saunter, followed closely.

Virginia, the donut and coffee in mid-transfer, was so surprised she spilled the drink on the man and dropped the donut. She could not recall being treated so rudely by anyone she had barely met. For a brief moment she thought about reporting that rude young man, *what was his name, "Hofer?"* to General Eisenhower himself.

CHAPTER ELEVEN

The next day was another weather induced stand-down at the 334th, the morning's mission having been scrubbed because of dense fog over the Continent. Hofer was dozing in the 334th Hanger Ready Room, in his favorite ratty overstuffed chair, with one hand resting lightly on Duke, who was dozing comfortably as close to Hofer as he could get.

The peaceful scene was disrupted by Scudday bursting in, as he seemed apt to do every so often; as usual, very excited, on a mission, and oblivious to his disruption.

"Mr. Hofer, Colonel wants to see you, *right now!*"

Peering at Scudday, still a bit sleep-addled, Hofer said, "Whatever it is, I'm innocent."

He looked down at Duke, who had raised up, with his feet on the arms of the chair, so he could get either his chest, his muzzle, or his head rubbed, as was Hofer's prime duty upon awakening. Hofer smiled at the big goofy grin on the dog's face, silently wondering who was training who in the relationship. He grabbed the dog's muzzle and peered into his eyes in mock seriousness, scolding gently, "Did you raid the mess hall again, Mister?"

Duke grinned more broadly, as if glad to share his guilty secret. Hofer lazily pushed himself out of the chair.

Minutes later, after the usual crazy ride in Scudday's jeep, Hofer was gathering himself at the office door of Colonel Don Blakeslee. He gulped, looked at Duke for encouragement, and knocked.

Duke, by now used to the routine, simply laid down in his preferred position, facing the door, but maintaining his ability to keep an eye on the hallway at the same time. Nobody was getting to Hofer without going through Duke.

A muffled response came from inside, "Enter."

Hofer stepped in. The Colonel was at his desk. At a glance, Hofer judged Blakeslee's level of *Colonelness* at about "medium." That is, his brow was furrowed, so he had something on his mind, but his ears were not glowing red with anger, so it did not have the earmarks of a major ass-chewing.

Then he noticed they were not alone. Also in the room, seated with her back to Hofer, was a lady. She was wearing a somewhat mannish hat, dressed in a pants suit of some sort. Hofer tossed off his patented half-assed salute and advanced enough to get a peek at the stranger out of the corner of his eye.

Oh, shit, he thought.

He steeled himself and took a more casual posture. "Hey," he said in recognition of his dance partner from the party.

She stared icily ahead, and barely glanced at Hofer as he stood there awkwardly. She responded coolly, "Hey."

Blakeslee, feeling the chill, and wanting to get to something he considered more important, like the war, asked impatiently, "Do you already know each other?"

Stammering, Hofer tried to come up with a way to explain his attempted pickup that resulted in an embarrassing public flame out, coupled with the ignominious retreat upon realizing who she was.

"No, sir. I mean, yes sir. I mean, we've not been formally introduced. That is, yes sir. Well, sort of, sir."

Blakeslee just stared. He briefly considered reassigning this duty to some other poor sap, and maybe suggesting Hofer visit the clinic for a combat fatigue evaluation. But, brushing off the thought, because of the delicious irony of the lady's need for the escort, and Hofer's obvious discomfort over it, Blakeslee continued.

"Calm down, Sergeant Pilot. I told Ms. Irwin this morning that you were to be her escort on the base. She thinks that's a bad idea. She tells me you were rude to her last night. Were you?"

Hofer spat out another string of contradictory, confusing replies as he tried to match his answer to the expressions on Blakeslee's face.

"No, sir. Well, maybe, sir. Not on purpose, sir."

He looked down and asked, "Was I that rude, Miss...?"

She looked up at him coldly. "Virginia Irwin. And, yes."

Blakeslee gave him a dark look that was clearly designed to suggest he, Hofer, *shut the fuck up, you asshole, you're only making it worse.*

Tapping a pencil in agitation he asked Hofer, "What do you think I should do?"

Hofer, caught off guard at having been given an option instead of just another ass-chewing, hesitated for a moment. Reading the situation, it seemed like he may have a chance to make a better second impression and get himself out of Dutch.

He pulled himself up, took a breath and said, "Ah, give me a chance to make it up to her?"

He glanced at Virginia expectantly. She had been busily filing her fingernails, tapping her foot, and generally enjoying his discomfiture. But it was starting to become painful even to her, she was starting to feel a little sorry for him. But she wasn't ready to let him off the hook just yet.

Blakeslee had been enjoying Hofer's situation as well, but now, he was tiring of the wasted time, and just seeking a resolution that would get these people out of his office. But he had seen General Eisenhower's letter, too, so it was a matter of some political delicacy to handle it with firm charm.

"Brilliant," he said. "Miss Irwin?"

Toying now, her answer was non-committal; studying her fingernails, she said, "I don't knooow..."

Blakeslee shifted uncomfortably in dismay. He could feel his impatience and irritation beginning to rise. His tone hardened a bit, enough that it made Virginia look up, suddenly aware of where she was, in the office of a military leader, and she was playing the insulted schoolgirl.

"Miss Irwin, I'm going to ask this once, then we're going to move on to a different solution. What would it take for you to approve of Mr. Hofer as your official escort?"

It sounded like a question, but Virginia, looking into the steely eyes of the Colonel, realized she had pushed her position to its limit. She correctly deduced that trying to pit Colonel Blakeslee against her favored status with General Eisenhower would result in losing the advantages she was accumulating with her new-found friend, Kay Summersby. It wasn't worth losing the opportunity to consolidate her gains at Debden.

A little more timidly, she decided to make it easy, "Well, sir, an apology might be nice."

There was a moment of silence.

Blakeslee looked at Hofer, "What are you waiting for, Pilot, an gilded invitation?"

Hofer, shaken into action, turned to Ms. Irwin, and assumed his most gentlemanly posture. Smugly, she looked up to accept his apology.

Looking in her eyes, his contriteness suddenly became genuine.

"Miss Irwin," he said, "I very much apologize if I was rude last night. It was unintentional. Could I escort you at Debden?"

Emboldened, she added, "And a tour of the base?"

Hofer smiled and nodded. Suddenly warming to the thought of spending time with the lithe and lovely Missouri reporter, and adding more frosting to the cake, and continued, "And a tour of London, too, Okay?"

Hofer glanced at Blakeslee, who sighed and nodded.

"It would be my honor, Ms. Irwin," Hofer said.

Standing, Virginia looked at the Colonel, who was visibly glad this was over.

"Thank you, Colonel. Thank you, Mr. Hofer." She said.

As they turned to leave, Blakeslee stopped them to make sure that there was no doubt about his expectations.

"Hofer, your request for a second chance with Ms. Irwin is approved," he said, adding, "VIP status for her. Get her a base ID. Make sure I don't need to be involved over this assignment again. You follow?"

Hofer nodded, "Sir."

Blakeslee turned to Ms. Irwin, his tone a bit more diplomatic, but the message was clear, *end of leash reached.*

"Miss Irwin," he put a cap on the issue, "I want to thank you for accepting Mr. Hofer's apology. He's a good man, even if he is a bit rough around the social edges. I trust you realize he has my full support for whatever you need while at Debden, so we might not have opportunity to visit again. I hope you enjoy your stay."

Hofer opened the door for Virginia who winked conspiratorially at him as she passed into the hallway.

He closed the door behind them, glad to be out of the inquisition chamber, but suddenly very curious to know more about this mysterious woman, and the meaning of that wink.

Outside, in the hall, Duke raised his head as they came out of Blakeslee's office and looked quizzically at Virginia. Had anyone paid close attention, they would have seen that the dog recognized the lady from the dance and was curious as to her place in his world. Signaling the dog to heel, Hofer gave his usual terse command. "Hey."

Duke got up and trotted alongside, taking a position between them, looking first at one and then the other.

Waiting until they were well out of earshot of the Colonel's office, Hofer whined, "Okay, how was I supposed to know that 'big time reporter' and 'donut girl' are one and the same?"

"If this is going to work at all, you have to stop calling me *girl*, Mr. Hofer."

"Sorry, Madam Lady Reporter. What do you want me to call you?"

Before she could answer, they had arrived at the jeep. Sgt. Scudday was lounging and waiting for Hofer's report on the latest ass-chewing. The reports of Hofer's adventures before the Colonel were some of the best entertainment on the base.

As Hofer approached the jeep with a tall, strikingly beautiful woman, with dark brunette hair, and luminous blue eyes, Scudday did a double-take worthy of the Three Stooges. He awkwardly hopped out of the jeep and assumed something resembling "attention," but which anyone else would have called *Scudday staring at Virginia Irwin.*

Hofer couldn't help but chuckle at Sgt. Scudday's sudden, sloppy and entirely unbelievable, military bearing.

He introduced them, "Technical Sergeant Jim Scudday, meet Miss Virginia Irwin, consummate dance partner, and War Correspondent for the St. Louis Post Dispatch."

Virginia gave Hofer an appreciative look and offered her hand to Scudday, who tried clumsily to doff his cover and offer a handshake simultaneously. He stammered a response, "Ma'am." And under the circumstances, he was lucky to get that right.

Laughing, she attempted to make him feel more at ease, and the effect was immediate, "Call me Ginny, Sergeant. Ma'am is your momma."

Turning her luminous blue eyes and bewitching smile on Hofer, she said, "That goes for you, too, Mr. Hofer." And as she held his gaze, that was the lightning bolt that pierced his heart.

Instantly, Hofer was smitten and smiling as goofily as Duke ever could. He motioned for Duke to stand up. The great dog stood on his hind legs and placed his front paws on Hofer's chest, almost looking him in the eye. His tail wagged furiously at the attention.

"Ginny," he said, using the offered informal name for the first time, "meet Duke, the Wonder Dog."

Virginia walked close to Hofer to pet Duke. For the first time since dancing, Hofer was close enough to smell the fresh scent of her light perfume, her soft rich brown hair, and the sweet aroma of her breath. His heart rate suddenly picked up as she reached out to Duke.

Duke looked back at her, sensing Hofer's approval, and as she rubbed his head and ears with both hands they became instant bosom buddies. Hofer felt a small pang of jealousy. He never thought Duke would be anyone's dog but his.

Grinning, he bragged on Duke with his favorite compliment, "Duke's the kind of dog that if he was a person he would read good books, and drink fine wine. Any friend of Duke's is a friend of mine."

The moment passed and they all climbed in the jeep, Hofer and Duke in the back, and Ms. Irwin assisted into the front passenger seat by the suddenly chivalrous Scudday. Hofer pointed towards the Officer's Mess, and noted that for once, Scudday's driving habits were almost human, and humane. He smiled inwardly at the way Virginia's presence seemed to sooth the savage breast, and the impulses of virtually everyone she met.

"Sergeant, we'll get her a base ID later, let's start with the scoreboard."

CHAPTER TWELVE

Standing in the Officer's Mess foyer, Hofer, Virginia and Duke looked at the Group Scoreboard. The date was written in the upper left corner: February 24, 1944. In the upper right-hand corner was scrawled: "US 89 - THEM 203."

Virginia, studying the list, asked, "What is this?"

Hofer said, "The gen. The scoreboard. This shows who's doing what to the Jerries. That's *our total*," he said, pointing at his group's tally, "and that's the total of Zemke's Wolfpack."

THE COLONEL	7
ANDERSON	4
BEESON	12
CARPENTER	6
CLARK	4
FIEDLER	3
GENTILE	12
GLOVER	2
GODFREY	4
GOODSON	8
HOFER	4
HIVELY	4
MCKENNON	3
MEGURA	4

MILLIKAN	3
MONTGOMERY	3
NORLEY	3
SCHLEGAL	3

And the list continued with various singles. Virginia, being a journalist, still had questions, "What's a gen? What's an e/a? What's a Zemke?"

"Gen is General Information; the scoop if you will. E/A is Enemy aircraft. Colonel Hub Zemke is the CO of the 56th Fighter Group. They're based about 30 miles from here, and they're our biggest rival in the ace race. Colonel Zemke is the only Fighter jock in the ETO that's in the same league with Colonel Blakeslee."

"Why do you care what they're doing?"

Hofer grinned, "Out motto is 'Fourth but First.' The Wolfpack is full of top notch pilots and aces. They like to win. So do we. The race can get pretty intense. Discussions sometimes spill over into the bars in London."

Virginia turned.

"Who are Beeson and Gentile? They seem to be way ahead of everyone else."

"Yep, 'Bee' and 'Gentle', they're tied in the race to break Rickenbacker's WWI record. Reporters and photographers meet them after every mission to scoop each other on what's happening. It's a big story."

"What's the record?"

"Rickenbacker got 26. First man to 27 is America's new Ace of Aces."

"Who is Mr. Goodson?"

"Ah, that's 'Goody'. He's from Canada, flew with the Eagles. A terrific pilot. Next to Duke, he's my best friend. I'm his wingman."

"The Eagles?"

"Americans in the RAF." Hofer gestured at his own uniform as he explained. "We got in the war before everyone else. Left side, U.S. Army Air Corps. Right side, RAF. I was in the Royal Canadian Air Force."

"Can I meet any of them?"

"Sure, you'll meet 'em all. Colonel's ordered the red carpet out for you. You're not just getting press credentials, you're getting a base ID. That allows you access all the time, and you don't have to go through the P.R. guys. I'm sure Major Hall will love that."

"Are you on the list? Oh, yes, there you are. Are you an Ace?"

Hofer grimaced, "Not yet. You need five. But it won't be long."

"Why five? Why not three, or six, or 10?"

"That's a very good question. The Germans require 10 to be an ace. But the English established five in the Great War, and we adopted that standard, too. Why they decided on five, I don't know, but every pilot is shooting for Ace status, and very few make it."

Hofer paused, reflecting, and then changed the subject as they turned to return to the jeep where Scudday was waiting. He helped her into the front seat and he and Duke hopped in the back, Duke putting his left front paw protectively on Hofer's right leg.

"So," he asked Virginia, "what's the plan? What's your angle?"

"The people back home want to know what it's like for the fliers over here. There's lots of press coverage for the bombers, a bit less for the fighter groups. So, I want to report specifically on the 4th Fighter Group. Flying and fighting with the 4th. What you guys do on duty, off duty, visiting London. Whatever you guys like to do, I'll tell the folks back home all about it."

Glancing at his watch, Hofer offered a plan, "It's dinner time. Sgt. Scudday will take you to get your base ID, and we can meet in the Officer's Mess in about 20 minutes. After we eat, we'll have time to get to Audley End, and chuff down to London on the 1320 train. Sound okay?"

Virginia beamed at the English slang, "Perfect. I've yet to 'do' London."

Hofer walked around to Scudday and spoke in a low tone, giving instructions. Scudday shook his head and then did a double-take. Smiling and nodding at the unusual addendum to the directive to get her base ID, he slipped the jeep into gear, and drove off at an uncharacteristically sedate pace.

Hofer smiled at Duke, who smiled back, and they sauntered off to the Officer's Mess to await the arrival of their charge. To Hofer, the prospect of "babysitting" the inimitable Miss Irwin, was turning out to not be the "shit detail" he had originally expected. He could tell that Duke was okay with it as well, and that Miss Irwin had already become a member of the inner circle of persons under Duke's protection.

Later, as Scudday was dropping them off at the train station, he slipped a small envelope to Hofer, who put it in his shirt pocket. Waiting for a moment when Virginia was distracted, Hofer opened it and confirmed the desired contents, then slipped it back in his pocket.

Audley End Station was crowded and Scudday couldn't get them very close, so they would have to stroll through the crowd. Standing on the station platform, waiting for the train, Hofer noticed that Duke had started taking up a station not just beside him, but between him and Virginia, so that no one could get to either of them without going past, over or through the dog, giving them a slim chance at best. He smiled to himself at the unspoken declaration that Virginia now belonged to Duke too. They had become as bonded at the Three Musketeers in a matter of hours.

Once the train arrived and came to a stop they climbed aboard and found seats, with Duke lounging in the aisle.

The train was full of servicemen, officers, and civilians from Debden and Audley End, most of whom were aware of Hofer's status as the leading enlisted fighter pilot in the ETO, and most of whom also had heard of the dog, who was a minor celebrity everywhere he went, which was everywhere Hofer went, night or day, pass or no.

Less than an hour later they arrived at Liverpool Station, London. They disembarked, and Hofer hailed a taxi. When one came to a stop for them, Duke rose up and stuck his muzzle up to the cab driver's window to "inspect" him. The driver didn't recoil or scream, but laughed in a friendly manner, thereby passing Duke's test. So, they got in the back seat and Duke stuck his head out the window, eagerly anticipating the ride.

"Where to, Mate?" asked the cab driver.

"Camden Town, please, Regent's Canal. The short route," replied Hofer.

They arrived at the canal a short while later, and Hofer, Virginia and Duke walked around enjoying the ambiance of the centuries old stores, and markets. Virginia was always on the inside of the walk, Hofer on the outside next to the road, and Duke on point, patrolling and clearing the way. Everyone approaching noted that the dog, who seemed to be guarding the couple, himself required a bit of distance and respect.

All kinds of artisans had wares on display in small stalls and shops, from leather merchants, to street wear vintage clothing from before the war and the limitations of wartime quotas, to pubs that had been serving brew since the time of Charlemagne.

Hofer was the consummate host, showing Virginia the sights and places of interest, historical and modern, of one of London's oldest boroughs.

Wandering along Regent's Canal, they strolled slowly, immersed in the views, with Duke barely resisting the temptation to chase birds and explore the park without his human companions. But he remained on duty.

Walking up a horse path towards Islington Tunnel, Hofer explained how the horses walked across Islington Hill while the boats traversed the canal in the tunnel. As he spoke, Virginia gradually became aware of his overall familiarity with the area and was impressed by his knowledge of the history of this vital part of London's transportation and barge industry.

After walking the path up to the entrance to Islington Tunnel, Hofer suggested they stop at a pub for a breather. Virginia readily agreed.

He steered her into the "World's End" at 174 Camden High Street. They found a table on the mezzanine balcony overlooking the street and settled in to watch the afternoon and evening strollers and shoppers.

Duke was relaxed, but vigilant. He placed himself between Hofer and the door so that no one could approach without being casually staked-out by the great dog's subtle maneuvering.

Virginia marveled at the ancient stone floor, the mahogany decor, and the laid-back atmosphere, complete with chatty, friendly, staff and bartenders, but mostly she was taken by the sheer size of the pub. The waiter came over and noted with a smile the added bowl of milk to accompany the pints of Guinness.

"Ralph, I never saw a more massive pub in my life," Virginia marveled, still taking it all in.

"Well the *World's End* has been here since the 1700's and is one of the largest public houses in London. My understanding is that on weekends they can cram over 1,000 people in here. And a few pilots as well. It's quite a landmark in London, but it's more for showing the tourists than giving you the inside scoop on fighter pilots."

"So, where *do* the fighter pilots go?" queried Virginia.

"It's a surprise, but you'll see it soon enough."

"This is absolutely beautiful, Ralph", motioned Virginia, referring to the entire Camden town area, "I never knew it existed."

The waiter returned with the drinks and a bowl of milk, which he placed on the floor in front of Duke, who waited for the waiter to retreat before looking up at Hofer, waiting.

Hoisting his pint, Ralph scolded gently, "If I can call you Ginny, you can call me Kidd. My friends do."

They tapped mugs, then Hofer looked down and gave Duke the "OK." Duke immediately began to politely sip his milk, and Hofer took a long drought from his beer.

Taking a sip herself, Virginia smiled playfully, "Who said we're friends?"

Rubbing the great head of his beloved canine, who responded with a milk-tinged lick of his hand, Kidd answered, "Duke."

Virginia reached down and added her hand to Hofer's, rubbing Duke's head and scratching behind his ears. They were quietly enjoying the moment and the link Duke provided between them, when her hand briefly brushed against his. He was startled by the electric surge he felt at her touch, but he didn't withdraw. He looked up to see she was watching him. They smiled shyly at one another, both aware of the moment that had just occurred.

Virginia, mildly flustered, tried to diffuse the sexual tension by raising her drink once more. Hofer raised his to meet hers and they clinked mugs again. In a sarcastic imitation of Humphrey Bogart, she said, "Well, Kidd, I think this is the beginning of a beautiful friendship. What's next?" They laughed, and Duke, ever the wingman for anything that smacked of fun, barked his agreement.

Hofer smiled, and enthusiastically suggested, "Where else? Next stop, Piccadilly!"

Exiting their cab in the early dusk, Piccadilly was packed with servicemen scurrying in every direction using their small flashlights. It reminded Virginia of jars full of fireflies caught in the early Missouri evenings of her childhood.

Once out of the cab, Hofer steered her into a pub at 14 Denman Street, just around the corner from Piccadilly proper.

As they entered, Virginia noticed there were scribbled signatures on the foyer wall, and soon they were inside the dingy, crowded pub. Pilots with fifty mission crushes, brightly colored nose art jackets, and uniforms of every known allied air force packed the rooms. A few of the pilots recognized Hofer and hollered after him and Duke. One group of pilots, who were rising to leave, motioned to Hofer and Virginia to take over their table. Grateful for the offer, they slipped into the corner and surveyed the organized chaos of wartime London pub life.

Duke quietly assumed his guardian position, but now had picked a place and an angle that would allow him to protect them both. Hofer didn't fail to notice.

They continued to chat until a cute little waitress came for their drink order. She stayed respectfully distant from Duke, but as Hofer was a regular, she knew the drill. In a few minutes she would return with their drinks and more milk for Duke.

"Where are we?" Virginia asked, while trying to take in the odors and ambiance of a pub several centuries old full of the boisterous personnel of the hottest fighter groups in the European Theatre of Operations.

"You wanted to know where the fighter pilots go... *This* is the Cracker's Club. I know it's a dingy little hole, but it opened in 1736. There's a gym upstairs, but I've never been there. Every fighter pilot in the ETO comes by here and signs the wall. The action always starts here, baby."

He cringed a little at the unintentional familiarity, but Virginia didn't even notice.

Finally, turning her attention to Hofer, she asked sweetly, "So what's the gen on you, Kidd?"

Hofer was temporarily unable to form words as he gazed into her soft blue eyes. But once he regained his tongue, he said, "Awww, not much to tell. That's the truth. I was born in Salem, Missouri. My birth name was Ralph Halbrook. Got no siblings. My Dad died when I was 8, and my Mother remarried a guy named Hofer. He and I didn't get along too well. I got his name but that's about all."

The waitress brought the drinks and set a bowl of milk down next to Duke. As in the Debden Officer's Club, it was emblazoned with the dog's name.

The waitress left, after first giving Duke an appreciative head rub, and Hofer continued, "We moved from Salem to Chicago, where I was raised, but

I've always considered Salem my home. After I graduated from high school, my Mom moved away with my step dad. I don't know where they are now. I stayed in Chicago, won a Golden Gloves title, played some semi-pro football, and eventually became a pilot."

"What about the rest of your family?"

"Well, my Dad's family is still in Salem. But I really don't have much family. Mom was pretty much it." He sipped his pint, reflectively.

Realizing that Hofer was essentially alone in the world, Virginia grew silent for a few more moments, pretending to study the room and wondering how it would be to give him a hug. Surprising herself at the warm attraction she realized she was already starting to develop for the fresh-faced young man 13 years her junior, she decided things were getting too somber and changed the subject.

"Have you always wanted to fly?"

Hofer, still lost in thought, didn't answer for a long moment. She allowed him the space to gather himself. Finally, the long silence startled him from his reverie, so he resorted to humor. Feignin1g a British accent, "Actually, no, my dear. I rode horses a lot as a child. Mine was named Duke, as well. Ironic, isn't it?"

Duke, hearing his name, interrupted his milk sipping and gave them a huge grin.

Hofer reached down to scratch his head.

"After I played some semi-pro football, they let me keep my jersey, so I wear it when I fight. I think it brings me luck. I also have my lucky snake ring."

He stuck out his right hand and showed her the ring on his right ring finger.

"How did you wind up a pilot?" she continued.

"Well, after my football adventure, I tried boxing, and went a few rounds with Billy Cohn. He babied me, but it convinced me boxing was not my forte either, even though my trainer thought I should stick with it."

He paused to take a drink before continuing.

"In '42 I went to Detroit, because I was planning to ferry a car to California for an auto dealer. To be honest, I was planning to try my luck in the movies. While I was there, in Detroit, I took up with a bunch of crazies and they coaxed me into going over to Windsor, Canada. I just tagged along to see what all the fuss was about. I went with them to the RCAF recruiting station. They all disappeared, I don't know where. A doctor came out and asked if I was there for a physical. I thought, sure, why not, so I went with him. One thing led to another, and before I knew it, I was in the RCAF, and training as a pilot. I really liked it, and I'm pretty good at it, so I stuck with it."

"How'd you become Kidd?"

"Remember, it's Kidd with two d's. When I enlisted in the RCAF, they wanted a middle name. I didn't have one, but I liked Kidd from my boxing days, so that's what I told 'em."

"Just like that?" marvels Virginia. "And, by the way, from what I hear you're more than pretty good at it."

"Yeah, pretty much. I loved flying right from the start. It just seems natural to me."

"Do you like the Army?"

"Army Air Force," he corrected, "it's OK, I guess. A fighter pilot has the best job in the world, but the military stuff is kinda silly, I think. The Colonel thinks I'm a maverick just looking for glory."

"Are you?"

Shifting uncomfortably as the conversation took a more personal turn, Hofer hesitated. "No, I don't, but this is my chance to be somebody. Don't you want to be somebody?"

Chuckling at the question, Virginia deflected it deftly.

"I'm the reporter here, buddy. No questions."

"Why not?" persisted Hofer, "I don't know anything about you. Are you married?"

She took another sip and reflected on whether or not to answer. She found herself drawn to the earnest man-child from Missouri, "I'm divorced, if it's any of your business."

He ignored her attempt to maintain some distance, "Any kids?" he continued.

"No." She said reflexively. The she set down her beer with a distinct clunk on the centuries old table top. "Say, how did this get turned around? I'm supposed to be interviewing you."

With a twinkle, Hofer continued to play, "Fair is fair. You're the one that used donuts as an excuse to get over here so you could interview me."

Blushing slightly, it was her turn to correct him, "I didn't come over here just to interview *you*. I came over here to be a war correspondent. You just happen to be my first interview."

Hofer took a drink and studied her over the edge of his glass. Virginia stammered a bit, "All's fair in love and war."

"Is this considered love or war?" Hofer asked with a grin.

"For a single woman, it's always war in the workplace."

"You sound like you have a bit of a chip on your shoulder."

"It's not a chip. It's bitter experience."

"Personal or professional?"

Tiring of the inquisition, Virginia's tone hardened just a little, "Can we change the subject? This is really none of your business." Shifting her legs,

Hofer caught another glimpse of her slender, well-turned legs.

"So, tell me, Mr. Hofer, are you a maverick looking for glory?"

Realizing he shouldn't push any further, Hofer went along with the new formality.

"Nah. But we lose guys almost every mission. Bobby Hobart bailed into the channel, was rescued, but died in the hospital of exposure. Pete Lehman was killed in a flying accident. Bobby Siefert just disappeared after a frantic May Day call. We won't ever know what happened to him. My number could come up anytime. I've already had three planes that were assigned to me get shot down while they were being flown by other pilots. I could have been the pilot that bought the farm instead of the poor sap that just happened to be in the cockpit when fate hit."

They fell silent in the midst of the pub's din. A small area of the floor was reserved for dancing and a few tipsy couples were jostling each other and the surrounding drinkers. Hofer heard the song playing on the radio; it was "We Three" by the Ink Spots.

To lighten the stiffening mood, he suggested, "I love the Ink Spots. How about a dance?"

They danced slowly, gradually drawing closer, the lack of room on the small dance floor to encourage their attraction for one another. Virginia and Hofer were a natural fit, and she drew herself up tightly in his strong arms, and eventually allowed her head to rest on his shoulder.

"You're a good dancer," she murmured.

Whispering back to her, he acknowledged the compliment, "Jocks know how to move."

Ignoring the suggestion and wanting to know more about this enigmatic man, she looked up into his eyes.

"Do you have a girlfriend?

She raised her eyes to meet his, saw his lips were pursed. It was a fair question, but she hoped he wouldn't think it too personal or forward.

"No." He said, finally. I have a friend named Susan from Salem. I named a plane after her, but I think she's in love with a pilot from the 56th Fighter Group, who is also from Salem. She almost never writes."

Silently, they danced another circuit around the floor.

Hofer drew back a little, so he could gaze into her eyes again, "You volunteering?" He asked, her last question still hanging in the air.

She looked up, licked her lips, and looked at his, contemplating what a kiss would be like. Surprised by the thumping of her heart, she was afraid he could feel it. At the same time, she hoped he could. She had known this man less than a day and he already made her feel electric.

"I thought the rule was *never volunteer.*"

Beginning to think he had a chance, he reassured her, "That's for bad duty. Good duty is Okay."

She looked at him with mock seriousness, "Are you good duty? Am I good duty?"

Hofer thought he saw his opening and pulled her closer. He tried for a kiss, but she turned her head and pulled away at the last moment.

"Wanna find out?" he pushes just a little.

"No."

With a firm and unequivocal response, the moment passed.

Trying to make light of the rebuff, Hofer smiled. "Good. Escorting you around is punishment enough."

She knew her rejection must have stung, but his response was a little hurtful too. She attempted to regain their earlier playful repartee by pouting her lower lip, batting her eyes, and cooing sulkily, "Being with me is punishment?"

He heard the note of genuine hurt and squeezed her reassuringly. Smiling as warmly as he could manage, "I don't know. Yet."

The music stopped.

"You wanna see some more of London?" he asked.

She smiled back. Their banter had gotten off track a little, but it was salvageable.

"No, not tonight," she said, "I still have Red Cross duties, too. Take me home?"

Without returning to their table, Hofer looked at Duke, who had been crouched watchfully, keeping an eye on them. He called to him with his one-word summons. "Hey."

They left the pub and walked into the blacked-out city. Hofer waved his flashlight to hail a cab.

He opened the cab door. Virginia gathered her skirt to sit, flashing a beautiful leg in the beam of his diffused light. She flipped the hem down again. Hofer looked at her, and she returned the look, and in the brief instant their eyes met, electricity passed between them. Both were surprised, the feeling was entirely unexpected, but undeniable.

Resigning himself to the inevitable, Hofer said softly, "Goodnight, Ms. Irwin."

"Goodnight, Mr. Hofer," she quietly replied. She looked at Duke, "Hey."

Duke stepped up and allowed her to pet and cuddle him one last time for the night. In the moment that Duke responded to her *Hey*, they became a threesome, knitted together by their love for the big dog and the amazing chemistry of knitted souls.

As the door shut, Hofer was contemplating how quickly serious romance had reared its lovely head amid the chaos and emotional turmoil of all-out war. The taxi pulled away, and Duke and Hofer just looked at each other for a moment. Then he turned and went back into the Cracker's Club. Fighter pilots work later than others. *It's a tough job,* thought Hofer, *but somebody's got to do it.*

CHAPTER THIRTEEN

MARCH 3, 1944

The last 10 days had been a bit of a blur. Between missions, it seemed Hofer always found himself in the company of Virginia Irwin. This morning, in the 4th Fighter Group briefing room, the pilots were lounging and talking. Hofer was sitting in a front corner and, after looking around to ensure that no one could see what he was doing, or was paying attention to him at all, he pulled the small secretive envelope Scudday gave him from his pocket. And while the rest of the pilots were comparing notes on dates, leaves, and missions he removed the copy of Virginia's base ID photo and gazed at it with genuinely developing affection.

Blakeslee entered and strode to the front. Stepping up on the stage, he pulled the curtain back to reveal the day's mission map.

It was a map of *The Continent*. There was a heavy, black crayon line extending from Debden to the heart of Germany. The Colonel turned to face the assembled pilots with a look of prideful determination and anticipation.

Quickly sizing up the direction and length of the black line, Hofer blurted out what had also registered with virtually everyone simultaneously.

"Berlin!"

Smiling grimly, Blakeslee pointed first at Hofer, then at the map with his pointer.

"Right. Today's the day. Big "B" at last. The Mustang is the ship. The 4th is at the tip of the spear. Jerry can't hide anymore. We've got seven league boots and we're going to crush the Huns."

From the back of the room came a voice from an FNG. "But when do we learn to fly the Mustangs?"

Blakeslee practically purred; it was meant to be reassuring. "You can learn to fly them on the way to the target. We'll be back before supper, and everyone can see their girlfriend."

He didn't care if they believed him or not, it would have no bearing on the mission. They were going, and they would learn.

Turning to Goody, Pappy Dunn, looking for a little extra reassurance asked a question in a stage whisper that practically everyone could hear, "Hey, Goody, I've got a hot date with a cute little Wren from London. Are you sure we can make it back before supper?"

Suppressing his own inner doubts, Goody smiled at Pappy and slapped him on the shoulder.

"Aw, sure, Pappy. No problem. It's probably gonna be a milk run anyway. Jerry doesn't know we can go all the way now, so he probably won't be ready for us.

"Hop to, you slackers."

The chaos of final preparations, dressing, donning survival and pilot gear, climbing into cockpits of planes lazily warming up on the tarmac led inexorably to the group's departure, with pilots and planes seemingly lining up and departing in a haphazard manner. But there was method to the madness as everyone knew exactly where they were in que, who was supposed to be on which wing, so that leaders and wingmen found each other, to become the proper elements, which then joined up into flights of four, which then quickly formed into the correct squadrons, cruising in proper formation en route to life or death 5 miles up.

Soon, the 4th was cruising east southeast at fighter altitude of angels 25, intent on rendezvousing with the bombers just before their run to the target. As had become his habit since meeting the enchanting Ms. Irwin, Hofer had the picture of Virginia stuck to his instrument panel with a piece of chewing gum, centered just below the gun sight.

Ahead, a formation of black dots grew into the silhouettes of P-47 Thunderbolts on a passing course, headed west.

Goody, known for having eyesight that would make an eagle envious, recognized the cowl markings first. "Hey, it's the Wolfpack."

In the lead of the Wolfpack, Zemke recognized their nemesis and radioed his feelings over the open radio/transmittal for all to hear. "Oh, shit. It's the 4th."

As they passed, at a combined speed of 500 miles an hour, there was little time for conversation or gestures, but the groups managed to accomplish both.

"Hey, guys," prodded Hofer, "Filler up, and check the oil?"

A millisecond later, Goody added insult to injury, "Say, Wolfpack, the war's behind you."

Zemke, shooting everyone in the 4th the finger, responded tersely, "Fuck you."

Blakeslee, rising to the occasion, came back with the ultimate response, "Sorry, don't have time for a date. We're going to Berlin. *With* the bombers."

It was just the comic relief to get everyone's mind on the task at hand, and to quit worrying about flying into the fight in a new untried (to them) fighter. Only Blakeslee had any combat time in the Mustang; everyone else was on a steep learning curve fostered by time, circumstances, and their commanding officer's guarantee to the general, although none of them knew about the last factor.

Everyone in the 4th was grinning ear to ear as they returned the middle finger salute of the frowning pilots of the 56th, all in the scant seconds it took for the two groups to flash by one another.

It wasn't long until the bombers and their new escort reached Berlin. By then, the 4th was starting to hear lots of German radio chatter, which by all accounts was expressing both amazement and irritation that the old tactic of waiting for the escort to peel off before attacking was not going to work. When it became apparent the bombers would have escort all the way to Berlin, the defending Luftwaffe had no choice but to challenge and fight.

The black specks gradually took the form of attacking fighters and rained down from above; Goody and Hofer climbed together. Neither one had any fear of losing. They were supremely confident in their aircraft, in their training, and in their superiority as members of the 4th Fighter Group, the heirs to the pride, ability and reputation of the Eagle Squadrons. Now that they were finally able to hand deliver the bombers to the target, they intuitively knew the kills would come.

They joined up with the bombers over Berlin near the beginning of their bomb run.

The Luftwaffe was waiting. But the 4th was ready as well and eager to prove themselves now that they had mounts they believed matched their skill as America's best.

Then, the German fighters attacked, and the unimaginable brawl of aerial combat exploded around the clashing groups; organized squadrons of expertly piloted planes became an angry chaotic swarm as a myriad of swirling dogfights filled the sky in a morbid dance the inexperienced eye couldn't even fathom.

The Mustang promptly showed its true colors. Having a tighter turn radius, and the performance edge in speed, maneuverability, acceleration, high speed stall, low speed stall, and pilot protection, the battle quickly turned into a bloodbath for the Huns. Every Mustang group in the fight won and won decisively.

The fight was surprisingly one sided in favor of the 4th. Nineteen German fighters were shot down. The 4th lost only three personnel. One killed, two POW. But the bombers got through largely unscathed and as they all turned for home, the bomber crews were waving ecstatically at the 4th, expressing their heartfelt relief and joy at having their *little friends* protect them all the way in and out, and realizing that the days of being mauled while unprotected by fighters was permanently over.

On their way out, the next fighter group rendezvoused with the bomber stream, relieving the 4th. Blakeslee waggled his wings a few times and the 4th accelerated for home, leaving the bombers in the very capable hands of a P-38 group. Every man of the 4th was exhilarated at the unqualified success of their first Mustang mission. Pilots who had worried about their ability to fly the P-51 now felt a growing pride and unshakeable confidence that they were good, they would win, and the defeat of Germany was just a matter of time.

Reflecting on a boast made by Field Marshal Goering regarding the ability of the Luftwaffe to keep Allied bombers away from Berlin, Blakeslee broke radio discipline to take a stab at the German high command.

"Well," he said over the static, "I guess the Luftwaffe is now run by Meyer."

There was an eruption of laughter over the R/T. Having started the fun, Blakeslee held his tongue as his group joined in with their own assessments and jokes about their donnybrook with Germany's finest.

As usual, after air combat, the group returned in small sections, even some singles finding their way home after getting separated in the melee of aerial combat. Hofer, as one of the singles, came barreling down the runway at high speed, barely 15 feet off the deck. He pitched up, dropped flaps and gear, and made a tight turn into a perfect three-point landing.

After taxiing up and shutting down, he carefully removed the picture of Virginia and tucked it safely into his pocket. He pulled back his canopy and while unstrapping, took a moment to pet Duke, who had jumped onto the wing.

As he jumped to the ground, followed by his faithful companion, Hofer noticed a small crowd around the tail of his plane. Walking back, he was surprised to see that his rudder was essentially shredded, hanging perilously by just a couple of bolts.

Shaking his head in amazement, Sgt. Scudday stated the obvious, "Mr. Hofer, you lucked out. If that rudder had separated during that high-speed pass, we'd be cleaning you up with a mop and bucket."

Hofer grinned, "I thought she was performing a little rough. Can you fix it?"

"Sure Kidd, *a miracle a day* we always say. She'll be ready when you are."

Hofer nodded, "Is everybody okay?"

Understanding what the question actually meant, Scudday gave the mission gen, "Gentle got two. Beeson got two. They're still tied."

"Great. Anyone else?"

"Mr. Herter is MIA. Pappy Dunn ran outta gas and is a guest of the Reich. So is Vermont Garrison, he got hit by flak."

"That's too bad. Did Pappy's Wren show up?"

"Yessir, she did. Misters Godfrey and Gentile are consoling her. Misters Goodson and Beeson are trying to help. It all seems to involve a lot of drinking."

Scudday waited a moment, and then asked the burning question, "How'd you do?"

"One. Shared with Goody."

By the time Hofer got cleaned up and made it to the party, it was in full swing and a brilliant moon was on the rise. In the game room, the Craps contest was already full of pilots and their dates, and some big bets to keep the adrenaline from the afternoon pumping.

Passing into the ballroom, Hofer looked around for Virginia. He spotted her standing in a corner, caught her eye and nodded towards the back door. Pursuant to their plan, she smiled and winked conspiratorially, then headed towards the ladies' rest room. Once inside, she entered the end stall next to the wall, but instead of sitting, she climbed up on the toilet, opened the window, and climbed out.

Hofer was already there in the dark shadows outside the window to help her down. They quietly jumped into an idling jeep with shaded headlights, barely illuminating the road, driven by Sgt. Scudday, who was waiting with Duke. For once, he slipped the vehicle into gear and quietly creeped out of the shadows, heading towards the flight line. As they disappeared towards the hangars the Master Sergeant in charge of the MP's appeared out of the shadows, smiling, and watching.

They arrived at the apron of the 334th where a P-47 was warming up. In the light of the full moon the markings of Hofer's former plane were clear. Scudday parked in the shadow of the hangar.

As they got out of the jeep, Hofer turned to Duke, "Duke, stay." The big dog stopped, looking quizzically at Hofer, but unquestioningly obedient, sat to wait.

Scudday hurried to the plane with Virginia and Hofer. Hofer jumped in and sat down, sans parachute, shifting his position to make room for Virginia. Scudday helped Virginia up onto the wing so she could climb in and sit on Hofer's lap. She wiggled provocatively as she sat and Scudday strapped them in.

Duke, from the shadows, was watching carefully to make sure his two charges were not in danger from anyone.

Scudday offered a last caution, "Mr. Hofer, this is bad juju. You could get court-martialed."

Hofer dismissed the warning, "Relax Sergeant. Just a quick hop. And only you know I have a passenger."

Scudday hopped down, pulled the chocks free and signaled a thumbs up to taxi. Hofer pulled the canopy shut, barely clearing Virginia's hairdo. She had to lean back on his chest to make it work. That placed her head almost on his left shoulder, and he could, once again, smell the warm feminine fragrance she favored. Being with her, and her willing participation in one of his patented peccadillo's, made him giddy. It was these unauthorized adventures that kept him constantly on the edge of real trouble, but maintained his growing reputation as a maverick, and raconteur.

With that, Hofer gently advanced the throttle to keep the noise down, taxied slowly and as quietly as a Pratt & Whitney R-2800 Double Wasp could be operated, out to the north end of the north-south runway and did his pre-flight mag check, calling the tower at the same time.

"Tower, Hofer, slow timing, check pass on maintenance flight."

"Roger," said the tower guy, apparently awakened by the unexpected call from anyone at this time of night.

"Runway 18 clear. You're cleared for takeoff."

With that, Hofer gunned the engine and the plane picked up speed. Sooner than Virginia expected they lifted off the runway. He and Virginia laughed out loud as they felt the plane lift off and heard the gear thump solidly into the wings. Hofer banked back towards the north and headed towards the coastal area of swamps and tidelands known as "The Wash." Since it was nothing but swamp there were no targets to attract the Germans, and no flak batteries to interrupt a flight with friendly fire. A safe area for illicit fun.

Yelling over the engine noise, Hofer said, "If we can find a target, you can shoot. But be ready, it's loud."

Virginia leaned back to yell in his ear over the throaty hum of the big fighter. "Oh, Ralph, you're crazy. I could get fired. You could get thrown in jail. I love it!"

Hofer performed some gentle banks and turns and maneuvers, just to give her a feel for what the plane could do. Spotting a derelict barge half-submerged in the mud and muck, he entered into a shallow, gentle dive. As he lined up on the smudge in front of them, he reached up to activate the N-3 gunsight, which illuminated a reticle in front of them with a rather typical set of cross hairs, and range circles. Descending slowly, and steadily so as not to frighten his passenger, Hofer, spoke into Virginia's ear.

"Lean over a little to the middle and look at the cross hairs inside the lighted circle. "When I say now, press this button. OK, now!"

Virginia squeezed the red tit on the stick and jumped with surprise as the Jug bucked and flames shot from the wings as the eight .50 cal machine guns roared, spewing tracers out and down into the dark outline of the target.

"Eeeeeek!" she shrieked and let go of the trigger, so she could cover her ears.

Hofer pulled into a gentle sweeping turn, banking slightly as he turned back to the south. Time to go home.

Virginia wiggled with excitement, her soft curves sensuously pressing against him, and turned to give him a quick kiss on the lips, for which he was not really prepared. Then, pulling back, she looked at him for a moment in the full moonlight. Her feelings for this man, this boy, this enigmatic alpha male, rose in her chest. She leaned in and slowly and deliberately kissed him again, pressing her soft full lips against his, pressing her firm derriere into his lap, and letting her mouth slightly open so their tongues could gently caress each other. She could feel the passion rising for both of them.

Returning to base, Hofer made a smooth, gentle landing, and taxied slowly in the moonlight, not wishing to attract attention with the landing or taxi lights. From out of the darkness came the shadow of Scudday's jeep, occupied by Scudday and Duke. Scudday signaled somewhat frantically for Hofer to stop.

Scudday scrambled up on the wing, taking care to avoid the idling prop, and leaned in so he could be heard. "Mr. Hofer, the Colonel's at the hangar."

Hofer unstrapped quickly and help Virginia off his lap and on to the wing, "Whoops! Here, Ginny, go with Scudday. And don't worry, everything will be fine," he said to her concerned look. She slid down the trailing edge of the left wing and was caught by Scudday; as quickly and quietly as possible the jeep rolled into the darkness in a different direction, taking the back route to the Officer's party.

Hofer turned on his landing lights and taxied slowly up to the 334th apron. He cut the engine and as soon as the prop stopped turning, pretended to be surprised when Colonel Blakeslee jumped on the left main gear, and appeared on the wing, peering into the cockpit.

"Hey, Colonel. What's up?"

Blakeslee peered closely at Hofer, "Where've you been, and why have these guns been fired?"

"Well sir, you see, this kite just came out of maintenance, and I just took it up to do a little test firing with the guns."

"Were you alone?"

"Alone? Of course. Yes, sir. Oh, you mean Duke. He doesn't like to fly at night."

"Since when does Duke wear perfume?"

Blakeslee leaned in to get closer to Hofer, his uniform saturated with the aroma of the beautiful reporter.

Unable to come up with any good explanation, Hofer was left with only one option— act dumb.

Trying to be as wide-eyed and as innocent as a new borne babe, Hofer gave it his best shot: "Sir." He said, "I don't know what you're talking about."

Realizing he had no evidence, and that Hofer had escaped justice again, Blakeslee squinted at him, and observed dryly, "Hofer, you're the luckiest SOB in the group. But one of these days your luck is going to run out."

Realizing the danger had passed, Hofer shook his head and repeated his mantra for whenever he was warned about the dangers of combat flying in the ETO.

"Sir, the German pilot doesn't exist who can shoot me down."

The Colonel's eyes narrowed at Hofer, feeling sure he had been duped, then he slid off the wing, turned on his heel and walked away.

CHAPTER FOURTEEN

The ready room was full of bored pilots trying to fill a *down* day with some meaningful activity until passes were issued at mid-morning. Hofer, sitting in the big overstuffed chair he tried to shanghai at every opportunity, was "studying" a girlie magazine. Duke, apparently just as interested, was peering over his shoulder. The general din increased in volume as the pilots tried to be heard over each other.

Suddenly, the room dropped to virtual silence. Hofer, sensing the change, looked up, expecting to see the brooding presence of Blakeslee. Instead, it was Virginia Irwin with two photographers; Frenchy, a disheveled Midwesterner, was carrying still cameras; and Ski, an equally disheveled Texan, who was toting all the movie camera gear and tripods any one person could possibly carry. But the biggest surprise was the second lady: a slim statuesque redhead in the military uniform of a Lieutenant in the British Motor Corps. Hofer instantly realized it was none other than General Eisenhower's chauffer, and private secretary, Kay Summersby.

Hofer, suddenly sensitive about his reading material, quickly hid the magazine in the folds of the chair and stood up, while Duke, always glad to see his female wingman, greeted her with a warm wag of the tail, presenting himself for hugs and rubs.

Speaking to Hofer but directing her comments to the entire room of pilots, Virginia explained, "You've been promising me pictures of the nose art of the 4th, and the 50-cent tour of the flight line. Colonel Don told me the group was standing down today, so I brought Frenchy and Ski down to document your mugs, and your planes. I also brought my friend, Lt. Summersby."

While not everyone recognized her, except for Hofer, everyone knew the name, and were instantly impressed, surprised, and intrigued that their very own "Ginny" had high-level connections that most of them could only dream about.

Murmurs and the exchanged looks of mild surprise were traded among the assembled pilots, not at the thought of having their pictures taken, or the prospect of a woman on the flight line, but the characterization of their iron-willed C.O. as "Colonel Don." If ever they needed confirmation of the exalted status of Ms. Irwin, they just got it. The added presence of General Eisenhower's chauffeur truly elevated Virginia's status to the near mythic proportions of her Sergeant Pilot friend from Salem, Missouri.

Since many of the pilots had never met Virginia personally, had only seen her at dances, or around the base and only knew her via rumor and gossip, Hofer realized it was time to make a formal introduction.

"Gentlemen," he said, standing, "the one and only Virginia Irwin, ace reporter for the St. Louis Post-Dispatch."

Virginia took the cue and gracefully introduced her guest.

"Gentlemen," she said, gesturing to Kay, "meet Kay Summersby. The General is in conference all day with the Prime Minister and gave her the day off. She called me this morning to see if I wanted to meet for lunch, and I told her about my photographic mission.

She decided meeting you guys was more important than just a lunch, and here she is. Please give her a Debden welcome like you've given me over these past few months."

The pilots gathered around, greeting Kay, Virginia and her photographers warmly, always willing to meet a pretty girl, and equally glad to get a little publicity for the folks back home. Getting this close to the very top brass was also an unexpected, and thoroughly delightful treat.

Kay acknowledged the warm greetings. "Thank you, gentlemen. Your reputation as the premier fighter group in the theatre precedes you. I think you all know that General Eisenhower has a soft spot for the Fourth, but if you tell him I said so, I'll have to call you a liar to your face. The General tries to make everyone feel appreciated and is loath to let his little secrets out. So, this remains between us girls, OK?

They all chuckled and smiled in appreciation, nodding their agreement to keeping the General's predilection for the Fourth a confidence.

After a moment, Virginia continued, "Thanks fellas. I'd like to get a picture of each of you with your nose art, and a little detail about the story behind it. Frenchy is taking still photos for your scrapbook and the newspaper, but Ski is filming for the newsreels, so please be sure and introduce yourself to Ski and explain your nose art."

"Let's go gents, don't keep the lady waiting," Hofer said. He motioned for the ladies and the photographers to follow him, and led everyone out on the apron, where the various planes of the 4th were sitting, being washed, maintained, or just admired.

The gaggle of flyboys jumped up and filed out of the ready room. They moved to the apron and gathered around the first fighter they came to, the P-51 flown by

Howard "Deacon" Hively. Complying with the requests of the photographers and standing in front of his Mustang with nose art depicting a backwoods country preacher, complete with halo and whiskey bottle, Deacon spoke up when signaled by Virginia.

"Howard Hively, Norman, Oklahoma. Go, Sooners! My nickname's "Deacon," and Norman is just a small town with a college located south of Oklahoma City, so they created a country preacher for me. The halo is my good luck charm."

Deacon gave the image a look of mock disapproval, "I don't know why they added a whiskey bottle."

Catcalls, whistles and laughter followed the well-known, hard partying Captain Hively's declaration of innocence.

Next in line was Pierce McKennon, the intrepid pianist, lyricist, raconteur, and ace fighter pilot from Arkansas.

"Pierce McKennon, Little Rock, Arkansas. What else are you gonna use besides a razorback hog, and call it *Ridge Runner*, right, Don?" He turned to admire his plane and its victory markers.

Next, posing by his nose art, the image of a cartoon bee holding twin machine guns, was the slightly built, somewhat thin, ace from Boise, Idaho.

"Duane Beeson. Boise, Idaho, is my home. My nickname is 'Bee,' so we created the Boise Bee, complete with .50 caliber machine guns. It's even on my flight cap." Beeson held up his Type C Leather Flight Cap, displaying a cartoon bee on the forehead of the cap.

Next in line was the famous P-51 of Don Gentile, with a large red and white checkerboard, an image of the Fighting Eagle from the RAF, a 15-foot scroll with victory markers, and the name "Shangri-La."

"Hi, Miss. Don Gentile, Piqua, Ohio. This is the fighting Eagle from the RAF, and you know about the mystical paradise of 'Shangri-La,' right?"

Ginny and Kay both nodded and smiled in acknowledgement.

Last, but not least, was Johnny Godfrey, accompanied by a beautiful black and white Cocker Spaniel named Lucky sitting on the wing next to him, standing next to his nose art picture. The painting on the cowl was of a golden horseshoe, with a picture of Lucky inside, and the label "Reggie's Reply."

"I'm Johnny Godfrey, from Woonsocket, Rhode Island. My dog, Lucky is my lucky charm."

Gently, and with great affection, he petted the dog, who grinned with delight.

The two women reached up to pet the dog also, "This must be Lucky."

"Right. Lucky, meet Miss Virginia Irwin and Miss Kay Summersby."

Lucky obediently stuck out his right paw, offering a shake, which was accepted with grace and amusement by the totally charmed reporter and the equally impressed Ms. Summersby.

Noticing the name on the plane, Kay asked about it, "Who's Reggie?"

Godfrey became somber at the thought of his brother, and of his mission of revenge.

"My brother," he said. "He was a merchant marine seaman killed when the Germans torpedoed a civilian freighter called the Vancouver Isle."

Genuinely touched, Kay reached out to hold his arm sympathetically. "I'm sorry, I didn't know."

Ginny put a comforting arm around his shoulder briefly. "I'm so sorry, Mr. Godfrey."

Godfrey softened at their apologies, and smiled shyly, "No offense taken, Ma'am, this one's on the Krauts, I'm here to give 'em what for."

Kay noticed that Godfrey's plane had the red and white checkerboard pattern on the cowl behind the engine, painted in a flag at least 3 feet tall, and 6 feet long. It dominated the silhouette of the fighter.

"Why the checkerboard?" she wondered aloud.

"Well," Godfrey explained, "if you'll notice, Gentle has it, too."

She glanced at the other plane which had an identical pattern.

Godfrey continued, "It's so we can find each other quickly in the air and operate as a team. Teamwork is what it's all about, you know."

While Kay nodded appreciatively at the gem of fighter pilot wisdom, Virginia glanced at Hofer, who had suddenly dropped to one knee and began petting and stroking Duke's muzzle. Speaking in a slightly raised voice, specifically designed to call attention to the comment, Virginia said, "That's what the smart pilots tell me."

Looking at Hofer, she inquired after his nose art, "Where's yours?"

Looking up, Hofer explained, "I'm getting new nose art. When it's ready, you'll be the second one to see it, I promise."

The publicity tour at an end, Goodson offered the next stop on the fun tour, which was greeted with approval by all.

"Anyone for a train to London and a show?" he said loudly.

Kay shook her head in disappointment. "The General will be looking for me in a couple of hours, I better get back. I can ride the train to Liverpool station, where the car is, but then I must go to Number 10 Downing. Raincheck, maybe?'

Assuring her of her continued status as a welcome guest at Debden, Hively smiled, and confirmed, "Of course, Ms. Summersby, you are welcome any time your duties permit. We look forward to seeing you again."

Hively pinpointed their destination, "All aboard for the Windmill!"

The whoops and hollers from the pilots hinted something special was in the air. At least special to the men.

Virginia thanked Ski and Frenchy who retreated back to their jeep and began to load up their equipment, then she turned to Hofer for an explanation.

"Why are we going to a Windmill?" she asked.

Hofer smiled broadly and chuckled as Duke barked happily, aware that a mobile bachelor party was getting organized. Everyone was getting boisterous as they organized themselves and started pairing off for transportation.

"You'll see," he said, mysteriously.

Goody headed inside the hangar to use the phone, "I'll call Ms. Henderson, and ask her to save us the front rows."

Virginia, accompanied by Kay, was quickly swept up with the others. They stuck close to Hofer and Duke as jeeps and trucks were being commandeered for the quick trip to the "chuff station" at Saffron Walden.

~~~

A short while later, at Leicester Square in the shadow of Piccadilly, several taxis pulled up to 1749

Great Windmill Street, London, just down the street from the Cracker's Club.

Piccadilly was, as usual, swarming with people, most of whom were wearing the uniform of some allied military force. The street party was spilling over into Leicester Square. In front of the building was a large sandwich board sign on the sidewalk: WE NEVER CLOSE.

The group got out of the taxi with Duke leading the pack, so to speak, and entered the club. In the lobby, Mrs. Henderson, a typical English matron in her 60's, was greeting the pilots with familiar hugs and kisses. She was obviously very glad to see each and every one, knowing that some she had greeted before would not be coming back, and for some she greeted now it could be the last time.

She bent down to greet Duke, "Whoa, Duke," she sniffed in mock disgust, "What have you been eating?" Smiling, she rubbed him playfully and he tried to lick her appreciatively.

The Windmill Club was in a very old, intimate, English Theatre with narrow seats that crowded a small stage. A balcony and a series of loges hung over the performance area, the chairs covered in worn red velvet. The theatre was very clean, but shabby chic, but its ambiance and appearance were of no importance to the pilots, who headed down the right-hand aisle behind Mrs. Henderson until they reached the front three rows, which were reserved for them with a golden velvet rope. Mrs. Henderson removed the rope and the pilots filed in boisterously.

Virginia sat in the second seat from the aisle, and Hofer took the end, with Duke in the aisle, apparently just as excited as any of the pilots at the coming spectacle.

When it was apparent that the third row was vacant, the men behind it immediately began climbing directly over the seats in front of them, until those seats were filled. Then each row behind them moved up, creating a wave of people climbing over seats.

Virginia was amazed at the lack of decorum, "What on earth are they doing?"

Hofer explained, "Oh, they're just doing the Windmill Steeplechase. It happens most every night at every show. Best seats are in the first six rows."

"Why the first six rows?"

Adjusting for the start of the show, Hofer, again with an air of mystery, replied, "You'll see."

The lights in the house darkened; the stage was equally dark. Then the curtain started to rise. As the house lights came up a bit, Virginia could see three small cupolas around the perimeter of the stage. Each was protected by a curtain of its own. From the wings, 5 to a side, came 10 striking young women, tap dancers, all in their twenties, dressed in revealing burlesque costumes vaguely suggestive of railroad oilers. Their breasts were almost bare, and the best word to describe their coveralls was "skimpy", or perhaps "cover-little." They entered in a chorus line, tap dancing and singing to "Chattanooga Choo Choo."

The routine became something reminiscent of a "Busby Berkley" routine, but bouncy as, one by one, the cupola curtains were drawn open, revealing more statuesque dancers. However, in each of the cupolas, posed on a rotating platform and standing statue still was a totally nude woman painted in silver or bronze, as if they were made of metal. Each was posed discreetly and artistically with oil cans, various hats, or tools to conceal their pubis mons, but their breasts were left bare. The sight of nipples in public jolted Virginia like a slap in the face.

Properly shocked, she whispered to Hofer, "Oh, Ralph, if I cared about my reputation, it's officially ruined now."

She tried to look away, but the dazzling intimacy of the nudity was impossible to ignore.

Hofer squeezed her arm, and leaned in to whisper, "Nuts, Ginny. Now you're officially "one of the boys. We wouldn't bring you here if we thought you were some snooty biddy that was going to tattle to our Mothers, or our commanding officer."

Smiling and chuckling, Virginia confessed she was experiencing a guilty pleasure at the scene, "I feel like a den mother to a bunch of naughty cub scouts."

She and Hofer winked at each other and squeezed each other's arms as they enjoyed the spectacle until the curtain fell and the next act began.

It was an Abbott and Costello-like comedy routine.

A little over an hour later, the curtain rose and it was again the Chattanooga Choo Choo number, signaling the end of the show cycle for the pilots of the 4th. Goody stood and motioned to the group.

"C'mon boys," he said, "this is where we came in."

He headed for the lobby, followed by the others. As their seats became empty they are quickly filled by the Windmill Steeple Chase. Virginia watched in amusement as the ripple followed them back along the aisle on their way out.

"Now you know why the Windmill Steeplechase is the most popular race in town," Hofer said as he and Duke hustled Virginia out of the theatre.

Standing outside, waiting for cabs, the pilots listened as Hofer and Goody compared notes to decide the next destination on the agenda.

"Where to, Goody?" someone asked.

"Whadayathink, Kidd? Has Ms. Virginia seen the Cracker's Club?" asked another.

He looked at her, "Yep, but it's still the best place in town for a fighter pilot to get a pint, and she's not been there on a Saturday night."

Goody and Hofer grinned conspiratorially at the prospect of exposing her to one of the wilder spectacles of London military party life.

Amid all the laughing and joking and jostling as they climbed into a caravan of cabs, Virginia got separated from Hofer. Taking advantage of the Kidd's oversight, Goodson and Gentile waylaid her, sweeping her into their cab, scrunched in between them. Hofer, Duke, Beeson and Hively grabbed the next cab. Far from being jealous, Hofer was glad they were making her feel included.

Virginia decided to take the opportunity gather more grist for the paper mill. She asked a question that had been rolling around in her mind ever since she had the opportunity to observe and compare the way Blakeslee treated Hofer versus other *miscreants* under his command.

"So, tell me boys, why does Colonel Don ride Ralph so hard? she asked, looking back and forth for who would choose to answer.

Goodson was first to respond, "Two peas in a pod."

Virginia wasn't sure what he meant by that. "What?"

Elaborating, Gentile took a turn, "Colonel Blakeslee sees himself in Kidd."

"You mean they're both pilots?"

Shaking his head, Goodson clarified, "Nope, rebels."

Gentile explained, "Colonel Blakeslee has always been a hell raiser. A non-conformist. He's trying to be a leader, and doing a damned good job, but there's this party animal inside that he rarely shows anyone outside the Eagles."

Taking up the thread, Goodson continued, "About a month before the Eagles got transferred from the RAF to the Army Air Corps, Colonel got busted from Squadron Leader to Flying Officer. That's the equivalent of Major to First Lieutenant. Big scandal. Very harsh."

Now Gentile took it again, forcing Virginia to look back and forth, as if she were watching a Ping-Pong match. Both pilots began to smile at the punchline Gentile was about to deliver, "When the Army was assigning ranks to us at the transfer, Don's demotion came to the attention of General Monk Hunter. General Hunter wanted to know why Don got busted."

Now both men were barely suppressing their laughter, and Gentile continued, "The reason was the station commander at Martlesham had caught Blakeslee red-handed, after hours with two women in his room."

Virginia was astonished. "Two? Colonel Don?" she asked incredulously.

"Two!" They said in unison.

Goody added the twist that made the story so good, "When General Hunter was told why Don was busted, the General said, "Two Women? Hell, I'd make him a Colonel.""

Virginia laughed, even though she wasn't quite sure she should. Two women in one officer's room was completely scandalous. Her opinion of the Colonel was enhanced. This apparently was a man of many talents.

Gentile continued, "All's well that ends well, I guess. Don was transferred as a First Lieutenant, promoted to Captain the next day, made Major in less than a month, Lt. Colonel shortly thereafter. When Colonel Peterson got kicked upstairs, Don was promoted to full Colonel and given command of the group. Now he's a bona fide hard ass..."

Virginia nodded, glad to be let in on the Colonel's story.

"...and a secret hell raiser." Goody finished.

CHAPTER FIFTEEN

Entering the Cracker's Club, the tension in the room escalated as the group from the 4th found that most of the revelers already there were members of the 56th Fighter Group. Every pilot in the room, which was virtually everybody, was keenly aware, or involved, in the rivalry-cum-feud between the 56th and the 4th.

Even Virginia noticed. Looking around the room she saw, to her surprise and consternation, that Colonel Don Blakeslee was present, sitting in a corner, in conversation with none other than Colonel Hub Zemke, the CO of the 56th. She marveled at their civility, given the extreme competitiveness of the two groups in determining who was best.

Hofer, Beeson, and Company bellied up to the bar and tried to get the attention of the barkeep. Beeson elbowed his way in by pushing aside a large Sergeant from the 5th, one Brian Cox.

Duke, also picking up on the tension, was in a state of high alert, ready to pounce if necessary to protect his self-appointed charges. Hofer and Virginia again lucked out and slid into a table just being vacated by Bomber Boys who sensed a Fighter Pilot riot in the making and didn't want to get caught in the melee. Hofer could see and hear the conversation between Cox and Beeson. They ordered, watched and listened as the encounter escalated.

Cox taunted, referencing victory totals of the two groups, "Well, short stuff, when are you guys gonna join the air war?"

Beeson bristled. "You guys are the ones with no gas. The air war's over Berlin, buddy."

He signaled for a pint and simultaneously placed his middle finger a half inch from the Sergeant's nose.

"Watch that finger, bub," Cox squared up, his temper rising.

"My finger goes anywhere I go, *buddy.*"

Cox warmed up to the prospect of kicking an Officer's ass, "How'd you like your finger to go up your ass when I put your lights out?"

Beeson was not intimidated, "I'd say you better bring your lantern and a sack lunch, asshole, 'cause it's going to be an all-day job."

They were seconds away from coming to blows when Hofer stepped between them with his back to Cox.

"Bee," Hofer said, "let me talk to the Sergeant."

Beeson glared over Hofer's shoulder and made a half-hearted attempt to get around him.

"Talking's done." he said. "Now it's time for that asshole to get a beating."

Around the bar, the members of the two feuding groups began to gather behind their respective champion, getting ready for the first blow to open the ball. Duke rose to his feet, at the ready, the hair on his back standing up.

As Hofer continued to reason with Beeson, Duke interposed himself between Hofer and Cox. Cox looked down and recognized a threat he was unprepared to meet.

"Maybe so, Bee," Hofer was saying, "but an officer fighting with an enlisted man results in a court martial. Then who's gonna race with Gentle for ace honors?"

Hofer patted Beeson's shoulder then turned to speak to Cox. Glancing down, he saw Duke already between them and ordered him to stand down. "Duke, no. Go. Sit."

He motioned to the table where Virginia was sitting, anxiously observing what was promising to be as big a donnybrook as any fights over the continent, and the dog looked at him for confirmation before obeying. Hofer gestured back to the table and Duke obeyed, but maintained a vigilant attitude, waiting to be summoned if needed.

In the corner, Zemke started to rise to intervene and prevent the altercation, but Blakeslee stopped him. Zemke gave him a questioning look, unsure as to why Blakeslee wanted Hofer to get his ass whipped by the noticeably larger man. Blakeslee had heard of Hofer's pugilistic skills, and this seemed like a good time to see for himself. He whispered something to Zemke, who nodded, grinned at joining the conspiracy, and sat back down.

The room had fallen silent, everyone was on pins to see what was going to happen. Almost without exception, everyone expected Hofer to get his ass royally kicked, which would then require a response, which would then generally escalate into a riot, which would result in busted heads, and lots of visits to the Chaplain to get T.S. cards punched, not to mention some serious discipline. The men of the 4th had also heard rumors of Hofer's ability with his fists, but no one had ever seen him attack anyone or defend himself. So, everyone in the room was in a state of expectation.

Hofer broke the silence with sarcasm, "Flight Officer Ralph Hofer, 4th Fighter Group, at your service... *buddy*."

'*Buddy*' was delivered with such open disdain that the only response was to throw a punch. Almost everybody in the room, except Cox, noticed that Hofer had casually assumed a boxer's stance—but with his hands at a low ready—and was waiting for Cox to respond.

Cox turned away as if in disgust, but it was a feint to disguise his attack. He whirled back around, threw his massive fist, and was utterly surprised when Hofer, his hands loose and ready, dodged, wiping the punch to one side with an amazingly fast right hand, and let the potential haymaker slip past him.

Cox wound up for another and threw a punch that had obviously resulted in a knockout many times in the past.

Hofer ducked easily and slapped Cox on the cheek with his open hand, which moved so fast, Cox never saw it coming.

A clear slight, Cox became even more enraged. He lunged at Hofer, who sidestepped the attack deftly, pushing and tripping the big man, causing Cox to crash into a table, upsetting the pints and occupants, who scattered to get out of the way.

Cox regained his feet and tried his best to attack and land a punch, but Hofer casually and quickly danced away, shielding himself and slipping in slap, then ducking away, generally exhibiting a real boxer's grace, with professional quality footwork, and demonstrating that compared to the cat like grace and quickness of the enlisted pilot, Cox was a lumbering, ineffective fool.

Hofer, smiling confidently, and playing with this opponent, who was grievously over matched, continued to land harmless slaps at will.

It was obvious that if Hofer was serious, Cox would be unconscious in a matter of seconds. Finally, even Cox realized the futility, and stopped, dropping his hands.

"Why don't you hit me?"

Hofer dropped his guard and addressed him like a figure of authority, "Because, we're on the same team."

Cox couldn't hide his surprise. The comment put him and his rage in his place better than any scuffle could. After contemplating the truth of the observation for a moment, Cox smiled, acknowledging he had been fairly bettered. Sticking out his hand, he said, "Then how about I buy you a pint?"

Hofer took the proffered hand, shook it warmly and turned with Cox to the bar. Bee still thought the big asshole needed a major ass whipping.

"Cheers, then," he said, giving a deflated Beeson a wink.

Peace being restored, and Hofer's gentle respect for his fellow combatants soothing ruffled feelings all over the room, the evening conviviality resumed. Hofer got his pint, thanked Sgt. Cox with a pat on the back, and headed to his table. As he passed Blakeslee and Zemke, he smiled, and lifted his pint in salute.

Zemke was duly impressed at the unexpected outcome, which preserved the honor of both groups, avoided a riot, and kept him from having to bust anybody for bad behavior.

Blakeslee was impressed as well but frowned a little; he was hoping to see Hofer's reputation as a genuinely talented brawler properly on display. And in a way, it was. Blakeslee could see along with everyone else that Cox was outmatched and had only lived to fight another day because Hofer permitted it. He smiled to himself, grudgingly, thinking that he was, now even more so, glad to have Hofer as a member of the

"*Blakesleewaffe*," he thought to himself, *the man's a real warrior on the ground, and in the air.*

Hofer rejoined Virginia at their table. He reached down to pet his beloved Duke, whose smile seemed to say, "you're welcome," and then resumed sipping his usual bowl of milk.

Sitting back a little, Virginia studied her young charge with enhanced respect. Not only at his fighting skills, but his tact, diplomacy, and uncommon good sense in handling a large half-drunk enlisted man without it resulting in jail, a beating, or court martial. There was obviously more to this young man than just flying fighter planes. She smiled. Hofer, unaware of her internal dialog, smiled back.

They sat silently for a while. Hofer sipped at his drink while Virginia let hers sit on the table untouched. She was studying Ralph, finding these newly discovered nuances about his personality immensely appealing. Hofer shifted uncomfortably, aware that he was being openly scrutinized by a beautiful woman, 13 years his senior, but not a hundred percent sure why.

"You've done that before," she observed.

Self-effacing, Hofer, shifted again, "What, that? Yeah, a little, I guess."

"Just a little?" she gently chided.

"Well, I won a Middle Weight Golden Gloves crown in Chicago. Once I went four rounds sparring with Billy Conn. But he babied me," Hofer admitted a little shyly.

"I'm surprised," she said. "You've mentioned Billy Conn. But the Golden Gloves title is new. What else have you hidden from me? I thought you were just a hot shot playboy who flies fighter planes."

Hofer glanced at her to see if she was deliberately insulting him. He concluded from her smile she was teasing.

"Nothing. It's really not that important to me anymore."

"What is important to you?"

Hofer ruminated a bit before offering a half reason, "Goody. And getting Jerries, I guess," he grinned sheepishly.

"Goody said I should ask you about your tactics," she said. "What's he talking about?"

"Oh, he's being cute. He knows I don't use tactics, or deflection shooting or all that fighter pilot stuff. I don't aim my guns, I aim *myself* at 'em. And I've got my lucky ring to help me."

Virginia continued to question him. "So, you think your lucky ring is the main reason you score?"

Hofer acknowledged other factors. "Well, that and Goody," he chuckled.

"Why Goody?" she asked.

Hofer gazed over at Goody, holding court at the bar, surrounded by his mates, obviously in his element and enjoying himself immensely. Hofer could appreciate a fellow raconteur.

"Goody's my best friend in the group. He stood up for me with Colonel Blakeslee. I owe him a lot. If it hadn't been for him, I wouldn't have had a chance to stay with the group and enjoy the success I've had."

He took a drink.

Looking at Goody, Virginia tried to pin Hofer down. "So, what's the most important thing Goody has taught you?"

Hofer turned his attention to Virginia. The twinkle in his eye told her she was about to get an evasive answer.

"That depends on who you ask," he hinted.

Taking the bait, she followed up, "What would Goody say?"

Hofer, teasing, chose to kid on the square. Alluding to the troubles with the Colonel engendered by his recklessness in the air, and cavalier attitude on the ground, he said, "How to avoid the Colonel when he's mad at me," he grinned on one side of his mouth.

"What would you say?"

He broke into a big smile, "How to avoid the Colonel when he's mad at me."

Sitting back, defeated, Virginia, reproached him, "You're incorrigible."

Noting that his pint was empty and hers was basically untouched, Hofer changed the subject, and the location.

"Moon's full. Want to go for a walk? The park is close, and Duke's on duty. No bombers, and the weather's mild for a change."

She nodded, and they rose and headed toward the door.

Turning, Hofer called out, "Hey!"

Minutes later, they were strolling in Hyde Park, Duke out front, Virginia on his left, Hofer on the street side as any Victorian gentleman would do. She put her right arm through his arm as they strolled in the quiet of the early night.

She looked at him soberly, "So, who are you really?"

Continuing his casual approach, he replied flippantly, "Jerry's worst nightmare."

She pulled up, stopping him.

He turned to look at her, surprised at the shiver of desire that coursed through him looking at her in the moonlight. She was serious. He listened.

"No. Really. Who are you?"

Acceding to her appeal for honesty and discarding the facade of humor he normally used to keep it at bay, he responded directly.

"Really. Jerry's worst nightmare. I've got dreams, Ginny. Scoring victories will help me get there. Haven't you noticed the reporters hanging around Bee and Gentile and Godfrey? Like flies around a fresh pie. After the war being an Ace will help me in a career. I might even stay in the Air Corps."

Not entirely satisfied, but relieved that she was able to get a genuine response, she turned to resume their walk.

"So, you have to be a lone wolf to score?" she asked.

Stubbornly, Hofer maintained his stoic attitude, "There's no time for baby-sitting up there in air combat, Ginny."

"But how is teamwork considered baby-sitting?"

"You snooze, you lose. Things move fast in the air. If you don't see them first, you can be dead before anyone hollers *break*. When I see a Hun, I'm going after him before he comes after me. You're either predator or prey in a fighter plane. I'm not anyone's prey."

"It seems to me that Gentile and Godfrey do all right *babysitting*. Bee, Goody, isn't there anyone you want to fly with?"

"I like flying with all of them. The 4th is chock-full of great pilots. I'm lucky to be able to fly with the best."

"But why the lone wolf routine then? Everyone thinks you're only flying for yourself."

"Let 'em think what they want. I'm just like everyone else. Fighting to survive. When the fighting starts, it's every man for himself."

"The Colonel wouldn't like to hear that. He preaches nothing but teamwork. Doesn't anyone suit you?"

"Goody, of course, he's my favorite. Frank Speer. He's good. Seems like he can read my mind. Frank's a great wingman. He's new, but he'll be an ace. I like Clemens Fiedler, from Fredericksburg, Texas. He speaks German and taunts the Krauts when we're approaching them. He's a great pilot. He'll be an ace someday, too."

Virginia squeezed Hofer's arm as he was listing his mates.

"Frank's a sweetie," she said. "I've heard Clemens in the Officer's Club imitating Hitler. He's funny. But I think Goody's my favorite, too. Except for you, of course." She laughed girlishly and gave him a playful peck on the cheek.

Hofer turned to face her, "Where's the nearest air raid warden?"

He leaned in to try to steal a kiss. Virginia pulled back, but it was different. It wasn't a refusal, it was a delay, as if she was saving it in payment for his being genuine with her.

"Tell me something else no one knows about you," she continued. "Why are the wings and the top of your fuselage painted olive drab?"

Hofer wasn't paying attention, in answer to her question, but he thought of something and laughed at the memory, "My picture is on a billboard in a Coca-Cola ad in the states."

Genuinely surprised, Virginia looked at him to see if he was exaggerating or joking. "A Coca-Cola ad caused you to paint your wings and fuselage olive drab? No."

"No, of course not. What? Oh, the paint job. I painted the wings and fuselage olive drab, so I could hang out at low level and catch the Huns doing their split "s" and trying to bug out for home. When they come down, I'm waiting for 'em. I blend in with the ground clutter and they can't see me until it's too late."

"What's a split 's'?"

"German's favorite evasive maneuver," he gestured with both hands as he tried to explain. "Roll over. Dive. Pull back. Reverse direction. Head for home."

She nodded in understanding, "How did you get into a Coca-Cola ad?"

He chucked, "I was driving a lady-friend down Michigan Avenue one afternoon in my RCAF uniform, and at a stop light this guy jumped out and hollered at me. I thought for a minute it was her husband or something."

Virginia ignored the implication. "Was it?"

"No, it was some Ad man. He says I'm just what he's looking for, and would I pose for some pictures for Coca-Cola."

"And you said yes."

"Yep. So, I pose for some pictures, and they come out on a big billboard with me and this guy in a U.S. Army Air Corps uniform, with the slogan 'Thirst knows no boundaries.' It was kinda neat."

"So, you're a star. Has Hollywood called?" she laughed.

Hofer stopped and looked up at the moon, then back at Virginia. His expression had turned somber. He hesitated a few seconds, then answered, "Nope. But I've got one more lucky charm."

Hofer reached in his shirt pocket and pulled out the wrinkled copy of Virginia's ID photo he had been sticking to his instrument panel. He showed it to her and she was genuinely surprised and moved by the revelation.

"You don't want an old lady like me," she scoffed.

"You're not old," he countered. "And besides, no one understands me like you."

She pulled her arm free from his, "I'm not living in anyone's shadow," she said defensively. "I want a career. I have things to do, places to go, people to see. Being married didn't agree with me."

Hofer gently took hold of each arm to emphasize his question, "What happened to you? Are you mad at every man? Or just me?"

Virginia looked at Hofer determinedly, "I got tired of being the little woman. *Honey*, bring me a beer. *Honey*, fry me some chicken. *Honey*, come to bed. It became insulting and demeaning."

"What about a man who appreciates you?" Hofer tried to put his arms around her.

"Please, don't. I told you, I'm not living in anyone's shadow anymore."

"Virginia, I'm not talking about shadows. I'm talking about a partnership. You're smart. You've got strength, courage. We'd make a great team."

"My teammate let me down. I don't trust anybody but me."

"Being a wingman is all about trust, baby. I know what I'm doing."

He put his hands on her arms and looked deeply into her eyes. She squirmed half-heartedly and looked away but allowed him to pull her a little closer.

"Maybe after the war, Ralph, but not now. I don't like to gamble on long shots."

"Ginny, every day is a gamble, particularly for a fighter pilot. There's no guarantee of tomorrow for either of us. Now is all we've got. Every heart beats alone unless you give it to someone."

He gently pulled her closer and she protested weakly. Finally, he kissed her tenderly. His lips were warm, caressing hers gently. It was a soft, sensuous moment, and they slowly, and deliberately, part their lips. As they kiss, she caressed his lips with hers, and slid her arms around his neck, returning his rising passion.

The "Kidd" - Killed in Action - July 2nd, 1944

Lt Ralph "Kidd" Hofer and his dog Duke standing on the wing of his P-51B Salem Representative

All photos courtesy of the U.S. Army Signal Corps

Virginia and the Kidd

Ace Aviator
Ralph "Kidd" Hofer

Virginia in her
Red Cross Uniform

Ace pilot with the 4th Fighter Group First Lt Ralph Hofer seated in cockpit.

Virginia Irwin of the St. Louis Post-Dispatch

Lt Ralph "Kidd" Hofer and his dog Duke

Lt Ralph "Kidd" Hofer at Debden describing a mission.

Lt. Ralph "Kidd" Hofer, of Salem, Mo., being debriefed after a mission.

The Kidd poses by Capt. Archie W Chatterley's
P-47C California or Bust. Hofer was flying
this P-47 on his first combat mission on
8 October 1943 when he shot down an Me109
over Zwolle, Holland.

Lt Ralph Hofer (on the wing) and Major James A "Goody"
Goodson tied at 30 kills.

Colonel Don Blakeslee, March 4, 1944, led the first mission of the 4th Fighter Group escorting bombers over berlin.

Captain John "Johnny" T. Godfrey of the 4th Fighter Group. (Right)

Major Bob Johnson (56th FG) and Captain Don Gentile (4th FG), the two highest ranking aces at the time.

Major Duane Beeson inspects P-51B tail feathers, struck by flak while strafing.

Major James "Goody" Goodson in the cockpit of his P-51B Mustang, May 1944

1st Lt. Pierce McKennon and Lt. George Green answer questions upon their return to Debden after McKennon's rescue in Germany.

Major Howard W. "Deacon" Hively beside his P-51D Mustang "The Deacon." He became the 334th Fighter Squadron's CO immediately after D-Day.

Lt Ralph "Kidd" Hofer and his dog Duke, also the 334th FS mascot.

Virginia Irwin and Andrew Tully arrive in Berlin days before Hitler's death.

CHAPTER SIXTEEN

MARCH 18, 1944

As Hofer exited the 334th hangar's ready shack wearing his blue football jersey with the orange "78", and headed for his assigned P-51 fighter, Duke had trotted out ahead of him. When he arrived at the plane, he was surprised to find that Duke was standing in his way, blocking his access to the left main wheel he used to climb up on the wing and get in the cockpit.

After watching several attempts by Hofer to get Duke to move, Sgt. Scudday walked over curiously to investigate. "What's the problem, Mr. Hofer? You're about to be late for the mission."

"I don't know, Sgt. Duke won't let me get in the plane."

Duke stared at them but refused to budge.

Sgt. Scudday scratched his head, noticed the dog was standing right by the left main gear tire, a place he rarely stood while Hofer was strapping in. Usually, Duke would go behind the wing from where he could see Hofer for as long as possible.

Sensing a problem, he took a closer look at the tire and motioned for the standby cart. When it was in place, Scudday checked the tire pressure on the left main wheel.

He stood back and looked at Duke, "Boy, that's amazing, Mr. Hofer. That tire's just below safe pressure. It could've blown taking off or landing. We had a pilot last week killed on takeoff when his tire blew and the whole plane cartwheeled."

Hofer looked at Duke, who was wearing an expression of complete satisfaction. His warning had been heeded and Hofer was safe for another day. Hofer, well aware that he had been granted a reprieve due to Duke, knelt and hugged the dog.

"I guess we'll have to add ground crew to your list of accomplishments, big guy." Duke's response was his signature grin that, in this case, seemed to say *I told you so.*

The mission on this day would prove to be a tough one; escorting bombers all the way to Munich. After climbing into the cockpit and strapping in, Hofer stuck his lucky photo of Virginia on the instrument panel. He taxied out late in the sequence, lined up with Frank Speer on his left, and accelerated into the blue sky. They climbed rapidly as the landing gear of the two fighters came up simultaneously, kites 3 and 4 of a 4 plane section called Pectin White, meaning 334th Squadron, White Section. Speer was Number 3, and Hofer, the last plane in the flight element wingman to number 3, was number 4.

To visualize the formation, the pilots would often tell others to hold their right hand out flat and look at the fingernails. Speer was the ring finger, Hofer was the little finger. Being the last guy in the element made him "tail end Charlie," the *bait* for bounces (attacks) from their six o'clock. It was either the best place for combat, or the worst place to be, depending on your point of view. For Hofer, there was no position he'd rather fly. Sandbagging the Huns was a favorite pastime for the *Salem Representative*. After all, the German pilot didn't exist that could shoot him down.

An hour later, the Group was cruising at 20,000 feet on oxygen. Enjoying the beautiful view, Hofer couldn't resist a comment, "Gee, ain't the Alps pretty?"

Instantly, Blakeslee scolded him, knowing only one pilot would break radio silence for a travelogue, "Goddammit, Hofer, shut up!"

Hofer was suitably sheepish, "Sorry, sir."

Just then, Hofer's radio became staticky, popped, and stopped transmitting all together. He tested his comms.

"Pectin White 4 to Pectin White 1. Do you read?" He waited for a response. When none came he tried again, "Pectin White 4 to Pectin White 1. Come in. Anyone?"

The transmission was greeted with silence. Hofer assessed his situation. He decided his best bet, with no communications, was to stick with his wingman rather than break away, so he continued to hold his position. He considered moving up from slightly behind Goody's nine line to signal he had no radio, but before he could communicate anything, events intervened that burnished his reputation to a high gloss.

Blakeslee spotted enemy aircraft below and radioed to Pectin White 1, a transmission which Hofer couldn't hear.

"Pectin White 1, 109's east of Mannheim. Bounce 'em."

Goody peeled off and led a diving attack with his section of four. Hofer stuck with the other 3 and quickly ascertained the targets. He switched on his guns and lined up on one of the enemy aircraft. At 250 yards, he dropped his exterior fuel tanks and fired, getting strikes around the engine, and cockpit. The e/a started falling, black smoke pouring out of the engine. Hofer followed, this time with Speer on his wing, as Hofer had become "it", but separating from Goodson and his wingman, and continued his attack. The wounded German fighter entered into a vertical dive and augered in, crashing next to an airdrome. No chute was observed.

Now, being virtually on top of an enemy airdrome, there was no real option but to attack. Hofer swooped into a ground attack, with Speer on his left wing, the two of them strafing 4 enemy bombers lined up along the runway. As they streaked across the field, barely skimming the grass with their props and their guns blazing, German flack gunners from all four directions homed in on the attackers. The flak appeared as glowing balls which seemed to float up towards their fighters, gaining speed as they approached, and then whizzed by at blinding speed.

Amazingly, every round missed. Hofer couldn't help but wonder (a) how they could miss, and (b) if the German gunners were killing each other with cross fire. After all, the rounds that were missing his plane were landing somewhere, generally directly across the field from where they were fired.

He said a silent prayer of thanks. But during their strafing run, while jinxing and juking to avoid flak, Hofer and Speer got separated.

Climbing out, and looking for Speer, Hofer swiveled, watching for planes which may be lining up to attack him. He spotted another 109 off his left wing. Chopping his throttle, dropping 15 degrees of flaps, and hitting the left rudder, Hofer juked around, made a stall turn, and attacked. Dropping in behind the Messerschmidt, which had not seen him yet, Hofer fired, getting strikes along the wing and into the wing-root connection to the fuselage. The pilot of the stricken fighter popped his canopy and bailed out, abandoning his aircraft which spiraled out of control and exploded in the middle of the runway. The pilot's chute opened less than 100 feet above the ground. Better to die quickly in a bailing accident than burn to death in a fighter; but this time, the pilot's gamble paid off, for he would live to fight another day.

Hofer climbed back to 10,000 feet and looked around. Off to the east he spotted bomber contrails approaching Munich, but no fighters at all. Everyone, Frank Speer in particular, had disappeared into the vast sky. Hofer set his course for the bombers.

As he tried to climb higher he spotted two 109's above him. They obviously didn't know he was down there or they would be maneuvering to attack.

Advancing the throttle, Hofer was dismayed when his prop ran away, and he started to lose flying speed. Scanning his instruments and manipulating his prop and mixture controls, he saw he was experiencing dangerous amounts of boost and excessive RPM's. An engine failure was imminent. His plane wouldn't climb, so—perplexed—he drifted down to 5,000 feet and started going over his options.

He muttered to himself, "I've lost my prop. I can't get back to Debden."

He checked his compass, and mumbled to himself, "Hmmm, which way to Switzerland?"

He set his course south by south-west, but his plane continued to lose altitude and airspeed. He wasn't going to make it. That left only one option, bail out. That meant becoming a POW, Hofer prayed and prepared to bail.

He took the picture of Virginia off the instrument panel and put it safely in his pocket. Then he jettisoned his canopy and pulled up on the stick to steady the plane. He stood up, ready to jump, when suddenly, the prop came back.

He quickly dropped back into the seat, belted in and scanned his instrument panel again. All gauges were showing normal. Hofer was presented with risky choices.

What the hell? He checked his fuel. Low, but not red-lined. He looked around. Even at 5,000 feet the air was very cold, and with no canopy he was in danger of frostbite. He realized if he didn't think of something he would be spending the rest of the war as an intern in Switzerland.

He scoffed aloud to himself, "Bullshit." Then he thought, *If I don't get back, they'll never see my flight film. I won't get credit for my last two victories. I'm an ace now.*

He took the picture of Virginia out of his pocket and studied it for a second and returned it to the instrument panel. He smooshed it onto the gum that was still there, touched his gloved fingers to his lips, and transferred the kiss to her picture.

"Wish me luck, baby."

He banked north and set course at 320 degrees, the estimated vector to Debden.

With 600 miles of low-level flying over enemy territory ahead of him, he sat as low in the cockpit as he could get and hunkered down into his cockpit, drawing his coat up around his head to reduce his exposure to the frigid slipstream. Thinking of Ginny and Duke and regretting not getting those last two 109's, he leveled off for the flight home.

CHAPTER SEVENTEEN

Back at Debden, Blakeslee had returned from the mission and entered his office. He threw his flight gear in the corner and picked up the paperwork on his desk. A moment later, he looked up at a knock on his door.

His orderly stuck his head inside, "Sir, Mr. Hofer is not yet returned."

Blakeslee dropped his head, "Oh, God, no."

He glanced at the clock which showed 1415 hours. He asked the one question that was the basis of all estimates of return and status.

"Fuel?"

"About 90 minutes. After 1545, Mr. Hofer's down."

Blakeslee shuffled his papers absentmindedly. "He's always the last one back. Keep me informed."

The orderly departed and Blakeslee looked up at the clock again. He ran his hand through his hair and sighed deeply. He sat down and, with no action to take but wait, swiveled in his chair, and stared vacantly out his window.

Back in France, Hofer was skimming the ground, figuring a lone wounded fighter had a better chance at low altitude. His paint scheme, with the olive drab surfaces along the wings and fuselage, made him virtually invisible from above. Skimming along roads, and rhythmically rising and dropping between tree lines, he swooped up and over and almost dropped on top of a French farmer driving a horse drawn vegetable cart. But he was already gone as the horse reared frantically, spilling half the cart's load. Hofer couldn't see or hear the farmer waving his fist and cursing at the rapidly disappearing plane.

Approaching the coast, he saw the English Channel; and beyond, the thin line of the White Cliffs of Dover shining in the scattered sunlight 22 miles across the channel. The lowering ceiling caused him to reduce his altitude as he approached the unforgiving water. He again checked his gauges. Fuel was now showing red-line. Airspeed was 180 knots, making the crossing just under 7 minutes. Reducing his speed to 110 knots would give him a maximum fuel burn of about 6 gallons a minute. Maintaining 180 knots meant he had to have at least 12 gallons of gas left.

He crossed the coastline and headed out over the channel leaving France, or Belgium, wherever he was, behind. He watched the water slip past just 50 feet below. It frothed with whitecaps and looked cold, dark, threatening and ominous. The sky was darkening, and lightning was beginning to flicker around the northern edges of the clouds. A storm was building.

Hofer started to circle as he struggled to make the life or death decision to fly or land in France. *Could he make England? he wondered*, and thought out loud, "Do I have eight minutes of fuel left?"

He remembered the fate, just days ago, of Bobby Hobart. Bobby bailed out over the channel and was rescued by patrol boats in just a few hours, and still died that night of exposure.

Would Hofer be another victim of the frigid waters of the English Channel? Circling was wasting precious fuel, he must decide.

Recalling for a moment the stories about prisoner of war camps, and the hostility of German soldiers when they got a hold of one of the airmen that tormented them daily, it made death in the sea seem a better choice. And besides, there was that gun camera film.

So, regaining his course northwest, the Kidd set off across the channel, skimming the wave tops and disappearing into the lowering murk. With no radio, he had no way to alert the rescue planes or ships. There would be no chance if he ran out of gas. Being this low, there was no option to glide, and he couldn't climb for any altitude because he couldn't lose sight of the surface or burn the precious fuel he estimated he had. It was do or die.

In the Officer's Club at Debden, Gentile, Goodson, Beeson and others were standing around making subdued small talk or sitting in silent contemplation of the clock. It read 1530 hours. As the minutes dragged by the talk petered out.

At the piano, McKennon was plinking at the keys half-heartedly, but no one was encouraging him, and it was obvious everyone was anxious for news of their favorite maverick. He stopped playing and checked the clock. 1540 hours.

Blakeslee entered and walked up to the bar, next to Goodson and Gentile, and ordered a small whiskey. Everyone watched glumly as the clock inexorably passed 1545, the silence was heavy, the implications were grim.

Colonel Blakeslee sagged noticeably and looked morosely into his drink. Goodson and Gentile, on either side of him, turned to face the bar to conceal the moisture in their own eyes. The mounting grief was palpable as the men in the room contemplated the loss of the irrepressible Kidd Hofer. Debden would be a more tranquil place without the tales of adventures in London, the vivid stories of air combat, the jokes, the dancing, the pranks, and the ongoing contest of wills between Hofer and the Colonel. More than one pilot in the group thought that the only reason the Colonel maintained the upper hand was RHIP.

Then, the door opened and Blakeslee's orderly peeked in. "Sir, we just got word. Mr. Hofer landed at Manston with 1 minute of gas."

The whole room sighed, sounding like a giant deflating balloon. Blakeslee dropped his head, covering his eyes with one hand, and muttered to himself, "That son of a bitch."

Overheard by Goodson and Gentile, Goody grinned, "With the Kidd, that's a term of endearment."

MARCH 25, 1944

Everybody standing on the apron in front of the 334th hangar turned their heads at the sound of a fighter approaching at high speed.

50 feet off the deck, Hofer's P-51 shot past the crowd doing victory rolls. He pitched up, dropped flaps and gear, and made a showboat main wheels landing, keeping his tail up far down the runway as he taxied at high speed. Finally, bleeding off airspeed, he gently dropped the tail, made a smooth U-turn, and taxied up to the apron.

Accustomed by now to his antics and knowing he was just letting off steam and having some fun, everybody enjoyed the show. Whenever Hofer made a showboat landing, everybody knew there were going to be some good stories to go with the celebration.

Sitting in front of the hanger, Hofer cut the throttle, took the picture of Virginia off his instrument panel and kissed it, waited for the prop to stop, then slid his canopy back as the signal to Duke, waiting patiently behind the left wing, to jump up to greet his beloved Master. The big dog stuck his head in the cockpit, and licked Hofer affectionately. Hofer laughed and rubbed and nosed the dog affectionately, and with relief.

He climbed out and dropped to the deck just as Sgt. Scudday drove up with none other than Virginia Irwin in the jeep with him.

Hofer approached, and Scudday spoke before he had a chance to say anything, "Mr. Hofer, Colonel Blakeslee wants you to come directly to the parade grounds."

Hofer grimaced, "Good grief. Does he sneak into the tower watching for me?"

Hofer and Duke climbed into the jeep, Hofer still amused at the difference in Scudday's driving when Virginia was with him. It was almost insulting to base personnel. He smiled to himself and sat back to enjoy the ride, stroking the neck of the dog.

Hofer sat forward and spoke to Virginia, "What's up, buttercup?"

She smiled at her favorite nickname, one that only Hofer was allowed to use.

"All you need to know is that Colonel Don invited me. I know what you're in for, and I wouldn't miss it for the world."

Hofer grimaced again, "Aw, that don't sound good. If you think it's good, it must be very, very bad for me."

They arrived at the parade grounds and Hofer was surprised to see the 334th Squadron assembled. Colonel Blakeslee, Colonel Clark, Major Hively, and most surprisingly, General Jesse Auton himself, were standing on the steps of the Officer's Mess. Hively, the Squadron CO, motioned Hofer to front and center.

Hofer told Duke to stay by the jeep and then made his way over to Hively.

Into a microphone, Blakeslee barked orders to the assembled pilots, "Command, Attention!"

The squadron snapped-to in one movement, except, of course, General Auton.

Hofer sauntered up, faced the steps and stood loosely at attention, unsure of what was going on, and what to do.

Blakeslee made way as Auton stepped up to the microphone. Hofer tightened his *attention*, (which, for once, actually looked like attention), and tossed off what all watching recognized as the best salute he had ever mustered. Virginia's influence again.

Auton solemnly intoned, "Flight Officer Ralph Hofer, 334th Squadron, 4th Fighter Group, United States Army Air Corps, it is my pleasure and honor to award you the Distinguished Flying Cross for heroism and extraordinary achievement in aerial flight."

Turning, he addressed Colonel Blakeslee, "Colonel, do you have the citation?" Blakeslee handed the citation to the General, who read it into the microphone.

"Flight Officer Ralph K. Hofer distinguished himself by heroism and extraordinary achievement and displayed outstanding airmanship and skill while participating in aerial flight over enemy held territory on 18 March 1944. After destroying two enemy fighters in aerial combat, Flight Officer Hofer navigated his damaged P-51 600 miles across enemy held territory, without a canopy, at low altitude, crossing the English Channel at wave top level, in bad weather, and landing at Manston, England with 6 gallons of gas. In addition to scoring two victories, he saved his aircraft at a time when the Mustang Fighter is top secret, and in short supply, depriving the enemy of vital intelligence, a preserving a vital resource of the Army Air Corps. By his high personal courage and devotion to duty, Flight Officer Hofer has brought great credit upon himself, the 4th Fighter Group, and the United States Army Air Corps.

"Colonel, do you have the medal?"

Blakeslee handed the box to Auton, who opened it and removed the medal. He stepped forward and pinned the medal on Hofer's flying suit, shook his hand, then remounted the steps as Blakeslee came forward to congratulate Hofer himself.

Smiling broadly, he offered his hand, "Congratulations, Hofer. You scared the crap out of all of us, but you're one hell of a pilot."

Hofer, glowing, presented him with the second-best salute he had ever mustered, "Thank you, Colonel. It's nice to see you when you're not mad at me."

Blakeslee's expression sobered just a little, "It would be a pleasure to have you obey the rules, so I wouldn't be mad at you at all."

Auton let their moment play out, then spoke again to the assemblage.

"Gentlemen, Flight Officer Hofer is now officially credited with 7 enemy aircraft destroyed, one damaged, along with a flak tower, flak boat, and locomotive damaged. He is the first and only Enlisted Pilot Ace in the United States Army Air Corps. I know he's very proud to be a member of the 4th Fighter Group, and I think the 4th Fighter Group should be proud of him."

Led by Auton, everyone applauded.

Blakeslee stepped back up to the microphone, "Command, attention! Dismissed!"

The squadron began to disburse, but Hofer remained, basking in his moment. He was joined by Virginia, Duke, Blakeslee, Clark, Hively and General Auton offering handshakes, encouragement and backslaps.

"Son," the General said, "you do know that you're eligible for a commission, don't you?"

Not expecting the question, Hofer stammered, "Yes, sir, that's what I hear, but I've been kinda busy."

Auton looked doubtful, "Too busy to apply for an officer's commission?"

Blakeslee saw that Hofer was headed for a major faux pas and interjected, "What he means, General, is that we've been flying a lot of combat, and we're behind on our paperwork, right, Mr. Hofer?"

Hofer caught the hint and smiled, "Oh, yes sir, General, sir. I'll get my application turned in as soon as operations slack off just a little."

Satisfied, Auton offered a military perspective, "That's good son. The Army needs good officers and pilots that take care of their equipment. Dedication to duty, and respect for your aircraft is important at this point in the war."

Blakeslee, Clark and Hively, fully in the know regarding the Kidd's now infamous disregard for Army property, exchanged weak smiles and nodded in agreement. Hofer merely beamed and shook his head, as if acknowledging someone finally recognized his appreciation and stewardship of his Mustang.

Duke, ever-present, seemed to understand every word that had been said. He cocked his head, and gave it a shake, as if to say *bullshit*. This brought on chuckling across the board as the 4th personnel got it immediately, but Auton, not included on the inside joke, just stood there looking momentarily confused.

Virginia smiled at the General, and the assembled Officers, and put in a good word for her favorite pilot. "The application should be on your desk shortly, General, I know Ralph values the opportunity highly."

Hofer smiled at her, not realizing until just now that she was right. Being a commissioned officer would advance his goals and career aspirations, not to mention perhaps impressing his favorite reporter with a new "butter bar". Being an officer and a gentleman appeared to have its advantages both in war and with the ladies. And he was very interested in gaining favor with this lady.

CHAPTER EIGHTEEN

On the last day of March 1944, Virginia and Hofer, accompanied by the ever-present Duke, were sitting in the Officer's Club whiling away a quiet evening on the base. They were huddled in the corner, discussing the events of the last month. March had been frantic, with the 4th going out almost every day, and Hofer adding six aircraft destroyed to his total.

Blakeslee entered, and the noise level dropped appreciably. He was clearly not here for drinks. He walked to the center of the bar and opened a folder he was carrying. When he had everyone's attention, he spoke up.

"Congratulations," he announced, "we got 156 kills in March."

The room filled with wild applause, whoops, catcalls, and whistles, all the pilots began shaking hands and clapping each other on the back.

Blakeslee stood silent, watching. When everyone looked over enough to notice the Colonel's attitude the celebrations quickly died down.

"I want 200 in April." Blakeslee gave his "look" to everyone, turned on his heels, and exited. The room remained silent until he was gone.

Hofer and Virginia got up and joined Goody, Gentile, Beeson, and McKennon at the bar. Each paid homage to Duke, who moved from pilot to pilot for his obligatory head rub.

Hofer broke the silence, "How many do we have now?"

Virginia consulted her notebook, and Goody did a mental calculation.

She answered first, "Let's see, that means we're just over 250."

Hofer dug a little more, "What about the Wolfpack?"

Goody was ready, "They're pushing 400."

Virginia chimed in, "Where is everybody in the Ace race?"

Whereas most reporters asking that question would be considered impertinent, Virginia's status as a bona fide insider, and a favorite of everybody in the group, got a straight answer from Goody.

"Gentle and Bee are currently tied at 22," he said. "Kidd's got 13."

McKennon piped up, directing his comment to Goody, "What about you?"

Goody was vexed, "I can't remember, I'm too busy keeping up with you guys."

Hofer said, "For the record, gentlemen, our man Goody's got an even dozen."

They all hoisted their glasses in salute to the group's success.

Goody summed up the general feeling, "That's a hell of a nice gift for April Fool's Day."

Draining his mug, Hofer whispered to Virginia, "I'm on the board for tomorrow, so I need to hit the rack. Walk you out?"

Virginia smiled, "Of course."

Turning to her companions, she wished them all success, and a good night, and walked out with Hofer.

Before the Kidd had a chance, Virginia turned to Duke and said softly, "Hey."

Amazingly, Duke followed without hesitation. Hofer looked at him as if he had been betrayed, but secretly pleased, gave him a head rub as they stepped out into the soft spring night.

The walked slowly to her flashy little red MG parked in front of the Officer's Club. While still on the base they had to be wary of prying eyes, so they maintained a distance they didn't have to observe when they were alone. Hofer opened the door for her like a southern gentleman.

She stepped in and sat down. Looking up at him she said, "Thank you, Kidd."

She gave Duke an affectionate rub of the muzzle, "Good night, Duke. Take care of our pilot, Okay?"

Duke seemed to smile and nod, acknowledging "mission accepted."

Looking back to Hofer, she spoke softly, "Be careful tomorrow. You're in my prayers."

The look was "kiss me," but the location was "stop."

Hofer smiled as he looked into her eyes. He patted the shirt pocket where he carried her picture when it's not gummed to his instrument panel.

"I've got you with me on every mission, buttercup. Call you when I get back? Or will you be here?"

"I've got a meeting with Colonel Blakeslee tomorrow morning at 1000, but if it's OK, I'll stick around for lunch. Might be a pilot or two I can interview after the mission. Know anybody?"

They both laughed, knowing that the two of them together constantly was becoming the center of base "gen."

Hofer shut her door and stood by as she started the engine, gave him a last look, waved, and drove away.

He looked at Duke, who was also watching her departure.

"So, big fella, following her orders now, are we?" Then conspiratorially, he said, "Want to raid the mess hall?"

The big dog lifted his head and barked once. *Damned right!* in fluent Duke.

CHAPTER NINETEEN

The next morning, promptly at 1000, Virginia was standing at the door of Don Blakeslee's office. She was wearing a fetching lady's business suit instead of her usual military fatigues and was more than a little nervous.

Duke, in Hofer's absence, had taken up his self-appointed escort station for Virginia. She ruffled his head and said a small prayer to allay her fears. When she was ready, she knocked on the Colonel's door.

While waiting, she reflected a moment on the fact that she had not been in Blakeslee's office since the time she was introduced to Kidd Hofer.

A muffled invitation, "Enter."

Opening the door, she peeked in and was pleasantly surprised by the Colonel's cordiality. He rose and walked around his desk to offer his hand.

She offered her hand in response, "You sent for me, Colonel?"

He smiled warmly and escorted her to a comfortable easy chair in the corner, instead of one of the wooden chairs directly in front of his desk, reserved for those on the *hot seat*.

"Miss Irwin, how nice to see you. Thank you for coming."

Virginia smiled nervously, but was wondering why the schmoozing, since an invitation to the Colonel's office was not really a choice.

"I didn't know an invitation from you was optional," she said.

Blakeslee sat on the corner of his desk and clarified his summons, "Technically, you're not under my command, but I like to think you'd be interested in my thoughts on most things *base* related. Am I right?"

Virginia nodded, "But, of course, Colonel. Since you gave me VIP status on the base, everyone has been pampering me, including my own editor. You know I'd do anything for you."

Blakeslee pursed his lips, "Does that include some *unusual* public relations?"

Virginia nodded again, "Certainly, but I thought Captain Hall was your Public Relations Officer."

"He is," Blakeslee agreed, "and he's doing a fine job. But this assignment is more like *private* public relations."

Intrigued, but unsure, Virginia wrinkled her brow, "I don't understand."

A bit more seriously now, Blakeslee said, "Miss Irwin, I need to shell down the corn. Everyone on base knows you and Mr. Hofer spend an inordinate amount of time together."

Faced for the first time with the knowledge that their relationship was an open secret, Virginia stammered, "Well, sir, I, uh..."

Blakeslee waved her off impatiently, "Don't misunderstand. Whatever article you and Hofer are working on is fine with me. He's almost a triple ace, and sometimes I think he may even become an officer and a gentleman, thanks to your influence."

Virginia smiled weakly, "I'm afraid I still don't understand."

Blakeslee offered more assurance, "You must keep this conversation private, don't discuss it with anyone, specifically the Kidd. Agreed?"

"Well, yes, sir, if you insist."

Blakeslee continued, "Tonight is a big night at Debden. Virtually all the brass in the ETO are coming. Eisenhower, Spaatz, Doolittle, everybody's coming to supper. All our aces will be there. Except Ralph."

Understanding the implication, Virginia asked the obvious question, "Oh? Why not Ralph?"

Sighing, Blakeslee elaborated, "It's simple actually. No dark calumny. Rank has its privileges. We simply don't have enough chairs at the table to include an enlisted flight officer, even if he is only two hits short of being a triple ace."

Puzzled, but shrugging her shoulders, Virginia said, "Okay. How does that concern me?"

"I need a couple of things from you. First, I need you to explain things to Ralph, regarding this dinner, without him necessarily knowing that I put you up to it. He deserves to know that his absence is not a deliberate snub, just the natural result of his delay in applying for his commission.

"And, I also want you to use your influence with him to get him to get that done. He needs that commission. And, I'm hoping that he will start using *his* influence in the command to be a leader, not a disruption. Would you do that for me?"

Blakeslee stood and walked to the window, letting his request simmer a bit. Turning to Virginia, he waited.

Virginia was still processing the idea that everyone from Blakeslee on down knew they were involved, and now she had to deal with the fact that the Commanding Officer of the 4th Fighter Group was asking her to help with delicate personnel matters.

"Colonel, you know Ralph hates details, and loves to fight. But I'm willing to help if I can."

Blakeslee continued, "With his status as one of our leading aces, he could be a big help to his Squadron leaders, and everybody else, if he'd grow up and quit being such a kid. No pun intended. But I don't want him to know we had this conversation. If it comes from me, it's just an order, or a dressing down. You see?"

Smiling, Virginia sat back, "Consider it done, Colonel. I'll do whatever I can."

He took a seat at his desk and directed the conversation to more interesting business, at least from Virginia's perspective.

"Good," he said, "and thanks. Now get out your notebook and I'll give you some *scoops*, but you can't disclose them until after tomorrow's mission is over, Okay?"

Virginia dipped into her purse for her pen and notebook. "Okay, sir, I'm ready," she said, more relaxed now and in her element.

"The 4th has been credited with 90 victories in our last three missions," Blakeslee said. "We now lead the scoring race with 414 confirmed kills."

Scribbling quickly, Virginia smiled, "Like your motto says, 'Fourth but First.'"

Continuing almost faster than she could write, Blakeslee added, "Gentile now has 28 confirmed kills and is officially America's new Ace of Aces. He's got one final mission tomorrow, and then we'll make the official announcement. By the way, you're invited to the ceremony, of course. It will be held at the 336th hangar after he lands."

"Oh, thank you, Colonel."

"James Goodson is now the second leading ace of the group, with 24 kills. Johnny Godfrey, Gentile's wingman, has 13, and Hofer, too, is up to a baker's dozen. Tomorrow Eisenhower is decorating me and Gentile with the Distinguished Service Cross before the mission. When Gentile returns, he'll be named America's Leading Ace, and rotated home for a bond tour. That's all."

Blakeslee stood and walked to the door, and clearly conveying that the meeting was over.

Virginia hurriedly gathered her stuff to leave.

He said, "I'll see you tomorrow on the apron?"

"Wouldn't miss it!" She stood at the threshold waiting for him to open the door.

When he did, Duke was standing there expectantly. Blakeslee almost did a double take when he realized Duke was there to guard Virginia. He leaned over and petted the devoted dog, who stood still appreciatively.

Waving as Virginia and Duke disappeared down the hall, Blakeslee, realizing his dismissal may have been a little abrupt, called to her, "Thank you, Miss Irwin. See you tomorrow."

She turned, waved, and smiled back. Exiting the building, she climbed into Sgt. Scudday's waiting jeep, and Duke hopped in the back. He drove them to the 334th hangar where the pilots were waiting for her to continue their interviews. And to where Hofer would soon return.

~~~

Later, after the mission, Virginia and Hofer were talking at the Rose and Crown, a 14th century pub in the town square of nearby Saffron Walden. It's early afternoon in the middle of the week, so the pub is deserted, except for the couple in the back room, sipping pints, in earnest conversation.

"You see, Ralph, staying so busy with missions actually is hindering your advancement in the squadron. That's the reason you're not invited to the big brass supper, it's not anything personal, or from your disciplinary record, it's just a rank issue."

Still skeptical, Hofer said, "So, I'm not being excluded as punishment for not getting the application done?"

"It's a consequence, but not a reason. I have it on the highest authority," she assured him. "But, you must take the time and trouble to apply for a commission, so you can be included at these officer's functions, not just the pilot functions."

"Paperwork is not my strong suit. Will you help?" He hung a puppy dog face at her.

Smiling, but a sucker for being needed, Virginia readily agreed, with a condition.

She added, "If I help you become an *officer and a gentleman*, will you stop making passes at me every time we're alone?"

"Sure," he said, reaching across the table for her hand, "if you can convince me you really don't like it."

Coyly, but smiling, Virginia eluded him.

"See, already I'm not very convinced," he admonished. "One minute you complain, then you play. You may say 'no,' but your eyes say 'yes.' I think I'm good for your ego."

Virginia dismissed his comment, because he was right, and changed the subject.

"By the way, Colonel Zemke of the 56th contacted me. He's asked me to come over to Halesworth, and interview some of his pilots. Seems their public relations officer has been a little lax, in the Colonel's opinion."

Leaning back and feigning disinterest, Hofer scoffed, "Why are you telling me?"

"Because I've decided to spend a little time over there, and they've offered to put me up in the officer's quarters. So, you won't be seeing much of me for a little while."

Hofer had to quickly cover his surprise, and disappointment. He was also surprised to realize he felt a pang of jealousy. He didn't like the idea of "his reporter" being off on another base around other pilots. At Debden, the other pilots readily recognized the special friendship between Hofer and Virginia, but at Halesworth, and with the "Wolfpack"? They got the nickname not only from their ferocity in combat, but their somewhat lurid reputation around the ladies.

"Well," he said, as casually as he could, "if you're going to be an award-winning journalist, you have to go where the story is. The 4th is the story, but the 56th is our main competition. Be sure and talk to Sandy Ball. Tell 'im I said hello."

"Okay. Why him?"

Hofer became reflective, "Before the war I dated a girl from my hometown, Salem, Missouri, named Susan. Sandy Ball and I were both interested in her. I named my plane after her, but she wrote me a dear john letter just before I got to England telling me she had agreed to marry Sandy after the war. I just want him to know there's no hard feelings. To the victor goes the spoils, I guess."

Virginia studied him for a second. Perversely, knowing about his *lost love* seemed to have made him even more attractive, despite her efforts to keep things professional between them.

"Do you ever talk to Sandy?"

"Yeah, we run into each other at the Cracker's Club from time to time. We rib each other about the competition between the groups, but don't talk about Susan much. I think he's jealous, although I don't understand why. He won, after all."

"Was she dating both of you at the same time?"

"Yeah, but she was always a lady, and always honest. We dated for a few months before she met Sandy, and she told me she was seeing him, too. She never led me on. I think the world of her. Sandy's a lucky guy. Just wasn't my fate..."

Virginia could see that these memories were uncomfortable, maybe a little painful. She hesitated before pressing the matter.

Hofer took a long draught of his pint and leaned down to pet Duke, who, having polished off his bowl of milk, was dozing between the two of them.

"Well, maybe he thinks because of the war..." she started.

Hofer laughed, realizing what she was about to suggest, "He's wrong. She is and always was a genuinely classy lady. No wartime romance for her. I think she decided she liked a potential banker better than a potential actor."

This bit of honesty seemed to restore their equilibrium. Virginia smiled genuinely and nodded.

Hofer drained his pint, "I have to get back. Mission tomorrow."

Virginia reached over and squeezed his hand, "It's still early, can I see your new nose art?"

Hofer grinned, "Of course, let's go."

As they stood to leave, they said, in unison, "Hey!"

Duke stood up quickly, looking back and forth between them. They could not help but laugh. The trio left the pub and hailed a passing lorry for the short ride back to the base.

After being dropped off at the gate, they strolled in the still bright sunlight down the main boulevard towards the 334th hangar. Aware of the curious glances in their direction, and the knowing looks from passersby, they walked casually, careful to temper their closeness. It was a tacit strategy Hofer had been using to keep on her good side. By sticking to the right side of the road and staying on the outside, or street side, with Virginia on the inside, Duke naturally took on the function of chaperone by stoically placing himself at Hofer's right knee. This effectively kept the two comfortably separated, while looking natural to interested eyes.

When they arrived at the hangar office, they found Virginia's photographers, Frenchy and Ski waiting, Sgt. Scudday was napping, as usual. Scudday, Virginia decided, apparently lived at the hangar, as no one ever saw him at the barracks.

Scudday roused himself when they entered, and asked sleepily, "You guys coming to the party tomorrow night? Colonel Blakeslee got word this morning that the Group is officially over 400 victories. Big do, donchaknow?"

Hofer laughed, "Of course. 400 victories is great, but since when do we need an excuse for a party?"

Scudday agreed, "Right. But it never hurts to have a reason and getting ahead of the 56th is a special occasion."

"Came to show Ginny my new nose art, wanna come?"

They all stood and followed Hofer into the dark hangar. He flipped on the lights, and they made their way to his freshly adorned plane.

"We can't take too long," he warned. "Lights out at dusk because of enemy bombers."

Virginia walked up to Hofer's plane. It was a "B" birdcage razorback model with the modification of a clear bubble "Malcolm" hood from a British Spitfire and had a paint job which could only be described as "spectacularly garish."

The tires were white sidewalls. On the main gear door of the port main gear, was the word "Kidd" hand painted in crude, large black letters. The tops of the wings and top of the fuselage, both in front of the windscreen and behind the pilot's compartment to the empennage, were painted olive drab. Along the nose were "victory markers," 17 Balkan Crosses, the silhouettes of two full-rigged sailing ships and a train billowing smoke. In front of the red, white and blue roundel of the United States were the letters "QP," and behind was the letter "L," signifying the plane was assigned as aircraft "L" in the 334th Squadron of the 4th Fighter Group of the 65th Fighter Wing of the 8th Air Force.

Under the canopy, the *nose art* on the port side of the fuselage labeled the plane as the "Salem Representative," in red script. It bore a cartoon winged Missouri mule, emblazoned with a championship belt buckle, wearing golden boxing gloves and olive drab boxing shorts with a large "M." At the tip of the tail there was a golden horseshoe, hanging tangs down.

"Oh, Ralph, it's beautiful," exclaimed Virginia. "Explain it to me, please?"

Mindful of Frenchy's softly purring movie camera, Hofer became the willing docent; with exaggerated formality, "Of course, Miss Irwin."

"It's my life so far," Kidd continued. "The Missouri Mule is there because, of course, Salem, my home town, is in Missouri. The 'M' on the shorts is for Missouri. The golden wings for being a flier, the golden gloves and the championship belt buckle for the

Golden Gloves middleweight boxing championship I won in Chicago. That championship was the reason I got to spar with Billy Conn while he was World Light-Heavyweight Champion."

"What about the horseshoe?" Virginia asked.

Grinning, Hofer gently explained, "It's a *mule* shoe, obviously, and it's my good luck charm."

Being a farm girl herself, and familiar with the good luck charms of rural life on the farm, she blurted out, "But why is it pointing down?"

Hofer, slightly perplexed, looked at it closely, "What?"

Virginia, not thinking, continued, "You hang a horseshoe tangs up, so it will hold your luck. Yours is tangs down, so the luck runs out."

She stopped herself, horrified at what she had just said. She started to blush and stammer, "I mean, ah... you know, it's just an old wives' tale, it doesn't mean a thing..."

Hofer studied the horseshoe, then at Virginia and brushed it off.

Confidently, he said, "The German pilot doesn't exist that can shoot me down."

He grinned a mirthless grin and gave Frenchy the *cut* sign to stop filming.

As Frenchy searched for the off-switch, the whir of the camera was loud in the silence, and the silence when it stopped was poignant.

Virginia, eager to break the uncomfortable turn of events, said to Hofer, "It's a beautiful day, and still light. Can we get some photos outside?"

Scudday looked to Hofer for guidance, who gave him a slight nod. "Of course, Ms. Irwin."

Scudday turned toward the hangar office, wedged his fingers in his mouth and blew a loud whistle. Immediately, several enlisted men came trotting through the door.

"The lady wants pictures in the sunlight, gentlemen, can we oblige her?"

Without comment, a couple of them jogged over to open the large hangar door, while another one started the parking tug. When it was fully clear, they quickly moved the plane out on the apron.

The late afternoon sun was perfect for photos. For the next few minutes, Hofer and Duke posed as directed. Hofer in the cockpit with Duke leaning on the cockpit rail. Hofer and Duke next to the port main gear door, emblazoned with "Kidd" in black letters. Hofer standing next to the port gear, with Duke laying on the wing.

Finally, Ski made a suggestion that took Virginia by surprise, "Miss Irwin, would you get up on the wing with Mr. Hofer, and pose Duke in the pilot's seat like he was flying?"

Virginia blushed, but complied, and the picture of Duke staring forlornly out of the cockpit, like he couldn't wait to get back on the ground, with Hofer and Virginia in uncomfortable personal proximity was taken.

Hofer and Virginia tried unsuccessfully to make sure their budding but mutual attraction didn't become permanently recorded with photographic evidence.

Stepping down, Hofer assisted Virginia off the wing and back on the ground.

"Tomorrow is a big day," he said to Virginia, signaling the end of the photo session. "Decorations first, then a mission, then the 400 victory party. Are you going back into London today?"

"No. Major Millikan's wife Ruby is coming to get me, and I can stay with her tonight. Kay Summersby and I are hoping to spend some time together with the early medal ceremony, and all the activities at the base, I didn't want to miss anything. I will stay with Millie and Ruby until they come back to the party. See you there?"

"Yes, ma'am. You owe me a dance."

"I intend to honor that, but remember, you promised to wear your Class A uniform, and your medals, Okay?"

"Sure, Ma'am, you're on."

CHAPTER TWENTY

Early the next morning, at promptly 0800 hours, Eisenhower and his staff were on the flight line in front of the 336th hangar ready to decorate Gentile and Blakeslee. The ceremony was brief and concise. All the activity was centered on the day's mission and the big party set for the evening to celebrate 400 victories.

Virginia and Kay sat excitedly in the stands watching the awards ceremonies. It gave them a long-anticipated chance to "catch up."

"So, Ms. Irwin, word has even reached London that the inimitable Kidd Hofer is sweet on a certain reporter. What's your thought?"

Kay smiled at Virginia's reaction. She was still trying to accept the fact that their ruse wasn't working, and their romance had apparently become common knowledge.

"Oh, Kay, that's just a rumor. You know how things get blown out of proportion around a military base, don't you?" She looked directly into Kay's eyes to see if her denial was working. It wasn't.

Kay smiled. "Virginia, you mustn't lie to your new best friend. You know, General Eisenhower has spies everywhere, and when they report to him, I'm usually within earshot. Everybody on this base, from Colonel Blakeslee on down, knows you come out here to see Hofer, even if you do try to divert attention by interviewing other pilots, and taking pictures, and doing whatever else you do to try to keep it quiet."

Virginia persisted weakly. "Oh Kay, that's an exaggeration. Hofer is an interesting young pilot, but he's only one of the many stories I'm working on."

She looked at her friend, and the façade began to crumble. Kay's obvious knowing look and bemused expression quickly disarmed the story, and Virginia surrendered the truth.

"I don't know why," she gave up, "but that man is the most fascinating, intriguing man I've ever met. Every time I'm around him I learn something new about him. He's like a diamond shining in the sunlight, with sparkles coming from every angle."

Now Kay chuckled out loud. "That's more like it, girl. I've been trying to keep my feelings for the General in check for over a year, and it's hard work, believe me. A General is one thing, but when you have a crush on a fighter pilot, I say enjoy yourself."

Virginia, a little taken aback by the reference to a romance between Kay and the General, looked at Kay with undisguised surprise.

"Kay, you and the General?"

Kay demurred, "Well, not really, not like that. He's just such a wonderful man, and we have some pleasant conversations which help him cope with the enormous stress he's under. But he's very loyal to Mamie and has even asked that she be allowed to join him in England. I think General Marshall vetoed the idea. Too much of a distraction, I guess. But I have to admit, he's someone I adore, and admire as much or more than anyone I've ever met."

The roll of the drums, and the announcement for Colonel Blakeslee and Captain Gentile to step forward interrupted their repartee, and they turned their attention to the ceremony.

They watched from the viewing stand as the medals were awarded, and then stood by as the 4th mounted their aircraft, fired up the engines, and began taxiing out for the days mission. *It's a rhubarb to the French coast and promises to be rather short and sweet. Everyone should be back before lunch*, she was assured by more than one person.

Kay and Virginia hugged, and Kay departed to drive the General back to London, with promises to get together as soon as their duties would permit.

But everyone knew that the return of Gentile would be when the real news started, because he would be named Ace of Aces, and there would be interviews and photographs, and plenty of celebration around and on the flight line.

For the next two hours, there was little to do as the "mission sweat" for the ground personnel was just that, sweating out the return of the pilots with no clue as to what was going on at the "tip of the spear"—the point of aerial combat where lives were lost, or changed forever.

Virginia, not wanting to lose her connection with the ground personnel, hung around the 334th hangar, visiting with the men, and exploring tidbits and gossip for possible use in other stories. She asked about Hofer, and found he was universally admired by the ground personnel. They told her funny stories about Hofer and Duke, and how friendly Hofer was to the ground crew. Since he was an enlisted pilot, known as a "Pilot Officer" (or P/O), they thought of him as *one of their own*.

Of course, all the pilots appreciated and respected the ground crews. In her wanderings, Virginia had never found any stories about any of the pilots disrespecting the men who work so hard and so long to keep their planes in the air and ready for combat. But there was always the intangible difference between "officers" and "enlisted." It was still the Army, after all, and the fact that Hofer was "enlisted" like the ground crew did create a special bond. She hoped he would not lose that bond when he got his commission.

Finally, around 1100 hours, word filtered out that the Fourth was only a short distance away. Apparently, they had gotten into some kind of *mix up*, because they were coming back without wing tanks, which means they were jettisoned before a fight, and they were coming back in small elements of one, two, or three. Things happened so fast in the sky and the planes got separated so easily during combat that it often became "every man for himself" very quickly.

Virginia joined the large crowd of ground crew, newspapermen, photographers, brass, and base personnel at the base of the Tower. Even Blakeslee was there, the mission having been led by Lt. Col. Clark.

As each plane or group of planes came in, the conversation ebbed and flowed as it was identified: It was Goodson. It was Godfrey. It was Millikan.

Then the group got an electric notice.

Leaning out from the top of the tower, one of the air controllers shouted to the assembled group below.

"Gentile is next!"

The Photographers scrambled to get good positions, everyone watched expectantly to the east. And there it was, a small black dot at high speed and descending rapidly. He was coming in low, as promised, for the publicity shots everyone wanted for their local outlet.

Barreling over the runway at about 150 feet, the most famous P-51 in the European Theatre of Operations was easily identified. A big, red and white checkerboard on the engine cowling to make join up with Godfrey easy, a large picture of the "Fighting

Eagle" emblem of the 4th Fighter Group, and a large scroll down the side filled with Balkan Crosses for the 28 victories attributed to Gentile so far.

But as he approached the middle of the field, Gentile recalled his promise to really put on a show; to "beat up" the field with a really low, high speed pass. So, he came in even lower, at full power. Not realizing that his depth perception had not had time to adjust from high altitude he neglected to account for the rise in the middle of the field caused by bomb damage repair. He was not just low, he was too low.

Disaster.

In less than a second, right in front of the tower, Shangri-li struck the ground, and ricocheted into the air. The nose was impossibly high, on the verge of a fatal stall; the bent prop was spinning crazily. Inside, Gentile frantically fought for control. He shut off the throttle, worked the rudder pedals, pushed the stick forward to bring down the nose. It took every ounce of his concentration and every trick and skill he had ever learned—in training or in mortal combat—to regain control, avoid the stall, and the sure death that awaited in the event of total loss of control.

Incredibly, the mortally wounded fighter slowly returned to level flight, but without power. There was nothing to do but belly in to the mushy ground. The severely damaged bird careened off the runway and into a conveniently located field next to the runway.

In mere seconds it was over. The Shangri-li was half submerged in a small stock pond, with a broken back. The severely bent blades of the prop gave silent testimony to their collision with the ground while still under power. The most famous Allied fighter plane in Europe was a total irreparable wreck.

For a few seconds, as emergency personnel raced toward the wreck, there was no movement, and everyone feared the worst. But as the emergency crews descended on the downed craft the canopy flipped up and Gentile climbed out, roughed up, unsteady on his feet, but with apparently no broken bones. He walked out on the left wing and sat down in total despair. He had hoped to take Shangri-li back to the States for a war bond tour. Now he felt he was looking at a court martial, reduction in rank, and God knows what else Blakeslee would do.

Back at the base of the Tower, Blakeslee was utterly livid and apoplectic. No one had ever seen the towering rage exhibited by the Colonel. Not only had Gentile pranged a kite by showboating, the ultimate sin in the "Blakesleewaffe," he had done it in the most public and humiliating way possible, both to himself, and to the Fourth Fighter Group. A moment of supreme glory had been turned into a public relations nightmare.

There would be no interviews, and the news of the crash would be edited out of the stories about the new Ace of Aces. The evening's big banquet and 400 victory party would be heavy with the pall of this epic screw up, and the whole base would live under that pall for days. All because a pilot was trying to accommodate the press.

In the early evening, Ruby Millikan and Virginia were preparing for the 400 victory party. Virginia was sitting at the vanity carefully applying make-up, while Ruby fussed with various dresses, laying them out on the bed for Virginia's consideration. The conversation, having already run the gamut from Don Gentile's epic crash, Virginia's budding friendship with Kay Summersby, their respective childhoods and school, family plans, general history and future plans, finally turned to the subject most interesting to any woman; the man in her life.

Virginia inquired tactfully, "So how did you meet Millie?"

Ruby, a bride of only a few months, stopped to remember, the recollection brought on the blossoming of a radiant smile, "A flat tire."

Having expected something more mundane, Virginia was intrigued now, "A flat tire?"

"Yes. Believe it or not, I was returning from the market at Saffron Walden, coming down Water Lane, and had a flat on my bicycle. Millie stopped and helped me fix it. Honest to God, Ginny, by the time he was finished, so was I, but of course he didn't know that."

They giggled like schoolgirls.

She continued, "He started coming around and introduced me to his friends and fellow pilots. Eventually he started inviting me to the base parties, and before you know it, we were thinking about the future."

While listening, Virginia had grown pensive. She started brushing her hair, "What kind of future can you have with a war on?" she sighed.

Ruby smiled, "The same kind of future you have when there isn't a war. The one God has planned for you. Short or long. There are no guarantees, you know?"

Virginia continued brushing her hair silently.

It was Ruby's turn for a question, "So what's going on with you and Kidd? Everybody's talking about you two. How did you meet?"

Virginia glanced at Ruby in the mirror, the genuine surprise on her face made Ruby laugh out loud. Up until now, Virginia had somehow thought that only those really in the know suspected something between her and Hofer. Now, with Ruby's comment, it was obvious her little charade regarding Ralph wasn't fooling anyone.

Resigned to the inevitable, she tried to steel herself for a conversation she really wasn't ready to have, "We met the first night I was in Debden. I went to a party to hand out donuts and lemonade with the USO. He came to my table, but he didn't want either. He asked me to dance. I wasn't very impressed, I even thought he was a bit rude, but I felt it was my duty, so I agreed. Turns out he's almost as good at dancing as I am."

"Rude, really? Well, I heard that Colonel Don introduced the two of you."

"Sorta. The next morning, I reported to Colonel Don, and he informed me that Ralph was to be my escort when I was on the base. I didn't want to only be allowed on the base when escorted, that would've made my job much harder. I wanted to have carte blanche for interviews and base access, so I pouted, and told the Colonel I didn't think Mr. Hofer was suitable, because he had been mean to me. Worked like a charm. I was able to wrangle VIP status, with Ralph as my guardian, which I accepted reluctantly, by the way. And I guess the letter from General Eisenhower helped a little."

They laughed again like conspirators, at the successful application of her feminine wiles.

"Reluctantly, huh? So, when did you and Mr. Hofer decide you liked the assignment?"

Virginia turned to face Ruby, maybe realizing this for the first time herself, "When he introduced me to Duke, and Duke licked me, I just wanted to be with them both forever."

She paused, "Of course, he didn't know that. And I'm not sure I knew it either."

"Hmmm," Ruby said, and a face that implied supplication, "maybe guys got wiles too."

Virginia rolled her eyes and went back to brushing her hair, "Oh, they got wiles, just no training."

Ruby continued, "So are you making plans?"

"Absolutely not. I've already got a plan, and it doesn't include Ralph Hofer."

"Wait a minute. One second it's *forever*, and the next second it's *never*. What's the matter with you, girl?"

Virginia stared into the mirror. She wasn't sure how to answer that question, not only for Ruby, but for herself. Until now, she only had a perfunctory awareness of the conflict in her heart, but talking with Ruby had brought it more sharply into focus.

She sighed. "Oh, Ruby. I don't know. I came to England with a plan, and it didn't include falling in love with a hot shot fighter pilot, 13 years younger than me. The only thing we have in common is we're both from Missouri."

"That's not true." Ruby countered. "Everyone that sees the two of you together is dazzled by how you complement one another. You seem like a match made in heaven."

"Well," she turned away again in exasperation, "would heaven match me with a guy that wants a family, when I'm done with family life? Would heaven match me with a guy that's fighting for his life almost every day? Would heaven match me with a guy that constantly tries to derail my career? Would heaven match me with someone who makes me afraid of the future because I can't imagine my life without him in it? Ruby, everything's wrong, except I'm in love with him."

Ruby smiled and gave her a hug from behind, "Well, Ginny, you have to remember that when everything seems wrong, except you're in love, then everything is right."

They laughed again.

"Ruby, tell me how you decided to marry a fighter pilot. Don't you worry about him?"

Ruby took a moment to gather her thoughts before answering. Virginia realized it was a loaded question, so she waited.

"My heart is in my throat every second he's on a mission. But we have a signal. When he's back, he buzzes the house. I run out the door and he waggles his wings."

"But how can you live with the danger? With the uncertainty? And you and Millie are about the same age, aren't you? Hofer and I have a huge age difference."

Ruby softened for Virginia's sake, "Before the war, I had a beau. We decided to wait until the war was over. That was a mistake. We lost whatever days the Lord had planned for us. He was killed in the Battle of Britain."

The memory caused a lump in her throat, forcing her to stop. After a moment, she continued, "I never thought I would have that feeling again. But when Millie and I met on that road— we talked while he was repairing my bike. I felt a warmth and passion I thought I had lost forever. Just from talking. I made up my mind then and there that I would not let love pass me by again, no matter the risk, no matter the consequences. But you're right, Ginny, life is so uncertain, you must grab love when it comes, and hold it tight for however long it's yours."

CHAPTER TWENTY-ONE

After the excitement and humiliation of Gentile's spectacular blunder the victory party was delayed. The Debden Officer's Mess doors were closed. Guests milled around outside, and inside the pilots of the 4th Fighter Group waited on the arrival of Colonel Blakeslee.

Blakeslee slipped in the back door and took the stage. The murmur of conversation ceased.

The Colonel looked over his audience with a tight smile and steely-eyed fighter pilot's glare, "Men, congratulations on 400 victories. We *are* fourth but first."

The men applauded, cheered and slapped each other on the back; the fourth was finally in front of the 56th.

Blakeslee hovered in front of the mic a moment, allowing the men their celebration, "There's plenty more Jerries out there. I promised General Auton we'd have 500 by May. I want 1000 before we're done."

Among the men there was a buzz of agreement. He waited again, letting the praise for a job extremely well-done sink in.

"But there's too many people around here thinking we've got it made," he studied the pilots. "We don't. Do not relax. Wear proper uniforms. Observe mess hall hours. Show up for duty on time. No unauthorized use of Group vehicles."

Pacing to his left, he continues, "We're just beginning to go to work. The busy season is at hand. The invasion is coming."

He stopped at the corner in front of Hofer and Duke but looked towards Godfrey and Lucky.

"Keep your dogs out of the mess hall. Do not take them flying."

Both Godfrey and Hofer pretended to have something on their dog that demanded their concentrated attention.

The Colonel noticed, but let it pass, "The next few months will test the fortitude of a lot of people. I'm already hearing complaints about overwork, whining about rotations, promotions and petty problems. For these I have no sympathy."

He paced back to the opposite end of the stage, "I hope you stand the test. Let's get to work and keep the finger out..." Blakeslee gestured with the famous middle finger salute, "WAY OUT!"

With that, the men erupted into even louder cheering and applause as they got the *pep rally* spirit the Colonel intended.

The band struck up a jitterbug, and at Blakeslee's nod, the batmen opened the doors to the club allowing the waiting guests to file in. They quickly made their way to their respective hosts, asking what was going on.

After greeting the guests and helping to get the party started, Blakeslee and the pilots retreated to the Officer's Mess where the big shindig with Eisenhower, Spaatz, Doolittle, Auton, and all the rest would take place.

About an hour later, after their squadron dinner, they emerged to rejoin the party. Hofer, arriving earlier, had looked for Virginia, without success. When he finally found her he was stunned. He almost didn't recognize her. After weeks of running around in fatigues, ball caps, wadded hair, and combat boots, Virginia Irwin, the elegant lady from Missouri, had finally been revealed.

Intent on making *an entrance* she had arrived late, knowing the pilots wouldn't be joining the party until after the squadron dinner. As she walked in, the buzz of the crowd swept the room like a wave. Ruby had dressed her in an elegant red evening gown with white pearls around her soft neck, and her dark hair was beautifully coiffed to spill around her shoulders. Beautiful black patent leather heels on her delicate feet, vibrant red nail polish on her fingers, and toes which just peeked from the tip of her shoes, and a black patent leather clutch purse for her feminine essentials.

She, too, almost didn't recognize the Kidd; she had never seen him with his jaw on the floor.

She strolled up, smiling, "Want to dance?"

Dumbfounded, Hofer fairly whispered, "Ginny, is that you? You're beautiful."

Blushing, she batted her dark lashes at him, "Thank you, Ralph. Now you know why I asked you to wear your dress uniform and medals. Ruby Milliken convinced me to do it. I hope you don't mind."

"Mind? Of course not. You are stunning."

He stepped back and looked her over with genuine appreciation of her elegant beauty, and a deep and honest affection.

Raising his gaze back up to her eyes, he said, "I've got some good news, too. Weather's closed in, so tomorrow's mission has been scrubbed. I've got a 48-hour pass. Instead of wasting that dress on another Debden party, would you like to have a night in London? I made some phone calls this afternoon."

She was surprised, but game, "Well, of course, but I can't just sashay out the door with you in the middle of a big celebration. I'm a reporter, and I have to appear objective."

Hofer gave her a conspiratorial grin, "Yeah, right. C'mon, meet me outside."

Virginia looked around the room, checking to see exactly how much attention they were drawing. Everyone seemed to have become absorbed in the rapidly escalating festivities.

She conceded, "I wouldn't climb out of a toilet window in this dress for just anybody, Mister. This is going to cost you."

Hofer laughed and meandered towards the door, speaking to Speer and Clemens Fiedler as he tried to look inconspicuous.

Virginia watched him for a few seconds, then headed towards the ladies' room down the hall.

Just as she reached the entrance to the hallway, an MP Sergeant cut her off, "Miss Irwin?"

Virginia was surprised to be called by name by the Master Sergeant in charge of the party, as they had never been formally introduced.

"Yes, Sergeant?" she said, thinking she had been caught.

"Ma'am, that's much too pretty a dress to snag on a windowsill. Follow me, please?"

He smiled and gestured down the hall.

Virginia looked back. The celebration was in full swing, they were alone at the entrance to the hall, and no one was paying attention.

With a demure nod, she acquiesced and followed.

He led her down the hall, past the ladies' room, to the emergency exit at the end. He pulled the key to the padlock from his pocket, then turned to look behind them to see make sure no one was observing. Satisfied they were fully in the clear he unlocked the door and held it open for her.

Outside, the moon was shining brightly, with scudding clouds off to the south around London; she could hear the jeep idling around the corner of the building in front of the restroom window she was supposed to be climbing out of.

She looked at the Sergeant in befuddlement, "Thank you?" she said, timidly.

"Take good care of Mr. Hofer. He's one of our heroes you know," he said sternly, but playfully.

She broke into a smile at his request, curtsied deeply, and stepped out the door into the soft spring evening.

Looking back, she couldn't resist a final word, "Does anything really get past you guys?"

Smiling broadly, the Sergeant tipped his hat, "Not much, ma'am. G'night." Then he stepped back inside and shut the door behind her.

Slipping around the corner, Virginia creeped up to the jeep, intending to surprise Hofer, but Duke, always watchful, perked up and whined noisily at her approach. Even the great dog knew they were all on a mission of secret fun.

After the short ride on the train to Liverpool Station, then the cab downtown, Hofer and Virginia were seated at a window table at the Savoy Hotel. Duke, as always, loitered watchfully at their feet, guarding his two charges carefully, but casually. Only the most careful observer would notice that even though the dog seemed relaxed, with his head on his front paws, his eyes were watchful and alert. Duke took in everything around them, his ears pointed to each sound to insure it didn't constitute a threat. It was raining steadily, giving the black-out flashlights of the crowds a fuzzy, holiday feel.

Hofer was slightly discomfited by the attention the two of them had drawn. Apparently, he had been recognized, and being dressed in his Class A dress uniform with all his ribbons, and medals accentuated his status as one of the leading aces of the war. Virginia, more accustomed to attention in public surroundings, didn't seem to notice the envious looks from the ladies, or the lustful glances from the men.

"So, whadayathink?" Hofer smiled. "Is this worth climbing out a window?"

Virginia smiled, mostly to herself, knowing that Kidd didn't know about the MP and the VIP treatment she got escaping the party.

"I don't know yet," she said, "but remind me to give you a report on base security."

Not rising to the bait, Hofer said, "Wine or cocktail?"

"Wine would be nice. Are you planning a mission of some sort?" She teased.

Stammering a bit, Hofer, blushed, "No, of course not. I'm just trying to pamper you."

He turned to the wine steward and gave him an almost imperceptible nod. Virginia was duly impressed at the suddenly polished manners of the rough and tumble prize fighter cum tight end cum fighter pilot she had only begun to get to know. She mentally added one more contradiction to this remarkable boy-child, man, warrior, and joker.

The wine steward, a very dignified elderly English gentleman in his 70's, and wearing a tuxedo, approached. Leaning in, he listened intently as Hofer whispered in his ear; then he smiled and departed silently. Virginia sat quietly but was watching intently and studying Hofer as he imparted his secret to the older gentleman.

When he turned back to her his expression, for once, had little of the devilish charm that was his trademark, and seemed intent, serious, almost somber.

"Ginny, can we be serious tonight? No more witty repartee? I'd like to have a real conversation now that we're away from all the chaos of the base."

Virginia was silent for a few moments. It was obvious he had something to say that he thought was poignant enough to prepare her for, and she took a moment to weigh whether their relationship, such as it was, and herself in particular, could bear to hear it. Stalling for time, she picked up her napkin, carefully and slowly unfolded it, then she laid it in her lap. That would have to do. Inwardly, she sighed, and resigned herself to having to address this with Kidd now.

Finally, she answered. "Okay, sure."

She leveled her gaze at him and waited.

Now it was Hofer's turn to stall. His moment had arrived, and he didn't want to stumble again. "Do you think we might have a future? You're so different from anyone I've ever known. Surely you know that I adore you."

She knew she shouldn't joke. Kidd was in earnest, and his declaration of affection was anything but unexpected, but she was unable to resist adding a little levity to the moment. She laughed softly, "*You're so different.* That sounds like the snake talking to the garden hose."

"Please, Ginny, not tonight." he entreated her.

"I'm sorry, Ralph. Is that a compliment?"

"It's meant to be. I think you know it is."

"Then thank you. I accept. You're very sweet when you want to be."

The wine steward returned with a bottle and displayed it to Hofer.

"Mr. Hofer, I believe this would be a perfect accompaniment for any dining selection you make."

He waited expectantly.

Hofer looked at Virginia, "Ginny, I'm mainly a country boy from Missouri. Do you have any preferences or suggestions on our wine?"

Virginia, pleased at being consulted, gave him a warm smile, and then looked at the steward.

"Our steward is the expert, Ralph. Let's follow his advice."

The steward was mildly surprised, but very pleased to have these young Americans defer to his experience, smiled warmly, "Thank you for your confidence, Ms. Irwin. If for any reason you find my recommendation to be unsatisfactory, I will be happy to replace it at my own expense."

The steward expertly opened the bottle he had chosen, poured a sample into a glass, which Hofer swirled expertly. He sampled the bouquet and took a sip to test its flavor. Hofer approved, and the steward poured a glass for Virginia first, followed by Hofer, and then placed the bottle into an iced, table-side 300-year-old silver wine cooler.

Virginia looked at Hofer quizzically, "Ralph, how does he know my name?"

"Please don't think of me just as Kidd Hofer, last of the screwball aces," he said, and took a sip of wine. "I stopped by the restaurant a few days ago, and asked management to introduce me to their most knowledgeable steward and waiter. They introduced me to Christian. He's been at the Savoy since 1889, when he was 16 years old. I told him I really needed to impress a beautiful lady. And that was before I saw you in that dress. I called earlier this evening to confirm our table."

"Well? Why?" she waited, expectantly.

Hofer picked up his glass and took another sip, steeling his nerve and forming his thoughts.

"Ginny," he said, "I've never known a woman who seemed less interested in what I think about her. You act like you couldn't care less."

"What makes you think I don't care?"

"Do you? You never show it. I want you to be proud of me."

"I am proud of you. Very proud." She took a sip of her wine.

Christian came up and stood politely by, waiting for Hofer to acknowledge him. Hofer smiled at him, "Christian, you've been a godsend. The wine is perfect."

"Thank you, Mr. Hofer," Christian smiled at them, "What's your pleasure this evening?"

"Ginny, want to be surprised? Christian knows this menu, and what's available with wartime rationing, so he would be sure to take good care of us."

Virginia smiled serenely, "I don't want to do anything to spoil the evening. Let's be surprised."

Christian smiled and stepped away.

Hofer became more earnest, "Are you proud enough of me to stand by me, no matter what? I've got big plans. If I can reach my goal of being Ace of Aces, it will help."

"How?"

Gesturing with his napkin, Hofer waved expansively toward the room. "Ginny, after the war, the sky's the limit," he elaborated. "Flying. Education. I've thought about politics. And don't forget about Hollywood."

Frowning, Virginia observed sagely, "That's a shotgun approach, not a plan. When and how do you decide?"

Dismissively, Hofer answered, "Oh, I don't need to decide until after the war. My goal is to be number one. After that, I'll see what's up, what's available, what presents itself."

"Well, that might be a plan, even if you don't have a schedule," she said.

Christian returned. He had a single red rose and laid it on the table next to Virginia's wine glass. She smiled at him and glanced at Hofer.

Christian proceeded to supervise the service of prime rib au jus, baked potato with all the trimmings, early English peas, fresh baked yeast rolls, real butter, and water.

Virginia was surprised and couldn't help but question the steward, "Christian, what on earth? How in the world did you do it? I thought the maximum bill for a supper here was two pounds. This meal must cost three times that with rationing, and all..."

Christian gave her a sly look, "Well, Miss Irwin, whenever Mr. Churchill brings the cabinet around, it seems they always have a little left over for the staff. Once I told my team about Mr. Hofer's plan, everyone was glad to contribute a little— to make sure the evening was special for you. You realize Mr. Hofer is well-known, and admired in England, don't you?"

Virginia hesitated, for the first time realizing that Hofer's accomplishments tended to precede him. She was in the company of a VIP, not just a crazy fighter pilot from Missouri.

She gazed at Hofer for a moment, her impression of him changing by the minute. She recovered her casual demeanor, and said, "Of course,

Christian. Please tell everyone we are very grateful and express our deepest thanks."

As Christian slipped away, Virginia returned her gaze to Hofer, whose appeal, and interest had significantly increased for her.

"Ralph," she said, "you're such a puzzle."

Hofer sensed that Virginia was finally beginning to appreciate his status and notoriety and gave her his undivided attention.

"There's a piece of the puzzle missing for me," he set down his knife and fork for a moment.

Virginia pretended not to understand what he was getting at. "Oh?"

Hofer looked directly into her sky-blue eyes, "You," he smiled.

"I need someone I can trust," he continued. "To share my dreams. A wingman for life. It's your strength and independence that I love."

Virginia scoffed, "I'm not any body's wingman as you call it. I'd be a fighter pilot, too, if they'd let me."

Hofer continued, "That's why you're perfect for me."

Virginia, now confused, shook her head, "I'm divorced for a reason. I left a little nest in St. Louis to become a war correspondent because I don't want anyone telling me how to live my life. My career comes first, not helping hubby."

Hofer responded, "I would never get in your way. You're thinking *hubby works, mommy manages the house, raises the kids.* But that's not what I want. I'm talking about two meteors lighting up the sky. Together."

He tried to reach for her hand, but she withdrew it. "Lots of girls would die for you to talk to them like this. I'm not one of them."

He left his arm extended, with his palm up, inviting her response.

"I know," he assured her. "Look, I'm an enlisted pilot. Okay. Maybe I'll get that commission. But the reason I catch so much flak from the Colonel is that I think for myself."

He put down his napkin, "You know why I score so much? Because I know what the Germans are thinking. When the fight starts, everything up there disintegrates into a whirling mass of flying metal. Planes everywhere, going in every direction; bullets, tracers tracking everywhere. Shell casings falling. Planes exploding or coming apart. Parachutes, pieces of planes, bodies. The sky is full of garbage.

"I can always tell when a Hun has decided to run. Their favorite maneuver is a split S, and head home on the deck. And I'm ready for them. When they come down, I'm already there. They never see me because of the olive drab paint on the upper surfaces of Salem Representative."

"What if someone waits for you?"

She was somber, and serious, but Hofer scoffed, and tossed his napkin down.

"The German pilot doesn't exist that can shoot me down."

Virginia looked at him for a long second, she had heard that before, often. She looked away for a moment, deciding how much she wanted to reveal, then returned his gaze.

"I'm a woman in a man's world," she said. "Any man, you included, is baggage I don't want, don't need, and refuse to carry."

Hofer protested, "Ginny, we're both mavericks. We lead. We don't follow. We make our own rules. Some people like that, some don't. But the point is, we get things done."

For the very first time, she found herself agreeing with him. She felt herself weakening, so she asked the question that cut to the heart of the matter.

"Why take a chance on you? This war is far from over."

He, too, could see she was softening. He opened his palm again. She looked at him, and then at his hand.

He continued, "You're absolutely honest and truthful with me, even when it hurts. I need you, Ginny."

"Pretty words."

"Not just pretty words. I'll protect you. I'll nurture you, love you. I'll help you find your dream and live it. I'll have your 6. You know I will."

Virginia's eyes began to glisten. "Dreams have a way of slipping away. Especially if you trust someone else to help you do it. I guess every heart beats alone unless you give it away."

Hofer smiled at her use of his own bromide, "Trusting the wrong person can lead to heartache. Trusting the right one is a little piece of heaven. The two of us are a terrific team."

"Hearing you talk about teamwork sounds funny. Are you starting to listen to the Colonel?"

Hofer's hand inched closer. "I listen to you all the time. With my head and my heart."

She slipped her hand into his.

Later, at her apartment in Knightsbridge, they slipped into her room quietly, followed by Duke. The drapes were open, and the windows ajar, allowing them to hear the gentle rain falling on the rooftops. Blacked-out London was before them, bathed in moonlight. Distant searchlights crisscrossed the sky. Far, far away, the muffled rumble of explosions could be heard. The radio was softly playing "Body and Soul" by the Ink Spots.

Standing in the glow of the moonlight, they embraced, mere silhouettes to anyone watching from the street. They kissed deeply. As their hands gently, and sensuously began to remove each other's clothing they embarked on a mutual exploration long overdue, and passionate kissing. Soon, as the gentle breeze ruffled the lace curtains, she moved him into the darker shadows of the room and pulled him down onto the bed with her.

Duke laid down at the foot of the bed, looking for all the world like he was going to sleep, but he was ever alert, guarding the two people he loved the most.

April 22, 1944

A couple of weeks later, Hofer was lounging in his room, writing in his log book. Duke was napping on his bed.

There was a knock at the door.

Without looking up, Hofer answered, "Enter."

The door opened, and Goody peeked in, a big grin on his face.

"Goody, what's up?"

"Colonel sent me to get ya. He's over in the Officer's Mess."

Hofer stood and looked questioningly at Goody, "Am I supposed to come like this?"

Goody looked him over, "You just got back from a mission. Colonel usually thinks mission uniforms are Okay for visiting him. So, you're Okay. C'mon, keeping him waiting is never a good idea."

Hofer motioned to Duke, and they walked quickly down the hall towards the Officer's Mess. Stepping inside, Hofer was surprised to see the

Colonel, several other pilots, and Virginia. Everyone was smiling at him.

The Colonel spoke first, motioning to the carpet directly in front of them, "Hofer, front and center."

Looking around furtively, Hofer obeyed, but chose to keep his mouth and let whatever was happening play out.

The Colonel continued, "Hofer, repeat after me."

Hofer was confused but complied.

"I," the Colonel started, "*state your name...*"

Ralph picked it up, "I, state your name..."

Everyone chuckled, except the Colonel.

Hofer cleared his throat, waxed serious and continued. "I, Ralph K. Hofer..."

"...do solemnly swear that I will support and defend the Constitution of the United States against all enemies, foreign and domestic..."

Ralph repeated the phrase, hesitantly.

The Colonel continued, "...that I will bear true faith and allegiance to the same; that I take this obligation freely, without any mental reservation or purpose of evasion..."

Ralph said the same, but now he was more fervent.

"...and that I will well and faithfully discharge the duties of the office on which I am about to enter. So help me God."

Ralph repeated, and ended.

Everyone applauded, and Hofer stood there, somewhat stunned.

The Colonel handed Hofer a small box. Hofer opened it and saw that it contained the gold bars of a Second Lieutenant. He looked up.

Blakeslee extended his right hand in congratulations, "Mr. Hofer, you are now a second lieutenant in the United States Army Air Corps. An

Officer and a Gentleman by act of Congress. Congratulations, Lieutenant."

A smile grew across Hofer's face. Shaking the Colonel's hand, he stammered, "Thank you, Colonel."

The Colonel looked at Goodson, "I've got to go. Meeting with General Auton. Goody, will you fill Hofer in on the other news?"

Goody smiled broadly, "Of course, Colonel. My pleasure."

Blakeslee slipped out quickly, accompanied by his aide and Sgt. Minter.

Goody beamed at Hofer. Everyone was smiling expectantly. Including Hofer, who picked up on the Colonel's hint that there was something more.

"Kidd," Goody said, "Congrats, you've been made commander of "D" flight."

Hofer was truly astonished. "What? Colonel would never approve it."

"No kidding, Commander of "D" flight," Goody laughed.

"The Colonel not only approved it, he asked around before he decided. You've got friends you don't even know about."

Hofer shook hands all around, and then leaned down to give Duke a good ear and muzzle rub, "Whadayathink, Duke? Now we're leaders of men."

Everyone laughs at Duke's response, his patented, *I told you so* yip.

Hofer turned to the group, "Drinks on me, gang. Let's head over to the bar."

They all followed an excited Hofer, except Virginia, who remained in the background, and appeared pleased, but conflicted.

Dropping back, but urging the others to keeping going, Hofer tried to take her arm, but she pulled away, "What's the matter?" he asked.

"Nothing. I'm just busy tonight, so I'll head on back into London."

"If you want to wait until after the first round I'll escort you back. I'd like to, I'm not on the mission board tomorrow."

"No, that's Okay. I didn't want to miss this, but I'm in a hurry."

"Well, see you tomorrow? I know I don't have anything I can't get out of for at least 48 hours."

"No, I've decided to accept Colonel Zemke's invitation to visit Halesworth and the 56th. I," she stumbled, "I'll probably be up there for a few days."

"Are you mad at me?"

"No, of course not. Just busy."

"Too busy for me?"

"Afraid so. Duty first, right? Many things to do, and not much time. I've got deadlines for the paper. Your article is almost finished, so I'm getting the next story in the pipeline."

"So I'm just a story now?"

Virginia just looked at him, then turned and walked away, leaving him looking bewildered. Duke was watching her leave as well, then he looked up at Hofer, as if to ask *Where's she going?*

From the door Goody hollered, "Hey Hofe, you coming?" When he realized that Virginia was heading out the door and not joining them for the celebration he hesitated a moment. But the look on Hofer's face told him it might be best not to ask.

CHAPTER TWENTY-TWO

Two days later, Hofer was sitting in his Mustang with the engine idling, gaggled up at the base of the tower with seven other fighters. To his left was Frank Speer, and to his right were the planes of Clemens Fiedler and Steve Pisanos. Behind them were four other Mustangs, piloted by "FNG's." He looked at each of the experienced pilots taking a newbie up for their first combat mission.

Together, they formed "D" Flight of the 334th Squadron of the 4th Fighter Group; call sign Cobweb Green. It was his first mission as leader of "D" Flight. He looked down at his instrument panel, pausing for a moment on the picture of Virginia gummed to its usual place above the artificial horizon. Scanning all the dials he confirmed that all systems were hot and normal.

All gauges were in the green, oil and coolant shutters were open. Rudder trim tab 5 degrees right. Elevator 2-3 degrees nose up. Aileron zero degrees. Flaps up. Canopy closed and locked. Magnetos check. Mike check. Oxygen check. Guns on safe. Fuel switch on wing tanks.

Hofer keyed his mike, "Diction, this is Cobweb Green. Ready for taxi."

From the tower, called *Diction*, came a call from ground control.

"Roger, Green, Diction clears the runway. Taxi into position Runway 9, hold."

"Roger, Diction. Cobweb Green, taxi in file to Runway 9, combat departure, hold for my command."

From the other seven planes, in order, came the responses:

"Cobweb Green Two, roger."

"Cobweb Green Three, roger."

"Cobweb Green Four, roger."

"Cobweb Green Five, roger."

"Cobweb Green Six, roger."

"Cobweb Green Seven, roger."

"Cobweb Green Eight, roger."

Hofer gunned the powerful Rolls-Royce Merlin engine and the sleek P-51, with a 75-gallon paper wing-tank under each wing, surged forward. Hofer broke left and headed to the end of runway 9, meaning that the compass heading on the runway was 090, or due east. Towards Germany. Towards combat. Towards fate.

The other seven pilots, Speer (Cobweb Green 2), Fiedler (Cobweb Green 3), and Pisanos (Cobweb Green 4), followed in file. Their wingmen following them in the same order, each of the new guys understood his primary, overriding duty on this flight was to stick to his leader like proverbial flypaper.

Hofer broke hard right at the end of runway 9, made the necessary "U turn," and held fast to the left center of the runway. Speer taxied into position on Hofer's left. Fiedler taxied into position just to Hofer's right, with Pisanos to the right of Fiedler. They were in a combat four position, for simultaneous takeoff. The wingmen line up behind their element leaders.

Hofer signaled to his flight for the final pre-flight mag check.

Simultaneously, all eight men applied their brakes and advanced their throttles to 2,000 rpm. The sleek fighters shook with the harnessed power of 2000 horses waiting to be unleashed. The pilots consulted their instruments. Suction 3.75 to 4.25 inches HG. Hydraulic pressure 800-1100 lbs. per square inch. Ammeter under 50 amps. Oil Pressure 70-80 lbs. per square inch. Oil temperature 70-80 degrees. All eight check their mags at 2300 rpm, noting not less than a 100 rpm drop as each mag was turned off, and then turned back on. They cycled the propeller pitch, for not more than 300 rpm drop as it cycled between maximum and minimum pitch. Oil and coolant shutters were set on automatic. Wing flaps to 20 degrees extended. Fuel Mixture Auto Rich. Propeller in full increase RPM. Fuel booster pump on emergency, check for 14-19 lbs. per square inch. Generator switch on. The tail wheel was locked at zero degrees.

One by one, the pilots checked in with their Flight leader.

"Cobweb Green two all systems go."

"Cobweb Green three all systems go."

"Cobweb Green four all systems go."

All eight pilots reported ready, willing and able to take off.

"Roger, Cobweb Green." Hofer reported to the tower, "Diction, Cobweb Green holding on Runway 9. Ready for takeoff."

The pilots watched the tower, waiting for a single green flare. Finally, when it arched into the sky, brilliant and portentous, Hofer advanced the throttle. At first, he applied thrust slowly, then more positively, to 3000 rpm, making a smooth transition from holding, to rolling, to accelerating. At that same moment, signaled by the flare, Speer and Fiedler turn, eyes glued on Hofer; and Pisanos on Fiedler. Behind them, the new FNG's watched their section leader and prepared to roll as soon as the turbulence of the first four abated. Every man, despite some being more experienced than others, was a superbly functioning machine.

The four fighters in front advanced as one, carefully pushing their throttles to synchronize with the Section Flight Leader, maintaining almost perfect formation as they rolled toward V-1, tails up at 65 knots, accelerating on their main gear, engines roaring, heading for the moment of rotation (departure from the ground) and flying.

Seconds later, the second section repeated the identical process. "Gear up."

A second or two later, "Climb at 2700."

The pilots would then retard their throttles slightly, setting the engine RPM's at 2700, and climb out in perfect formation with Hofer.

In moments they were airborne at 110 knots, accelerating to climb out at 180 knots, with manifold pressure of 47 inches. The wingmen formed up on their respective element leaders so that the fighters aligned in a formation known by pilots as the "finger four" which for demonstration purposes resembles the fingernails of two outstretched hands, thumb to thumb. Hofer was the middle finger of the right hand, with an FNG as his wingman, flying in the position of the index finger. The Second element leader of the lead section was Speer, flying in the position of the right ring finger, with his wingman to his right in the position of the right little finger. The left hand had Fiedler as the middle finger of the left hand, with his wingman as the index finger of the left hand, and Steve Pisanos as the ring finger of the left hand, with his wingman as the little finger of the left hand.

They were headed for 25,000 feet, five miles into the sky. At a climb rate of about 2000 feet per minute, it would take them 10-12 minutes to get to their cruise and rendezvous altitude. In their combat configuration they had a range of just under 1200 miles. The distance to Berlin was about 700 miles. The bombers had a two-hour head start, but with the Mustang cruise speed of about 110 knots faster than the loaded, lumbering bombers, the fighters would catch up. Because of their long range, the P-51's were designated as the escort over Berlin, the farthest part of the mission, and thereby the most dangerous. Hofer wouldn't have it any other way. Neither would anyone else in the Fourth. They were killers looking for their prey—the Germans—who dared to challenge their mastery of the sky.

The bombers had their mission, but they were also functioning as bait to lure the Luftwaffe into the sky so that the allied fighters could engage and destroy. They called it the Rodeo to Berlin.

A little less than three hours later, Cobweb Green was approaching Berlin and all eyes were scanning the sky looking for the bombers. Hofer saw them first.

"Green, Big Friends 11 o'clock low," he said.

The others quickly spotted the contrails of the big bomber stream, and then the dots of the bombers themselves. Even from a distance they could see the tinier dots of fighters darting around the formation. Occasionally the bigger dots slowed and dropped lower or fell like leaves. The bomber boys were taking a licking.

Hofer squawked, "Green, drop tanks. Guns on. Follow me."

Flight "D" spread out into combat formation, roughly 200 yards apart, and their almost empty paper tanks fell away. Switching to their fuselage tanks, their endurance was now cut to about a ½ hour of combat, and fuel for home. They increased power and accelerated to the attack.

Index finger covered middle finger, little finger covered ring finger. Teamwork. Wingmen. Mates.

The eight fighters headed straight into the maelstrom. Death and destruction awaited, fate would determine the winners and losers, but to the pilots of Cobweb Green, it was about skill, determination, courage, and ability.

Diving at a shallow angle, the planes of *Green* rapidly closed on the formation of bombers. Hofer took note of a swarm of approximately 20 bandits gathering in the path of the bombers, obviously planning their favorite attack maneuver of head on, trying to knock out the pilot compartments.

He fed in a little left rudder and calculated his lead on the forward German fighter. Knowing that his tracers would leave contrails of their own and warn the Germans they were under attack, he radioed his flight.

"Green, I've got the leader. Everybody take the guy in front of you. Fire when I fire. I want to break up the formation before they can attack the big friends."

All eight acknowledged. "Roger, Green Lead."

As they closed the distance they could see that the German planes were Focke-Wolfe 190's, the best the Germans had. At about four hundred yards, Hofer gave the lead fighter a spurt of two seconds. Watching the tracers and contrails arc out ahead of the German, he observed some strikes around the cowl and along the right wing. The tracers of the other members of *Green* arced into the formation; the Germans now knew they were under attack by a new group of fighters. Hofer saw several strikes from Speer find their targets. Now on the defensive, the Germans broke into multiple elements, and dove, turned, or climbed away, giving the bombers a momentary reprieve.

Hofer and his wingman curved left after an element of six planes, firing short bursts to keep them on the run. Speer, Fiedler and Pisanos and their wingmen had disappeared into the darting mass of planes around the bomber stream.

One of the German pilots was obviously more experienced than the others; he kept his turns tight and was trying to come about and attack Hofer or his wingman. Several of the Germans had dived away and were heading home, choosing to live to fight another day.

Over the intercom, Flight "D" could hear the chatter from the bombers, whistling and hollering like cheerleaders at a football game as they watch the Mustangs break up the German swarm.

Three planes had chosen to stay with the German Experten in the lead, stalking the two-plane element of Hofer and the new guy. It was four against two. Hofer chose the leader, knowing that the leader would be choosing him, too. The two entered into mortal combat. Only one would see his base that night. Hofer said a silent prayer that his FNG could keep up.

Hofer's speed took him past the turning German, and he honked up into a vertical climbing loop, looking straight up through his canopy as his plane turned onto its back.

There. A black dot, with three others close behind, the German was still in horizontal maneuver, apparently losing sight of Hofer as he climbed into the sun. Hofer was aware that his wingman had stayed with him in the loop—*good*—and the two of them were coming down on the Germans from about 2,000 feet above.

Hofer rotated starboard, to level out, and saw, with satisfaction, that his wingman had followed him perfectly. Hofer made a note to write this guy up.

What's his name? He tried to remember, *Cowboy? Yeah, that's it, the new guy, Megura.*

Both planes rotated starboard and settled into a dive. Hofer had the leader in his sights. "Cowboy" Megura was setting up on one of the other four. Almost simultaneously, they fired several short bursts. They watched their tracers, using carefully coordinated, almost imperceptible movements of stick, rudder, and throttle to adjust their position, and bend their fire into the enemy. They wouldn't dive past them this time but would pull up and loop over them for a second attack. The Germans had missed their chance and were now chickens scattering to avoid the attack of the hawk.

Bursting spots against the wing-root and canopy of the Experten told Hofer his aim was true. The German fighter staggered in the air, pieces of wing and ailerons tearing off. The strikes walked into the belly tank beneath the fighter and in a flash, it was all over in an explosion that disintegrated the fighter, leaving a trail of black, oily smoke and debris that Hofer had to pull up sharply to avoid.

At virtually the same time, he saw strikes coming from hits from Megura's guns on the third German plane in trail. The German fighter turned on its back, and pulled into a dive, trying to get away. Cowboy was on him instantly, following him down, short bursts continued to get strikes along the tail, and right wing. In a mere second, Cowboy and the German had disappeared beneath Hofer's wing. Hofer let him go and concentrated on the last two.

The two remaining German fighters, seeing the death of their leader, and the imminent fate of his wingman, had enough and pulled the classic split "S", turning on their backs to dive away and head east towards home. Hofer followed them down, losing contact with Megura.

The two Germans were in fear for their lives. They firewalled their throttles and sped for home in a shallow dive, obviously trying to simply outrun the Mustang until fuel would cause Hofer to break off. But the Mustang had plenty of power and speed to catch up to the fleeing Germans.

As Hofer lined up on the *tail end Charlie*, he smiled grimly to himself and thought, *You should have run when you had the chance, Jerry.*

He lined up at the six o'clock position and marveled at how easy it was. This guy was not even trying to evade, just run. It was not going to work.

Lining up with the MK14 gun sight, Hofer uncaged the gyro, placed the sight reticle on the tail of the German, and worked the range dial to adjust the circle of the six sighting diamonds to the wingspan of the German. It was almost by rote, one smooth movement. Hofer squeezed off a two second burst. The German was flying straight and level. Hofer's two second burst threw approximately 320 rounds from the six 50 calibers, of which 64 rounds were incendiary; at least a third of them hit his target; they chewed into the tail, destroying metal, controls, and ultimately, airworthiness. The plane flipped over instantly, mortally damaged, and fell away. No canopy ejection, no chute; no chance. He was dead.

The other German, seeing his wingman killed, now tried some basic evasive maneuvers, riding his rudders to slip sideways and his stick to move up, and down, and rolling his plane in a corkscrew. Hofer sat back, stalking—following, carefully calculating the German's movements, learning his pattern. It was the dance of death for a greenhorn in the sights of a natural predator. In a second, the Hun would apply left rudder and roll to his port side. Hofer saw it even before it happened. He adjusted his sights and waited for the moment—

NOW!

Another two second burst arced out to the 190 with a perfect lead. The Mustang bucked from the recoil of the six 50's, and the German plane wiggled as the load of lead struck its target. Spots of fire danced along the fuselage and up forward to the engine nacelle. A big puff of black, oily smoke indicated to both pilots that the engine in the 190 was mortally damaged.

The stricken fighter pulled up into a sharp vertical climb, rapidly losing speed since it had no power; the canopy fell away, and a black figure tumbled out into the slipstream.

Hofer dodged the man, breaking into a port turn, and looked back over his shoulder at the black figure falling to earth. In a second or two, a dirty brown parachute blossomed.

Hofer rapidly checked his six, scanning every quadrant of the sky. Then he inverted the fighter in a slow roll to make sure no one was below him in his blind spot. Satisfied that he was alone in sky, he throttled back and circled around to the drifting parachute.

As he lined up on the figure, he saw the pilot tucking into a small ball, expecting to be shot. Hofer was not one to take an easy target, this pilot would live to fight another day. He moved his centerline to one side, and slowed down, assuring the helpless German that he was just doing a flyby.

The man untucked and hung in the chute, waiting.

As Hofer cruised by, he saw that the German was wearing a black leather jacket, gray trousers and shiny black jackboots. A sharp looking soldier. The pilot straightened up, and saluted Hofer as he passed. Hofer grinned and returned the salute.

Checking his gauges, he set course for home, 270, due west. A triple today. A good day.

Now that combat was over, Hofer called to see if anyone else was around.

"Cobweb Green, this is Green lead. Anybody around?"

Silence.

Hofer couldn't help but wonder how everybody did. Did Cowboy get his victory? Did he survive? Did the others make it?

It was about 2 pm, he would be on the ground in less than an hour. Fuel was just about right, provided he didn't see anyone, and no one saw him.

~~~

There were missions almost daily. Some were little more than patrols. Others were life-changing moments. For Kidd Hofer, some were just opportunities to vex his C.O.

On this day, Kidd lead his flight into the air, but before they got to the English coast, his radio crapped out again. Signaling for Speer to take over, he returned to base.

Landing, he taxied up to the 334th hanger, and cut the throttle. As soon as the prop stopped, his ground crew gathered around, aware that something was amiss, because Hofer never aborted.

Pulling back the Malcolm hood, he hollered at Scudday. "My radio quit. Take a look, will you?"

Scudday motioned hurriedly to the radiomen, who quickly analyzed the problem and found that it was nothing more than a fuse. It was replaced in seconds, and the radio was working perfectly.

Hofer figured he was not too far behind Speer, and that he could catch up. As soon as everyone cleared, he started his engine, got clearance, and took off for the continent, a one-man rodeo.

~~~

A few hours later, Kidd returned from the mission. He spotted his landmarks and pulled back his throttle to drop down to treetop altitude. Checking traffic, he saw that everyone was apparently already back, the sky was empty.

"Diction, this is Cobweb Green One, request clearance for landing."

"Roger One, pattern is clear. Landing runway 270. Winds 2 knots from the west. Cleared for landing."

A straight-in approach with no one else in the air was just too good to pass up. Now, just above the trees, he advanced the throttle, speeding up to 350 knots. As the runway appeared under his cowl, he put the agile Mustang into a series of three deliberate barrel rolls, the traditional signal for victories. Flashing past the hangars, and the tower, Hofer could see the ground personnel waving, and could imagine their cheers. The ground guys spent so much time working on the planes, and got so little of the glory, Hofer enjoyed putting on a show for them. They deserved all the credit the pilots could give them, and every pilot on the base knew it. They were genuinely loved and respected by every guy at the tip of the spear.

As he passed the tower, Hofer pitched up, retarding throttle as he climbed to bleed off airspeed. He quickly performed landing checks. Mixture auto rich. Oil and coolant shutters automatic. Fuel selector to fullest tank. Booster pump switch to normal.

As soon as his airspeed indicated 170 kts, he put the landing gear handle into the down position. He circled back to his left, keeping the hangars and tower in sight, and waited for the red lights showing the gear down and locked.

Full flaps. Hofer lined up on the runway, flared expertly, and touched down at 100 knots, making another perfect main wheel, tail up landing, and high-speed taxi, letting the speed bleed off until the tail gently settled to the ground. Only then did he apply brakes and slow down to "U" turn and taxi back to the apron in front of the 334th hangar.

Pulling up in front of the hangar, he motioned at Sgt. Scudday with three fingers, and everyone around was laughing and gesturing. Duke was waiting in the jeep, grinning from ear to ear, and his long tongue lolling around with the relish of treats from the mess hall. The Kidd was back, time for the party to begin.

But this time, when he taxied up to the hangar, Sgt. Scudday had a grim look on his face.

While Hofer unstrapped and climbed out into the loving welcome of Duke, Scudday waited by the jeep. Hofer walked up, knowing what was coming, but hoping he was wrong.

Scudday started to speak, "Mr. Hofer…"

Hofer interjected, "Let me guess. The Colonel?"

Scudday just nodded. Hofer jumped in the jeep and Duke followed, taking up his usual station.

Minutes later, standing at attention in front of the Colonel, Hofer listened to half the conversation as Blakeslee finished a phone call.

"Thank you for calling Colonel Graham. Yes, thank you. Goodbye."

Blakeslee hung up the phone and gave Hofer an inscrutable look.

Hofer was uncertain of his read and felt like a kid in the Principal's office.

After a few long seconds, Blakeslee spoke in a tone that was disarmingly placid.

"Hofer, you're going to be the death of me," he started. "I would have bounced you out of the group a long damned time ago, but your Squadron C.O.s keep speaking up for you. What the fuck am I going to do with you?"

Knowing the only thing Blakeslee tolerated when he was mad was adding to the luster of the fourth, Hofer volunteered some positive information.

"Well, sir, I got three victories today."

Nodding, Blakeslee said, "I know. That makes you a triple ace, right? Colonel Graham of the 357th just called and confirmed that you joined up with his boys today and had a good time. Know what *I* thought you were doing?"

Hofer shook his head, "No, sir."

"I thought you had aborted and crashed in the channel. Know how many Air Sea rescue kites were out looking for you today?"

"No, sir," said Hofer, feeling mildly guilty.

Blakeslee held up his hand, four fingers extended, "Four."

"Well, sir, when I had the problem, and came back to base, Scudday and the guys told me they could fix it real quick. So, I just waited about 15 minutes, and when they gave me the thumbs up, I thought I should go."

"You thought you should go? Hofer, do you realize that you're not a one-man air force? Who in the hell gave you permission to fly a combat mission alone?"

"I wasn't alone, Colonel. The 357th was out there."

"What if you hadn't found the 357th?"

"Well, there's always somebody out there." Hofer shrugged.

Wagging a finger for emphasis, Blakeslee scolded, "That somebody could be a flight of Huns looking for an easy single to kill."

Hofer donned a devil-may-care grin and started to spout his patented answer, "The German pilot doesn't..."

Blakeslee cut him off with a flourish of his hand. "I know, I know, he doesn't exist. But stupid risks are going to be the death of you. And make me an old man before my time."

Genuinely apologetic, Hofer said, "I'm sorry, sir. I thought pressing home the mission was the right thing to do."

Blakeslee, finding it hard to get mad at a pilot willing to fight and wanting to fight so much he takes off for combat infested European skies alone, turned to Hofer somewhat exasperated.

"Goddammit, Hofer, just when I think you're going to be a leader, you twist off and do something fucking stupid, fucking heroic, or both. You're the best we've got. Yet you keep doing crazy shit that makes me look like a goddamn idiot for putting up with you. Apparently even Goody can't control you."

Hofer was genuinely subdued, "It's not a matter of control, sir. I guess I'm just too eager."

Blakeslee smiled. "You're like a whore in Piccadilly," he said, referencing the Piccadilly lilies. There's a lot of war left, Hofer. I just hope you're around to help us win it. Get out of here."

He waved his hand, ass-chewing over.

Hofer gave his infamous half-ass salute and slipped out the door, rejoining his furry shadow, and heading for Sgt. Scudday's jeep.

Hofer was just jumping out of the jeep at the Officer's Club when Goody intercepted him.

"Want to fly another mission today?"

Looking at the sun, and estimating the time at about 3:30, Hofer jumped at the chance.

"Hell, yeah," he said, as Goody expected he would. "Maybe the altitude will put out the fire in my pants. Colonel just lit into me for going out by myself, even though I found the 357th and worked with them."

Goody just laughed. "One of these days you'll learn. Let's go see what we can find. I'm leading a flight and we're a couple short."

In a less than a half an hour Goody had assembled an ad hoc flight of eight planes and they were airborne, headed for the French coast.

The patrol was basically uneventful. Just at the end of their fuel endurance they returned to base, hopeful that they could get some more fuel and go back out again. But he learned upon landing that the Colonel had called mid-celebration meeting. Hofer turned the plane over to the hangar crew and went to freshen up.

In the Officer's Club, the party had started. The bar was already full of rowdy alcohol−soaked pilots reenacting their battle encounters with hand flying, informing each other of the current stats, mission numbers, MIA, KIA. Telling bawdy stories and jokes, and generally having a good time.

The din of fun abated quickly when the door opened, and Col. Blakeslee strode in and went straight to the scoreboard. He erased 414 and wrote 621.

He turned to the gathered pilots, all of whom were grinning expectantly. "Official word boys. 207 victories in April. We're over 600. Fourth but First!"

Blakeslee wore a tight, satisfied smile as he waited for the cheers, shouts and applause to die down. He had not walked away, so there was more.

"We celebrate tonight at the gym. The guests arrive at 1800 hours. We cut the cake at 1900." Then sternly, "Don't be late."

He turned and left, and the happy bedlam resumed with even more enthusiasm.

Over the P.A., signifying the party was "on!"— came the announcement, "There will be a small craps game in the game room."

Pierce McKennon started up a boogie-woogie version of "Rock of Ages," and the party was quickly out of control.

CHAPTER TWENTY-THREE

THE MERRY MONTH OF MAY

May Day, 1944. Hofer was on the mission board to Cologne. The usual pre-flight briefings, takeoff, form up, and flyover resulted in arriving late in the day, but with enough daylight for Hofer to score another kill, this time a ME 109.

Sixteen.

Standing down until May 12, Hofer shared another ME 109 adding a ½ to his score.

Same thing nine days later. Another shared kill over Rathenow A/D.

Seventeen victories.

May 24, 1944: Mission to Hamburg. Result: Two FW 190's killed.

Eighteen and Nineteen.

May 28, 1944: Mission to Magdeburg. One ME 109 destroyed.

Twenty. Quadruple Ace.

May 29, 1944: The Group attacked Mackfitz Airdrome and ran amok. Hofer got credit for four destroyed and two shared, for a total of five victories.

Result: numbers Twenty-one through Twenty-five. Making Hofer a quintuple Ace.

Hofer's name and fame were spreading far and wide, and many people were starting to keep scorecards for both the 4th, and for Hofer, waiting to see if he could become the leading American Ace of Aces, currently at 27.8 kills, held by Don Gentile, who had rotated home after pranging his kite.

May 30, 1944: Oscherleben Airdrome was destroyed. Hofer was credited with 2 ½ victories.

Twenty-six, Twenty-seven, and a half.

May 31, 1944: Luxeuil Airdrome in France was the next target, the Luftwaffe being reluctant to duel in the sky, the 8th took the war to the ground.

Hofer got three credits. Twenty-eight, Twenty-nine, Thirty, plus the half. His victory credits also included a damaged flak trawler in the Channel, a flak tower, an armed auxiliary vessel and three locomotives.

A marvelous month. Seven missions. Fifteen and ½ victories. At least one victory on every mission.

For Hofer, his giddy success was marred only by the fact that Virginia was nowhere to be found. He called several times to Halesworth, but for some reason she was always busy. He thought about flying over to Halesworth, but that was shot down over drinks with Goody and some of the others, who thought it was a monumentally bad idea for multiple reasons.

~~~

June 5, 1944: At the end of a mission, Hofer pulled up at the 334th, Scudday and crew greeted him on the apron. "What's the report, Kidd?"

"No report to report is the report," he said. "No encounters, no damned kills, it's eerily quiet up there, Sergeant. But Goody spotted a convoy, and we want to clobber 'em before the sun sets. Try to salvage the day. Get her turned around as fast as you can."

Scudday, surprisingly, shook his head, "Nothing doing, Lieutenant. We just got buckets and paint brushes, with orders to paint black and white stripes on every plane before midnight."

Hofer was puzzled. "Black and white stripes? What for?"

Scudday grinned, "Invasion."

That night, at the Officer's Club, Colonel Blakeslee and the pilots of the Fourth gathered around the radio to listen to the words of General Dwight Eisenhower.

"Soldiers, Sailors, and Airmen of the Allied Expeditionary Force. You are about to embark upon the Great Crusade towards which we have striven these many months.

The eyes of the world are upon you. The hopes and prayers of liberty-loving people everywhere march with you.

In company with our brave Allies and brothers-in-arms on other fronts you will bring about the destruction of the German war machine, the elimination of Nazi tyranny over the oppressed peoples of Europe, and security for ourselves in a free world.

Your task will not be an easy one. Your enemy is well-trained, well-equipped, and battle hardened. He will fight savagely.

But this is the year 1944. Much has happened since the Nazi triumphs of 1940-41. The United Nations have inflicted upon the Germans great defeats, in open battle, man to man. Our air offensive has seriously reduced their strength in the air and their capacity to wage war on the ground. Our Home Fronts have given us an overwhelming superiority in weapons and munitions of war and placed at our disposal great reserves of trained fighting men.

The tide has turned.

The free men of the world are marching together to victory.

I have full confidence in your courage, devotion to duty, and skill in battle. We will accept nothing less than full victory. Good Luck!!!!

And let us all beseech the blessing of Almighty God upon this great and noble undertaking."

At the mention of the air war offensive, the men began to quietly chatter with each other in appreciation, exchanging knowing glances.

Blakeslee turned off the radio. He looked at his men—his peers—for a few seconds before speaking somberly.

"This is it," he began. "Six missions tomorrow. Not every squadron will make every show. The first mission is the entire group. I'll lead. We press at 0300 hours. Remember who you are. Remember why we're here. Remember exactly who is depending on us. Those troops on the ground need all the help we can give. I know each of you will do your best."

He turned to leave, but added, "There's no curfew around here. Each of you is smart enough to know when to call it a night. Just make sure you answer the bell."

He left them to consider the significance of the mission. No one moved, the urge for a final drink was strong. Goody took the lead, motioning for Hofer, who followed him out, along with Duke. Watching the two leading aces of the group call it a night, the message was clear. Duty first.

The men began to file out and in just a few minutes the bar was quiet, and dark. Everyone had gone to bed.

June 6th, 1944
D-day

The next morning, at the break of dawn, the planes of the fourth were gaggled up and forming into their flights, sections, and elements for takeoff. With all three squadrons at full strength, Blakeslee was leading 108 fighters into action. By section, they ran through their pre-flight rituals, took off, and climbed east into a pink sky.

As they crossed the coast of England and flew out over the channel the cloud cover was 10/10, but flashes of reflected gunfire forewarned of the coming big battle.

After crossing the French coast, the clouds broke up enough that the ground could be seen.

Blakeslee keyed his mike, "This is Horseback. Cobweb, Caboose and Becky cover your assigned sectors. Divide into Sections for maximum coverage. If you encounter any large formations, your call sign for regroup and reinforcements is Alamo, Alamo, Alamo. Break on break. Three, two, one— break!"

At the signal, the three squadrons broke formation and diverged in their respective directions. The 334th (Cobweb) headed straight inland. The 335th (Caboose) headed north. 336th (Becky) headed south.

Each squadron had 36 planes, or nine sections of four planes. As they cleared their formations, each squadron prepared to divide into sections of four planes each.

Major Howard Hively, C.O. of the 334th, called for the break.

"Cobweb, break into sections and cover your vectored areas. Break!"

Hofer, in Blue Flight, was the middle finger of Blue Blue, meaning Blue Section of Blue Flight. Frank Speer as his wingman was the index finger of his element. They peeled off and headed to the northeast.

After a few minutes at a cruising speed of 180 knots to conserve fuel, Hofer saw the tell-tale smoke of a train on the distant horizon. He couldn't contain his excitement.

"Whoo, whoo, a train! Blue Blue, drop babies, and follow me!"

The four planes of the section dropped their wing tanks, pulled a wing over, and entered a shallow dive, automatically opening up into a line abreast combat formation.

As they approached, Hofer gave instructions. "Frank, I've got the tender, you take the engine. Three and four take the caboose and last boxcar. We want to disable it. Make it a stationary target. Watch out for flak cars."

As they closed on their target little yellow balls seem to float up towards them, floating and spinning, until they zipped by their canopy. *Flak.* Gradually, the outline of the AA mounts on every third boxcar could be seen and the streams of yellow balls crisscrossed in front of them, above, below, and past their wings.

At 600 yards, Hofer pressed the tit on his stick and his 6.50 calibers began to spurt their deadly rain. Using minute control of his rudders for slight, almost imperceptible changes in the angle of his fire, he raked the tender from stem to stern, watching in satisfaction as holes appeared and the holding tank inside began to spew water in huge gouts.

He took just a second to glance over and observed, with satisfaction, that Frank Speer was working over the engine thoroughly, causing it to slow. The Engineer and Fireman jumped from the slow-moving train before they could be turned into mincemeat by the big 50's.

The engine slowed and gradually came to a complete stop; Speer continuing to pepper it with lead. As they soared above the train and prepared to go around for another attack, Hofer heard, and felt, an explosion under his left wing. His plane rocked violently.

While the other planes of the element pulled out to the right, he cut left and Speer followed; they pulled up to 10,000 feet to regroup.

Hofer checked his instruments and saw that his fuel gauge on the left wing tank was dropping noticeably. He radioed Speer, "Frank, check me out. What's happening?"

Speer dropped beneath Hofer and looked him over. "Yeah, Kidd, you're leaking fuel from your left wing tank. You've had it, buddy."

"Shit", griped Hofer, "I'm RTB. You guys finish the train."

With that, Hofer vectored to 00, due north, and headed for Debden. The remaining three planes regrouped and prepared for another strafing run on the now helpless, stationary train. This time, they would attack in file, from engine to caboose, raking the boxcars and their AA emplacements as they flew over. After three passes from the Mustangs, it was likely none of the AA guns would be functional. .50 caliber bullets disable machinery effectively and encourage gun crews to scurry for cover in the surrounding vegetation. And if the train was carrying ammunition, or explosives, no one wanted to be close when it took a hit.

In less than half an hour, Hofer was back at Debden. He taxied to the apron in front of the 334th hangar and Scudday and his crew were waiting for him.

He cut the engine and threw his canopy open, "Sergeant, my left wing tank is damaged. Take a look will ya?"

He climbed out and dropped down to greet his furry welcoming committee. Scudday and a couple of ground crewmen looked under the wing to assess the damage. Coming back out with a smile, Scudday delivered the good news.

"It's not too bad, Lt.," he said. "We can get you back in the air today."

"Great!" Hofer grinned, but then sighed, "I'm missing the biggest show in history. Can ya hurry it up a little?"

Nodding, Scudday signaled to the others and they moved the *Salem Representative* into the shadow of the hangar.

Hofer and Duke stepped into the ready shack. He quickly curled up in his favorite chair. He was the only pilot around, so the ready room, normally buzzing, was very peaceful and quiet. Duke curled up beside him. Hofer scratched Duke's ears and they both nodded off in quiet bliss.

A couple of hours later, Hofer awoke with a start from the sound of a Merlin engine clearing as his Mustang taxied up; then the engine was cut. Hofer and Duke hurried out. Through the open hangar door, they could see Major "Deacon" Hively climbing out of his plane which was parked on the apron. Several other planes had pulled up. The pilots climbed out and headed into the ready shack.

Hofer walked up to his plane, where Scudday and others were working under the left wing.

"How's it going, Scudday?" He asked, and peered under the wing, noticing the wing tank sitting on a dolly.

Scudday said, "Aw, not as quick as we expected, Lt. We removed and repaired the damaged tank, but it didn't seal right, and started leaking when we added fuel. We had to drain and remove it and go scavenge a left wing tank from the bone pile. This one's gonna be ready in a little while, and it doesn't have any bullet holes, or cracks from getting chewed up by ground fire. But don't worry, we'll have you back in the air by 1600 hours."

Hofer headed back to the ready shack and hollered over his shoulder, "Great, Sergeant. Hurry it up, will ya? I'm counting on you."

Duke trotted alongside, intuiting Hofer's excitement and anxiety.

Inside the ready shack, Hively and several others were talking excitedly, comparing notes on the invasion. Hofer tapped Hively on the shoulder.

"What's happening, Major? Am I missing all the fun?"

Hively turned and grinned, his face oily and grimy, except for the white around his eyes protected by his goggles, and the area on his nose and cheeks covered by his oxygen mask. He smelled like sweat and fear.

"I'll say" he laughed wickedly.

"We got four FW 190's outside of Evereux. The Germans are coming out more as the day goes on. I think they weren't sure where the actual invasion was this morning. But they know now. We're kicking their Teutonic asses right now."

At that, there was more laughing and excitement among the pilots.

"Sergeant Scudday tells me he'll have me ready to go pretty quick," Hofer said, and asked anxiously, "Can I go back out again?"

Hively slapped Hofer on the back, "Sure, Kidd. We need everyone up and out as often as possible. Colonel is leading 334 and 335 on a Rhubarb at 1800 hours. 334 is full with spares, but you can attach to 335."

"Thanks, Deac," he said, shaking Hively's hand enthusiastically.

A few hours later, Hofer was airborne with 48 other planes, the full squadrons of 334 and 335, led by Colonel Blakeslee.

As they formed up at 10,000 feet over Rouen, France, Colonel Blakeslee radioed Hofer. "Caboose Blue Section, you get the spare. Caboose Blue Five, you read?"

"10 x 10, Colonel. Roger," Hofer slipped over to the designated section of four aircraft, joining the formation as the extra little finger on the right hand. He was *tail end Charlie*, the guy most likely to catch it in the ass, but Hofer was just glad to be back in the fight.

Blakeslee issued more instructions, "Caboose Blue Section. See that convoy to the east of Dreux? Paste 'em."

The Caboose Blue Lead Captain Bernard McGrattan, of Utica, New York, acknowledged the transmission, and instructed his section. "Roger, Horseback. Blue Section, drop babies. Follow me."

The five Mustangs simultaneously dropped their wing tanks, peeled off from the main formation, and dove down line abreast, Hofer on the starboard end. The rest of the group continued their patrol, gradually turning south.

As they neared the convoy, McGrattan cautioned Hofer, who was the closest plane to a line of low hanging clouds over the little village of Neubourg.

"Hofer, watch those clouds on the right. Caboose Section, line abreast at 2,000 feet. Fire when I do. If the convoy stops, vertical loop and continue attacking. If they keep moving, bank left, and we'll make another pass from the other side."

He got acknowledgment from each plane and the section continued their approach. Hofer looked to his right, checking the clouds. He looked at his picture of Virginia, "Roger, Mac, I've got it."

He thought to himself as he patted Virginia's picture, *wish me luck, baby.*

At 600 yards, McGrattan fired, and the others all joined in. The roar of 30, 50 caliber machine guns firing at once was deafening. The impact of 900 shells per second on the convoy was utterly devastating. Trucks exploded, veered into the ditch, caught fire, and scattered, as driver's slammed on brakes and bailed out of their cabs to avoid them turning out to be their coffins, trying to survive the onslaught.

Just as they stopped firing, and passed over the convoy, Hofer looked right, and just as he turned, out of the cloud bank popped more than 15 Jerries, FW 190's and ME 109's, guns winking.

Hofer yelled as he broke right, directly into the attacking planes.

"Caboose! Caboose! Blue Section, break right, break right! Jerries 3 o'clock high!"

Pursuant to McGrattan's instructions, the other four planes were already starting to break left, which placed the attacking Germans right on their six o'clock position, dead astern. A fighter pilot's dream. A target's nightmare.

Hofer watched over his left shoulder as several Germans attacked each of the fleeing Mustangs. They were low, slow, and turning, easy meat. There was nowhere to go.

A P-51 exploded in mid-air from the hail of cannon fire into its fuselage fuel tank from the two lead FW 190's. A second Mustang lost a wing from multiple hits, augered in and exploded. The third Mustang tried to reverse his turn and come back right but flew into a deflection crossfire stream from several Germans and was riddled with shells. The plane flipped over on its back and crashed canopy first into the unforgiving ground, a giant explosion scattering debris over a wide area. The last Mustang tried to add emergency power and climb out but stalled and slipped back into the bullets of several Germans, causing the wings to shear off. The wingless fuselage dropped to the ground like a lawn dart, exploding on impact. The combat was over in five seconds. Swift, fierce, violent and fatal.

Hofer whipped violently starboard, gunning his engine with emergency water injection power, and headed for the cloud bank from whence the Germans appeared. The cover they came from was now his only hope for survival.

Now that the others were all dead, he was the sole target for a dozen Jerries intent on a clean sweep. Fate would determine if Hofer could reach the cloud bank before the Jerries converged and got in range.

He reached the cloud bank just as tracers started whizzing past his canopy. After stooging around in the cloud bank for 15 minutes, Hofer gingerly poked his plane into the edge of the murk, looking around, and ready to duck back in at the first sign of trouble. No other planes were in sight. The sky was completely empty. He set course for zero zero, due north, and headed for Debden.

The sun was setting in the far western horizon as Hofer flared for landing. No hot main gear landing this time. He was physically exhausted and mentally overwhelmed. Losing four fellow pilots in one engagement was devastating.

Hofer taxied up to the 334th hangar, again the last man of the group to get back, his engine exhaust was glowing brightly in the semi-darkness. He cut his engine, slowly opened his canopy, removed his helmet, rubbed his eyes and pushed back his hair, then he slumped forward, shoulders shaking.

The *longest day* was over.

Duke, instead of waiting on the ground by his left wing, jumped up, and pawed up onto the canopy rail, nosing at him. Hofer, uncharacteristically, ignored his great friend.

Scudday hurried up to the plane and climbed on the wing, peering in at the trembling pilot.

"Mr. Hofer, are you all right? Mr. Hofer? Mr. Hofer? Duke, get down."

Duke obeyed and hopped off the wing but circled nervously close by. Hofer had never behaved this way, especially to Duke.

Hofer slowly looked up, his face drawn, his eyes red, dark shadows of fatigue under them. He took the picture of Virginia off the instrument panel and looked at it for a long moment. He slipped it into his shirt pocket, and slowly and painfully rose as Scudday helped him with his safety belts.

"They're dead. All dead." Hofer looked blankly at Scudday.

Scudday asked, "What happened, Kidd? Who's dead?"

"McGrattan, Sobanski, Caboose Blue Section. Everyone but me. Dead."

Scudday repeated, "What happened?"

Hofer, speaking slowly, as if in a fog, tried to gather his thoughts and describe the carnage he witnessed.

"I was flying Caboose Blue Section Five, McGrattan leading."

"Captain McGrattan?" Scudday asked, but he knew. He shook his head. "He was done. He didn't have to go. His bags are already packed. He was due to rotate home today. But he didn't want to miss the invasion."

Hofer hesitated, the bitter irony of being killed while volunteering for a mission you didn't have to fly slowly washed over him. He thought about Captain McGrattan's family, a prominent banking and political family in New York. How sad to lose their son and heir when he had already done his duty.

Hofer slowly continued, "We attacked a truck convoy near Dreux. Just as we cleared, a dozen or more Jerries popped out of cloud bank and bounced us. I yelled *break right*, but it happened so fast..."

Scudday asked, "You're the only one?"

Hofer looked pleadingly at Scudday as if to get absolution from some great sin. The question was not meant as an accusation, but Hofer couldn't help thinking there was at least at tinge of it in the asking.

"I saw four fireballs," he said. "We were cornered."

"How'd you get away?"

Hofer looked down, tears falling on his hands, "God only knows. I broke right, and everyone else broke left. The Jerries had perfect position. We were slaughtered before we could do anything."

Hofer climbed down and shuffled into the ready shack like an old man. He dropped into his chair and Duke took up a position right next to him, nosing his hand. After a few moments, Hofer finally ruffled the dog's scruff affectionately, as if seeing him for the first time. In his other hand, he held the picture of Virginia, which was the last thing he saw before slipping into an exhausted slumber. Virginia's picture slipped out of his fingers and fell to the floor. Duke saw the picture and laid down with his paw on protectively over it, protecting both the pilot and his good luck charm.

Scudday, watching the scene sympathetically, turned to the ground crew of Salem Representative.

"C'mon," he said, "we've got to get this plane ready. He goes out again in six hours. This invasion is becoming a meat grinder."

CHAPTER TWENTY-FOUR

The next day, after the morning missions, Hofer was leaning on a corner of the bar, Duke was dozing at his feet. He sipped his pint in silence. The other pilots were aware of his presence, but no one was saying anything. The atmosphere was subdued.

Suddenly, the door flew open and Blakeslee stomped in furiously. He stalked up to Hofer and confronted him. Hofer was shaken from his reverie by the volume of Blakeslee's fury.

"What the fuck happened?" he roared.

Hofer was almost too stunned to respond, "What?"

"Five guys get jumped, and you're the only one that gets away? How the hell did you do it? Were you off stooging around by yourself again instead of watching out for your wingmen?"

Everyone else in the room could only pretend not to be paying attention.

Hofer pleaded, "Colonel, I swear, there was nothing I could do. It was a perfect ambush."

Stepping closer and leaning into Hofer's face, Blakeslee continued to rage. "Hofer, if I find out that you were fucking around and got four men killed with your glory-hound antics, I'm going to court-martial you."

Hofer continued to protest, but he was too hurt and broken to rise to anger himself, "Don, those men were friends. I wish I could trade places with them."

Blakeslee spun on his heel and stomped back to the door, making a parting declaration. "I don't give a goddamn if you are the leading ace in the group. If I find out you got your wingmen killed, you're going to wish you were dead, too."

The door slammed in the wake of Blakeslee's anger and the silence left behind was palpable. Hofer looked around the room hoping for some sympathy, but everyone looked away or down at their drinks.

A few days later, Hofer was laying in his bunk, next to Duke, sleeping an exhausted, troubled sleep. There were several knocks, progressively louder, until Duke finally woke up, and nosed his leg. Sleepily, he answered, "Come on in."

The door opened and Goody peeked in. Duke trotted over to welcome him. He rubbed the big dog's ears as he stepped inside. "How ya feeling?"

Hofer stuck his head in his pillow, "Beat. With a rubber hose."

Goody nodded agreement, "Understandable. The last four days have been a nightmare."

Hofer mumbled into his pillow, "I wish it was a nightmare. You wake up from nightmares."

Goody continued, "We've lost a dozen men in the last four days."

Hofer rolled over and peered at Goody, "Any word on Blue flight?"

Goody shook his head, "No. You're the only survivor. And that's not all. Eddie Scott, Don Pierini, Ken Smith. All killed. And Wee Mike McPharlin disappeared. I hope he turns up, his wife is due at any minute. I feel really bad about Mac McGrattan. His bags were literally already packed. All he had to do was leave, but he wanted to *make history.* Tragic."

Hofer nodded, "That makes me sick. Somehow you think the sons of rich politicians get a pass."

Goody smiled feebly, "Well, *some* good news. The Colonel has read all the reports. Some infantry on the ground saw what happened. He knows now there was nothing you could do."

Hofer groaned and flopped back on his pillow, rubbing his head and trying to clear his thoughts.

"How comforting," he said, almost angrily. "Is he going to come to the Officer's Club and apologize for my public ass chewing?"

Goody regarded him. "C'mon, Kidd, get your guts in a pile. Everybody's nerves are shot. Word'll get around. We heroes have to stick together."

Hofer continued to pout, "He owes me an apology."

Goody stood, "Go see the Chaplain and get your TS card punched. None of us get a pass right now. Any day can be our last mission. We fly two missions tomorrow. You ready?"

Hofer groaned, "I was born ready."

He flopped back on his bunk to sulk some more, but Duke, thinking it was an invitation to play, jumped up on his chest and began to lick his face mercilessly. In spite of himself, Hofer started laughing and playing with the irrepressible Duke, while Goody looked on approvingly, thinking, *that can only help.*

~~~

By midmorning the next day, Hofer, Goody, and the other members of their flight were cruising at 10,000 feet, looking for targets of opportunity.

Goody, with the eyes of an eagle, spotted a convoy. "Convoy. Two o'clock. Let's get 'em boys."

The squadron broke with polished precision into a line abreast of strafers and swooped in on the hapless trucks, guns hammering. Personnel scattered as they pounded the vehicles into shapeless wrecks.

As they pulled out, Hofer's plane rocked, and he immediately heard a hissing sound. He looked to his instruments trying to dope out the problem. They indicated his coolant temperature was rising rapidly, and, his oil pressure was dropping dangerously. He pulled up and called to Goody.

"Goody, I'm losing power. Whadayathink?"

Goody, looped over, beside and under Hofer, and came up on his left wing.

"You're losing oil. Head east. 10 miles. Be careful. Cheers."

Hofer turned east and flew for only a few seconds, then he saw a rough strip. He lined up for a straight-in approach, with only a moment to wonder whose field it was, but it was immaterial. He couldn't get back to Debden and he was too low to bail. It was a dead stick landing, or dead, period.

Prop wind milling, Hofer made a smooth dead stick landing and having no power to get off the runway, coasted to a stop at the end of the field.

Almost immediately, several vehicles emerged from the tree line along the runway. Hofer was initially anxious but as they got closer he could see the big, white American stars on the jeeps and was relieved to find that it was an Allied field.

The first jeep stopped at his left wing tip. Hofer climbed out and stood on the wing. It took him a moment to realize he was looking at a Major General. Hofer climbed down and started to salute.

Major General Ralph Royce, 44, walked up to Hofer with a big grin and an outstretched hand. No military formalities here. Hofer abandoned his salute and took the General's hand.

In the near distance, Hofer could hear the pop of rifle fire, the roar of artillery, and the chatter of automatic weapons, both ours and theirs. He had landed in the middle of a real battle.

Grinning at the unexpected warm welcome, Hofer said. "Hey, sorry to just drop in, but I lost oil pressure, and I needed a base, quick."

Continuing to shake Hofer's hand, the General laughed, "You're a lucky guy, son. This is the only Allied airfield in France."

"Thanks for the break, General."

Taking a closer look at Hofer's plane and Hofer himself, the General broke into an even bigger smile, and slapped him warmly on the back.

"Say, aren't you Kidd Hofer? Everybody's heard of *Salem Representative*. Welcome to France, son."

The other men crowded around him, shaking his hand, and welcoming him in true hero fashion. The infantry knows well how valuable the *flyboys* were with air to ground attacks. The story of the 30 victory Ace from Debden had been well publicized. Turning to his aide, General Royce barked some instructions.

"Captain, get our maintenance men to inspect this aircraft, and whatever it needs, get it done and get it done fast." The Captain saluted and scooted off to "get it done".

General Royce turned back to Hofer and made him an unusual offer. "Well, son, since you're going to be our guest for a while, how about the 50-cent tour of the battlefield?

Hofer grinned, "Great, let's go. But I gotta owe you. We can't carry money on missions."

Royce gestured to a grizzled Top Sergeant, the epitome of a combat hardened grunt. "Sergeant get this man a helmet, and rifle.

Another soldier offered his own gear and as Hofer put on the helmet, he looked at the rifle like it was a snake, "Wow, this is beginning to feel like a real war."

Royce climbed into his jeep and Hofer jumped in the back right behind him. The Top Sergeant got in behind the driver, and they headed east, bouncing in the ruts, towards the sound of the guns.

Passing the artillery battery, a salvo was fired. The concentrated concussion of the 10 guns almost caused Hofer to lose his helmet. Royce, his driver, and the Sergeant all grinned at the flyboy's discomfort, he had obviously never been exposed to the up close and personal aspects of war.

In less than three minutes they were into bocage country; hedgerows, furrows and pastures made travel cumbersome, but these soldiers knew the territory. Combat rubble was all around. Burned out tanks from both sides. Overturned and wrecked jeeps, trucks, and vehicles of all kinds. Dead horses, and other livestock. The stink of death. Occasionally they passed a dead German, but mostly for morale's sake, the American casualties had been quickly cleared.

At the instruction of the General, the driver pulled up to a destroyed German pillbox. Royce turned to Hofer.

"This was a particularly tough nut to crack. We called in the P-47's, and they took care of it. Wanna see how you flyboys are so much help to us?"

"You bet. Maintenance is always asking for details, and I don't know what to tell them. We just kill machines and rarely see much else besides a plane going down."

Royce cautioned, "Be careful, the demolition boys are not finished around here. Fighting's just ahead about a mile or two. Whew, obviously, graves registration missed someone."

Royce and Hofer gingerly stepped into the shadowy darkness, General Royce shining a flashlight to illuminate the dark wrecked interior. Just inside the door, his light revealed a dead German's face, eyes wide open, a bullet hole right between the eyes.

Hofer grunted with disgust, "Ugh."

"Looks different down here, doesn't it?"

"Yeah. Pilots kill planes, not men." Hofer, curious, approached the corpse a little closer. "Okay?"

"Sure, be my guest." he continued. "My advice, son? Never make that mistake. In every plane there's a man, in every tank and under every helmet. You forget that, and it becomes a game. For their side too, you're the man in the other plane."

As the General talked, the Sergeant looked over and around the body to make sure there were no booby traps. Satisfied, he stepped aside. Hofer stepped in and gingerly searched the dead German. He pulled a book from inside the man's tunic, then reached over and picked up the dead man's helmet.

"I guess he won't need his hat anymore. Hey, it's a copy of "Mein Kampf." Hofer modeled the helmet and put the book in his pocket. Then, noticing the German's canteen, he reached down, opened it, and took a whiff.

Drawing back from the pungent odor, "That doesn't smell like water. More like schnapps. Want some?"

Smiling and shaking his head, Royce opted out. "No, thanks. But you're welcome to it if you want it."

Hofer said, "I see your point, General. There's a story behind this stuff."

They returned to the jeep, and Royce turned to Hofer, "We're only about a mile from the front, but I think it would be prudent for you to get some rest, rather than taking chances with snipers and the dangers of the front line. How about some coffee, and a little something to eat back at my headquarters?"

Hofer appreciated the gesture, and said so, having had quite enough of the ground war.

After a quick ride back to the General's headquarters, and a couple hours of rest and relaxation, Salem Representative was ready, and he took his leave. Standing beside his plane, which was already warmed up, Hofer shook the General's hand, and those of this staff, including the Captain in charge of repairs and the Sergeant who had chaperoned his sojourn to the front.

The General's staff included a photographer, who asked Hofer to pose with the copy of Mein Kampf, and the German helmet he had liberated. Hofer, glad to accommodate the men who extended such generous hospitality and help to him, readily, and cheerfully complied. Another image to add to the luster of the greatest "screwball ace" of the war.

"Thank you for everything," he said. "If any of you guys ever make it to Debden, look me up. I know how to repay favors."

He stepped in, strapped down, and waved one last time before taxiing out and taking off. He set his course for Debden, his ETA was around 1600 hours in the afternoon.

CHAPTER TWENTY-FIVE

The afternoon had dragged for Virginia, who was lounging in her room at Halesworth, reviewing her notes, and mentally arranging them for reports, and articles on the 56th. She mused to herself that the 56th was certainly full of excellent pilots, and was scoring heavily on virtually every mission, but they did not have the sense of excitement, mystery and wonder of the 4th Fighter Group.

Colonel Zemke had extended every courtesy, and the pilots were equally gracious and engaging, but she couldn't help but ruminate about the crazy boys of the 4th, their impetuous youthful exuberance, and their sheer energy and enthusiasm for risking their lives 5 miles in the sky. It some ways it had been a very long month, and she mildly regretted not accepting any calls from Hofer or responding to any of his letters.

As she sat gazing somewhat vacantly out the window, a gentle knock came at the door. Without giving it much thought, she called out, "Enter," a mannerism she had picked up from Colonel Blakeslee.

The door cracked open slowly, and to her astonishment, Kay Summersby peeked in.

"Hey, you, whatcha doin'?" Kay grinned at the look of surprise and happiness on Virginia's face.

"Kay! What on earth are you doing? When did you get here?" She rose to take her friend in a bear hug, which was reciprocated, as they had genuinely become affectionate friends and confidantes.

"General Eisenhower came up this afternoon, and is having supper with Colonel Zemke, and some of his staff. I've got all afternoon, and we can have supper together if you're not busy."

"That's perfect. I'm just thinking about finishing my projects here at Halesworth and trying to decide what station to visit next."

Kay, astutely noting the lack of enthusiasm with which Virginia expressed the idea of going to another station, searched her face for some genuine emotion about her priorities and choices. Noting an unspoken yearning, she decided to—as she had heard Hofer say—*shell down the corn.*

"What's wrong?" She asked.

Virginia shook her head and glanced out the window. "Nothing, I'm fine."

Kay stepped in front of her and took her by the shoulders, forcing her gaze away from the window to look at Kay.

"If I didn't know better, and I do, I'd think you were missing someone."

Virginia, unprepared for a direct assessment, glanced away again, the tears quickly forming in her eyes.

"I'm just tired," she whispered. "I want to go back to London. I need a break."

Kay shook her head and hugged her friend gently and supportively. "That's not true, you need to let your heartache breathe. Tell me what's really going on with you."

Virginia shook a little as she fought back the tears, a month's worth of denial, worry, and emotional turmoil boiling to the surface, almost uncontrollable.

"Oh, Kay, I don't know what to do. I can't live with him, and I can't live without him."

Kay hugged her again, sat her on the bed, and pulled up a chair, so they could face each other. "By him, I presume you are referring to a certain screwball ace that drives everyone crazy in combat, and is the life of the party at every dance?"

Virginia put her head in her hands and began to sob. "Oh, God, yes. He's everything I've ever wanted, and the opposite of what I need."

Kay patted her knee, "There, there, sweetie, just let the tears come. They help heal your heart, you know."

She sat quietly for a minute or two until Virginia could gather herself again.

Looking up, and dabbing at her red eyes, Virginia mused, "I never intended to let him into my life, much less my heart. But one night in London..."

"Do you regret that night?"

Virginia sighed, "Yes, I do, but I wouldn't have missed it for the world. I've never been so completely loved, and I never have loved so completely as that night."

"Does he love you?"

"He said he did, but I thought it was just the moment, the atmosphere, his way of letting me down easy."

"So, did he ignore you the next day?"

"No, quite the contrary. He called me first thing, and when I got to the base, he wanted to see me that night. But I told him I was coming to Halesworth and would be busy for a while. I was trying to nip the commitment in the bud. How could I deal with the fact that seeing him made my heart skip a beat, I got a warm fuzzy feeling inside, and the thought of being with him again made me almost dizzy with desire? I thought I had to escape."

"Ginny, love is hard to find, and even harder to keep. A certain pilot I know has been known to say every heart beats alone unless you give it to someone."

Virginia couldn't help but smile at the reference to one of Hofer's bromides. It was amazing how that guy and his many idiosyncrasies got around wartime England.

"It's so strange," Virginia continued. "He thrills my soul, makes me want more, but at the same time, I feel a peace when I'm around him. He likes to say 'don't worry, you're under my wing'. I feel protected, and cherished when he's around."

Kay smiled. "Do you see the rest of your life when you look at him?"

Virginia's eyes watered again. "No, that's just the problem. All I see is heartache and a lonely life pining over the loss of the love of my life if something happened to him. I can't bear to think of losing him. I can't bear the thought of committing my heart to him. It's just too much of a risk."

"Is he demanding? Does he insist that you do everything his way?"

"No," Virginia admitted with a rueful smile. "He loves me for myself, or rather, in spite of myself. No one's ever done that before."

It was Kay's turn to smile ruefully. "I know what you mean. To love someone seems to mean that you tune out the rest of your life, and everything that's been important seems smaller. Why do any of us allow ourselves to get in a situation where you can't bear the thought of a day without the company of that special someone?"

Virginia said, "It was getting to the point that when he was on a mission, I was beside myself with worry. I was getting mission sweats just not knowing for sure if he was flying or standing down. That's why I kept bugging you for information about the mission schedule of the 4th."

Kay chuckled a little. "I knew your constant calls weren't really about scheduling interviews. The General's spies are everywhere."

Forlorn, Virginia looked at Kay, "What am I to do? I can't concentrate, I'm always distracted. The other day, I called Hub Zemke "Colonel Don". That didn't go over very well."

"I can only imagine. But the heart wants what the heart wants. You're fighting a losing battle, as you can plainly see. Your only cure is to be with him. You'll never get over him, even if you chose to live without him."

"I can't, Kay, I just can't." Virginia looked up, "Can I?"

Kay smiled her broadest smile. "Yes, of course. All you have to do is throw caution to the winds and remember that when you find that someone that is your heartbeat, your breath, your soulmate, the love of your life, that every hour with them is worth the risk of a lifetime without them."

"I was thinking about him today," Virginia said, "and started to try to remember how long he had been on my mind. Then it occurred to me that from the minute he walked up to my donut table, and asked for that first dance, he's never left my heart or mind. I've just been fooling myself by trying to resist the magnetism of our souls."

"So, what's next, then?" Kay searched Virginia's face for the answer.

Virginia looked at her with realization, her face suddenly serene. "I have to go to him. I have to be with him. His love gives me courage. His soul sings a song to mine that only we can hear."

Smiling, the two friends embraced, and they comforted one another in the secure knowledge that a life changing decision had been forever made, come what may, in God's grace, and will.

CHAPTER TWENTY-SIX

The next day, after an uneventful mission touring the continent looking for trouble, Hofer had just arrived back at Debden and, attracted by the small crowd around a new P-51D—the newest and hottest version of the Mustang—taxied up to the base of the tower. When he got close enough, he could see Goody sitting in the cockpit answering questions and posing for pictures. He cut his engine, removed the picture of Virginia from his instrument panel, and threw back the canopy.

All kinds of newsmen and photographers were milling about Goody's plane. When Hofer walked by, Goody motioned to him to join him. On the left cowl was painted 30 swastikas in six rows of five. He and Goody were tied at the moment. Walking closer, the newsmen spotted him, and recognizing the co-champion Luftwaffe killer of the Fourth Fighter Group, they too asked him to join Goody.

While Goody sat in the cockpit and Hofer sat on the left wing, cameras recorded the moment as they grinned at each other, Goody leaning out and pointing at the 30 victory markers.

For several minutes, Goody and Hofer answered questions from the reporters, and happily posed for photographs. Then Hofer spotted a familiar smile at the fringe of the crowd.

It was Ginny.

Instantly, his priorities changed. He quickly put the kibosh on the publicity op and made his way to her. He pulled her out of the crowd and into the ready room, which for once, was vacant, not even Scudday to disturb them.

"How have you been?" Hofer asked somewhat timidly, unsure of the kind of reception he should expect.

Virginia gave him a quick hug and smiled brightly. "I've missed you. I've finished my story on you. It's going out in the next couple of days. Want to see it?"

She handed him a mimeo of the article. He started to peruse it but didn't even get past the title.

Frowning, he asked, "Last of the Screwball Aces?"

"My editor came up with that. It's not an insult. I just means you're a maverick, which nobody can deny. Not even you."

He read some more. After a moment, she squeezed his arm warmly. "How do you like the lead about Missouri finally being shown? Fits you, doesn't it?"

Unsure but unwilling to risk wrecking her mood, Hofer nodded, "Yeah, I like that."

Virginia continued, "Your birthday is coming up on June 22nd, right? Can we celebrate?"

After missing Ginny for an entire month, it would be great to spend a lot of time with her, but among other things he knew the war was ramping up and it may not be possible. He hadn't counted on having to explain the *other things*.

"I don't know, Ginny. Gen has it that a secret mission is coming up."

"Are you going?"

"Well, I don't know." Suddenly he was regretting his behavior. A little embarrassed, he tried to explain, "Deacon's mad at me because I won't take my booster shots. Needles give me the willies. I've been restricted to base, and my privileges at the Officer's Club have been suspended. All I can do right now is fly combat. And pose for pictures. Can't tell you more."

They gazed at each other for a moment, aware of the awkwardness of the surroundings, and noisy nearness of other people, and all the things they've left unsaid.

Virginia broke the awkward silence. "Ralph, I'm sorry I've been gone so long. I've missed you terribly."

Hofer turned to go, but Virginia reached out impulsively and snatched his hand. Startled at the display of affection, he turned and stared at her.

"I'll wait for you," she offered. "When you can, we'll celebrate."

She smiled reassuringly, surrendering to the immutable fact of being in love with a man who was so much younger. "At least for a while there's only 13 years between us."

"What are you saying, Ginny?" Hofer puzzled.

"I'm back for good. If you still want to plan a future, I'm in. For better or worse. Till death do us part."

At the quote from wedding vows, Hofer grinned, relieved that the month-long separation seemed to not mean the end, but only Virginia's way of gaining space for thinking. Ignoring for the moment where they were, he pulled her to him, placed his arms around her, as she encircled his neck, and they kissed deeply, feeling the knitting of souls that only true love allows, and creates.

"You're a young soul, and I'm an old soul. I think we meet in the middle." He grinned a broad smile, sure for the first time that he and Virginia had a future and were truly committed to it.

She squeezed his hand and peered into his eyes, "Can you come see me before you leave?"

Hofer returned the squeeze, "I will if I can."

He leaned in close to whisper in her ear. "I'm sorry I can't kiss you or hold you close some more. I'll make it up to you when I get back. I love you, Baby."

"I love you, too, Ralph. Come home to me."

Shouting over the din of journalists and reporters and pilots, Goody summoned Hofer back, "Hey, Hofer, we need you over here."

Their eyes met for a long second, anxious for *forever together* to begin as soon as possible, but knowing the circumstances had no intention of accommodating them.

As they stood there, eyes locked in an emotional embrace, Duke was nosing their joined hands. They laughed and reached down, scratching the great dog's head, and acknowledging his place in the "family."

Virginia watched with an aching heart as Hofer and Duke reluctantly turned and walked back to the assembled news-hounds. The thought and possibility of never seeing him again caused an icy fear to freeze her heart. She's done the one thing she swore she would never do— she fell in love with a fighter pilot whose daily existence depended on the winds and whims of war.

The men in the briefing shack were abnormally subdued. Blakeslee had called a group briefing in the middle of the afternoon, a time when the pilots were either in the air or gone to London. Base rumors had been swirling for days about a secret mission of some sort, and it seemed the gen, for once, might be close to right.

Blakeslee entered and walked to the map wall. Instant silence. "At ease. Be seated."

Chairs and shuffling filled the room as everyone got comfortable.

"Men," he began, "we've been chosen for a shuttle mission to Russia. We escort bombers to Berlin, but instead of returning, all bombers and their escort fly on to Russia. We rest, refuel, and rearm in Russia, fly on to Italy, operate from there for a few days, and then return to Debden. Details are being worked out, and the weather and flak issues are a nightmare. Until we get the final go, we continue with normal operations. Any questions?" No hands go up, no one speaks out, the logistics and ramifications of such a mission would take a few minutes to sink in. "Good. Carry on."

After Blakeslee left the room excited chatter began to build until it filled the room as everyone discussed the mission. Everyone, except Hofer, who sat glumly in his chair contemplating his options. Reaching a decision, he rose and headed for Deacon Hively's office in the hangar.

Hively was in the small, closet-like office allocated for him as Commanding Officer of the 334th Squadron. When Hofer arrived, Hively's door was open to allow a little ventilation. Hofer knocked and Hively looked up. Seeing who it was, he motioned him in.

Hofer came directly to the point. "Deacon, I promise to take my shots. Just let me back in the bar and take me to Russia."

Hively smiled agreeably, glad Kidd had come around. "OK, Kidd. As soon as Doc confirms you have your shots, your privileges are reinstated. As for the shuttle mission, I don't know. I've already assigned Salem Representative to Preston Hardy."

Hofer scoffed, "I don't care. Just let me go. Sergeant Scudday won't send me up in a dangerous kite. Anything he clears, I'm fine with."

Hively shook his head, "All the slots are taken. All that's left is alternates in case someone aborts, but I'm not striking anyone to make room for you. You've been entirely too much trouble about this. And you realize you won't have ground crew, right? Have you learned how to load your own ammunition?"

Hofer pleaded, "Look, I'm sorry, Deac, shots make me sick. Let me back in the fight. Sgt. Scudday tipped me off that's what everybody was learning, so, yes, I know how to load. I'm not very good, or very quick, but I can do it."

Hively leaned forward to peruse a list on his desk for a moment, "Goodson is leading a fighter sweep tomorrow that's all filled up. But I'll put you down as an alternate to Russia. After that, I'll put you up for every mission if you want."

Hofer nodded, "I want. Thanks, Deac."

The next afternoon, Kidd Hofer was lounging in his overstuffed chair, thumbing absent-mindedly through a two-year-old Saturday Evening Post he had already read about 15 times, one hand on Duke's great head scratching his ears.

Suddenly, Sgt. Scudday burst in, a look of genuine distress on his weathered face. "Mr. Hofer, bad news. Major Goodson's been shot down."

Hofer jumped to his feet, instantly sick to his stomach at what could come next. "What? Where? When? Oh, no. Oh, shit."

Sgt Scudday continued, "He was strafing New Brandenburg Airdrome, and got hit in his coolant system. Bellied in. He was last seen heading for the woods. His mates shredded his new Mustang, so there's nothing for Jerry to salvage. Probably POW by now."

"Oh, no. Son-of-a-bitch. I can't believe Goody's down. Thank God, he's alive.

"One last thing. Official word, you know tomorrow's the Russia Shuttle mission. Sorry, you're just an alternate. But I've got a decent kite for you. Too bad you won't by flying Salem Representative."

"It's OK, Sergeant. Any thing's better than not going. I just can't imagine going without Goody. I warned him about strafing airdromes."

The next morning at 0700 hours, Blakeslee briefed the pilots of the 4th. "All right, men, I need you to listen closely. Everything has to be pansy. It's not what you do but what you seem to do. There will be no fighting on the way in. Do not drop your wing tanks. You will need them for the next leg from Pyriatyn to Foggia. Radio discipline. No bullshitting on the R/T channel. No one will abort because of oxygen. We'll be flying at 15,000 feet. You have no business with this Group if you need oxygen at 15,000 feet. If you get dizzy, drop down below the bombers for a while. This whole thing is for show. All alternates turn back at the French coast. Ok, we press in 30 minutes, depart at 0755. Any questions? Good. See you in Russia."

Everyone began filing out, but Blakeslee motioned to Hofer. "Kidd, follow me."

They went down the hall to the empty office of Grover Hall, the Group Public Relations Officer. Puzzled, Hofer followed. Blakeslee opened the door, motioned Hofer inside, and shut the door, leaving him alone in the office.

Hofer was surprised to see Virginia standing by the window. She turned and, even more than usual, took his breath away. She was dressed uncharacteristically stylishly, with a hat and fox cape.

"Ginny! What are you doing here?"

Virginia came to him and put her arms around his neck. "I asked Colonel Don to repay a favor, and he said Okay. Are you sorry to see me?"

"No, of course not, baby."

They kissed repeatedly and passionately.

Virginia took Hofer's face in her hands and spoke earnestly. "We only have a minute. I heard about Goody, and it made me think. There are no guarantees for anyone. Every heart beats alone. But when two hearts beat as one, you have to listen."

Hofer brightened, "By the time I get back, I'll have enough hours to rotate home. You'll go with me?"

Virginia giggled, "Yes, but only if we can take Duke, too."

Hofer grinned his biggest goofy Duke-like grin. "Of course, I wouldn't dream of leaving either one of my wingmen behind."

Virginia kissed Hofer gently. "I'll take care of Duke until you return. Ralph, you are my breath, my life, my heartbeat. I love you."

Hofer kissed her again, and repeated the phrase that had become his talisman, "Wish me luck, Baby."

"Good luck. And be careful, my love."

Hofer smiled, "Don't worry. Really. Between you, Duke, your picture, and my lucky snake ring, I can't lose. All of me loves all of you."

He kissed her one last time, turned and disappeared through the door. In 30 minutes, he was airborne, headed for Russia.

Less than a half hour later, the bright, wind-swept line of the French coast passed silently beneath the 45 Mustangs of the 4th, and 16 Mustangs of the 362nd

Group. They were at 15,000 feet and heading for a rendezvous with the bombers.

Blakeslee keyed his mike. "There's the French coast. Alternates return to base."

The six alternates circle back west, except Hofer's P-51, being last, hung back, circled to the easterly heading of the main body, and followed behind and below, unseen.

The Group, unaware of Hofer stealthily tagging-along, droned on east for another two hours, making rendezvous with the bombers at 1113.

About an hour later, the flight encountered a head on attack by two dozen ME 109's.

Hively spotted them first, "Tallyho, Horseback. Bandits 10 o'clock high."

Blakeslee cautioned, "Roger, Cobweb Green Leader. Watch 'em, but don't engage unless they attack. Remember your fuel status."

The Group engaged briefly, but because of mission limits, couldn't press any advantage and follow the Germans as they flashed through the formation.

Hofer, however, being as eager as any whore in Piccadilly, instinctively dropped his tanks and pressed the attack.

He uncaged his gunsight and fired at the nearest enemy plane, getting strikes around the wing root. But, simultaneously, enemy tracers flew past his canopy, warning him of bandits on his tail. Hofer pulled up sharply into an *Immelman* and dove briefly at the Jerries behind him. They scattered, and Hofer resumed his easterly course, but this time, thoroughly confused as to what happened to everybody. The sky was empty. There was no alternative but to call for help.

"Horseback, this is Cobweb Green Five. Where are you?"

Blakeslee, leading the group, could not believe his ears. "Cobweb Green Five? Hofer, is that you? What the hell are you doing here?"

"I'm sorry, sir. I didn't see the coast."

Blakeslee's anger could be heard by everyone. "You missed the entire fucking country of France? God damn it, Hofer, this is the last straw. I'll see you in Pyriatyn."

"Yes, sir. Ah, Colonel, could I have bearing and altitude?"

"Angels 15. Relative 100. Duration 4 hours."

"I can't make it sir. My fuel is about 3 hours."

The disgust in Blakeslee's voice was palpable, "Divert to Kiev. Relative 90."

Hofer set course as directed, and the Group droned on east, headed for Pyriatyn, Russia.

About two hours later, Hofer found himself in the vicinity of Kiev with no idea how to communicate with anyone. Taking a chance, he keyed his mike to a standard landing channel.

"Ah, Kiev ground, this is American pilot Ralph Hofer, 4th Fighter Group. American. American. Coming in to land. Don't shoot. Don't shoot."

Hofer made an unmolested landing and taxied up to the tower where he was immediately surrounded by soldiers with machine guns. Gingerly, he opened his canopy, his hands in the air.

"American, I'm an American, don't shoot, don't shoot."

A jeep pulled up filled with Russian officers who motioned him to the ground. Hofer got in the Jeep, covered every inch of the way by the machine guns of rough, and nervous looking Russian soldiers. As they pulled away, he noticed that they had formed a cordon around his P-51.

By the time the jeep reached the base of the tower and Hofer was escorted into the office of the Duty Officer, the Major on duty was on the phone, with Blakeslee. Hofer listened to the surprisingly fluent English of the Officer; he described Hofer's airplane, gave the tail number, then looked at Hofer and gave an accurate physical description of him to the person on the other end of the phone. The officer grunted and hung up the phone.

He turned to Hofer with a wry smile, "Mr. Hofer, you have been identified, and verified. Welcome to Kiev."

When the Officer stuck out his hand for a welcoming handshake, the tension in the room was immediately broken and the soldiers relaxed their weapons and departed silently.

"Your Colonel Blakeslee is not too happy with you. You and he will have some things to discuss when you arrive in Pyriatyn, I think. However, at his request, you are our guest here tonight, and we will rearm and refuel your plane, so you can go on tomorrow morning. Unfortunately, we are short-handed here and have no escorting aircraft available, so you will by flying alone, but your Colonel thinks that's okay, especially under the circumstances. Are you hungry?"

Nodding, Hofer was led to the mess hall and given beans and what Hofer thought was a Russian tamale, but was actually a pelmeni, a minced-meat filling made up of beef, pork, and lamb, wrapped in a thin dough with a little butter or sour cream on the side. Not bad. All washed down with strong black coffee.

After that, he was led to another small room in the headquarters shack—the duty officer's sleeping quarters—and bid goodnight. The room was bare and spare with only a cot and a small table, with a single light bulb hanging from the center of the room with a string to turn it on and off. *It ain't Debden, but it's not bad*, he thought, considering the alternatives of the sleeping arrangements of the soldiers outside, and the other personnel below the base commandant.

The next morning, Hofer was fed the same meal for breakfast that he had for supper and escorted out to his plane. In addition to being gassed and rearmed, the plane had been washed, and sparkled in the morning sun.

The Major bid him farewell at the left wing root before Hofer climbed in.

"Your course is 095," the Major informed him, "distance 160 km, or about 100 miles. Your Colonel asked me to call him with your departure time. At your cruising speed your Colonel tells me you should make it in less than ½ hour, so he wants to figure your arrival time since you are alone. The radio frequency at Pyriatyn is 99.85 for arrival. Got it?"

Hofer, in a muted mood, nodded and shook the Major's hand, grateful for the comfortable night, and the welcoming treatment, but dreading the confrontation with Colonel Blakeslee. He was so worried, in fact, that he forgot what day it was.

He climbed in, took off, and in 22 minutes was in the pattern and landing at Pyriatyn. He taxied up to the open slot at the base of the tower, cut his engine and climbed out, and was immediately greeted by Sgt. Scudday.

"Scudday, what the hell are you doing here?"

Scudday laughed as they embraced quickly, patting each other on the back.

"There's actually 33 of us sumpies along for maintenance, and emergency repairs. You *flyboys* can't be expected to keep your own planes running, can you?"

283

Hofer happily agreed as they walked over to Blakeslee's temporary office.

Pausing at the door, Scudday gave Hofer the gen, "You actually lucked out to some degree."

Surprised, Hofer asked, "Oh, yeah?"

"Yeah. After flying 580 miles, the group arrived exactly on time. It was, as Blakeslee liked to call it, pansy, and he is still tickled about it. Plus, your overnight delay gave him some time to cool off. He's seen reports and understands you were separated by chasing Huns and trying to score. Disobeying orders is bad. Chasing Huns is good. Plus, you distracted them from the main group. Being an aggressive fighter pilot under the Colonel counts for more than being a maverick. But you already know that, right?"

Hofer smiled as if one of his secrets had been exposed. But, it was time to face the music, so he took a deep breath, and knocked.

"Enter."

Hofer stepped into the Lion's Den, braced, and instead of looking the Colonel, stared out the window, waiting for the worst.

Silence.

Eventually, the silence was too much and Hofer moved his gaze from the window to Blakeslee's face, which was regarding him with a surprisingly benign look.

"You're probably the only pilot in the 4th that got a good night's sleep."

Hofer was puzzled and didn't answer.

Blakeslee continued. "The Germans blasted the hell out of the bomber base at Poltava, destroying 77 bombers, and things around here last night were a madhouse. Everybody spent the night in the trenches. There were chandelier flares and anti-aircraft all over the place. Utterly impossible to get any rest."

He stood and walked around his desk, perched on the front edge, and sized Hofer up. Hofer, not used to being at such close proximity for an ass-chewing, found himself beginning to sweat a little.

Suddenly, inexplicably, Blakeslee stuck out his hand.

Hofer, stupefied, looked at the hand, then at the Colonel, and tentatively, took it.

Blakeslee smiled, "By the way, happy 23rd Birthday, Mr. Hofer. Your present is you get a pass for disobeying orders and coming on this mission even though you were only an alternate."

Hofer broke into a relieved grin. He was genuinely shocked that Blakeslee knew it was his birthday. He had totally forgotten himself in all the stress of combat, and landing at Kiev.

"Thank you, Colonel," he said. "This is a most pleasant surprise."

"Well, we need hunters on this mission, and you're one of our best. Because of the success the Germans are having blasting the bombers, we're going to move the Mustangs to other bases in Zaporozhe, Odessa and Chingueue. It'll just be the pilots; the maintenance gang is staying with the bombers. So, go join your mates for the flight briefing and scheduling, Okay? And one more thing."

"Yes, sir?"

"I expect you to describe our meeting as the most royal ass-chewing you have ever received from me in your time with the 4th. I have a reputation to protect."

Hofer could barely suppress outright laughter. "Of course, Colonel. Your guilty secret is safe with me. And thank you again, sir. I will make sure you don't regret the mercy."

He snapped a pretty good salute, spun on his heels, feeling as buoyant as he could remember, exited. It was the first time he suspected how much Blakeslee liked him.

CHAPTER TWENTY-SEVEN

The base at Odessa had been the sight of many tank battles and bombings and all the craters had simply been filled in with dirt, which was too soft to support the 7 tons of a P-51 Mustang.

After landing, Hofer was taxiing to his assigned parking spot when he suddenly felt his plane start to sag into the ground. He quickly cut his engine. The plane continued to sink slowly into the ground, until it was supported by its wings, looking like it had just performed a perfect belly landing.

He stood on the wing, surveying the situation and mentally calculating what kind of equipment would be needed to pull the plane out. Then, a jeep with Hively and the Russian Commanding Officer arrived.

After explaining what happened, Deacon could see there had been no way to avoid it and nothing to warn Hofer of the danger, so he was off the hook. But there was still the problem of how the hell to get the plane out, since there were no jacks, shims, cranes, or any kind of equipment capable of raising that airplane.

As Hively and Hofer furrowed their brows and scratched their heads, the Russian Colonel, through signs and grunts, convinced them to leave the problem to him, and go get some chow.

That night, at the new "safe base" at Odessa, the 334th got very gracious treatment. Everyone got a GI sleeping bag, toiletries, and other goodies, and a GI pyramid tent large enough for four people, with comfortable cots to sleep on. And at the mess tent, there was GI food, as the Americans who helped build the base were still around.

Hofer joined the pilots and the enlisted GI's in marveling at the food, but even more so, the server at his table. A remarkably stunning, tall, statuesque long-haired brunette named Tanya, dressed in an officer's uniform without any badges of rank, a short skirt at least six inches above her knees, which displayed some truly spectacular legs, and stylish knee-high polished leather boots.

As they were eating, the enlisted GI's kept suggesting to Hofer that he ask Tanya what's for supper. Hofer, already eating, didn't understand, after all, he's eating it and knows what it is. GI rations.

"Go on, sir, ask her what's for supper."

"Come on Lieutenant, ask her what's for supper."

"Go ahead, sir, ask her."

Hofer suggested the GI's should ask her themselves, since they seemed so interested in the answer.

Finally, Hofer gave in. Catching Tanya's eye, he motioned her over, and said, "Tanya, what's for supper?"

With a great big beautiful, innocent smile, Tanya put her hands on her hips and said in surprisingly good English, "Same old thing! Fucking "C" rations!"

Hofer's jaw dropped as the table roared with laughter. The GI's had been teaching Tanya *English*, in their special ornery way. After the initial surprise, Hofer laughed his ass off.

The next morning, Hofer was roused by the arrival of a stocky Russian captain, accompanied by a 6x6 truck loaded with Russian soldiers. He jumped into the Captain's car and they drove straight to Hofer's stranded airplane.

As soon as everyone had arrived, the Russians climbed out of the truck with shovels and picks, and started digging. The Captain was simultaneously acting as the engineer, the foreman, and cheerleader, showing the men where to dig, encouraging them, shouting, patting people on the back, and cussing as the 40 or so men busily excavated a hole completely around the plane.

Surveying the hole, the Captain ordered his men down into it, apparently intending to lift the plane out. Hofer jumped, and frantically conveyed to the Captain that airplanes have specific, limited lifting points, and lifting elsewhere can break something. After showing the Captain where he could lift, he surveyed the hole, and ordered his men to enlarge and adjust the hole to fit the lifting points.

To Hofer, the whole effort seemed a complete waste of time. Seven tons can't be lifted manually, that should be obvious.

Finally satisfied with the size, and position of the excavation, the Captain ordered his men back into the hole, and carefully placed them at lifting positions according to the lift points provided by Hofer.

Hofer confirmed that he was satisfied with their positioning and then stood back to watch them fail, thinking, once that happens they could move on to other ideas. He nodded at the Captain.

The order given, the men started singing a little work song, and then, struggled in unison to free the plane, rocking it one direction, then the other. As each chorus came up the song got louder, the rocking got higher. On about the fourth verse, everyone gave it the old Russian heave-ho and the seven-ton plane was lifted up and walked out of the hole.

Except for all the mud, it seemed no worse for the incident. They pushed the plane to a wash stand where it was quickly cleaned off. Hofer, thoroughly impressed, climbed in, went through pre-flight, and she started right up! He was ready to go!

~~~

That afternoon, Hofer and the 334th joined the rest of the 4th's scattered squadrons to regroup and reform at Pyriatyn, where wing tanks were reinstalled. Two days later, the group, led by Blakeslee, formed up for a Penetration Target Withdrawal Support mission to bombers coming back from Poland. But Hofer, and three other pilots, had to abort and return to Poltava, Russia, while Blakeslee and the 4th headed for Foggia, Italy, to the join up with the 15th Air Force.

While Hofer and his three mates fretted at Poltava, Russia, waiting for parts and personnel, and suffering the fallout from the devastating raid of June 21, Blakeslee, along with the rest of the 4th began cooperative operations with the 15th Air Force in support of bomber operations into southern Germany around Saarbrucken and Leipzig.

To the pilots of the 4th, this war seemed to be less intense than the war over Germany. Little did they know that they were only days away from one of the bloodiest, hardest sky battles they would ever fight.

On 29 June 1944, Hofer was summoned to the ready shack at Poltava. Entering, he found Lieutenants Gillette, Callahan and Lane, his fellow aborts. They shook hands and waited for their briefing, while their kites were rearmed, refueled, repaired, and made ready for transition to Foggia, Italy, the new temporary home of the 4th.

The briefing was short and uneventful. Afterwards, the four pilots climbed in to their planes, and departed for Foggia, Italy. It promised to be a simple trip, in fighter pilot parlance, a "milk run."

But of course, when Kidd Hofer was involved, things tended to get complicated pretty quick.

Just about the time they skirted the Caspian Sea, Hofer spotted some German planes. "Tally ho, bandits, 3 o'clock low, let's get 'em!"

Gillette responded quickly, "Negative, Hofer, we're on a transition flight, not a combat flight. The Huns haven't seen us, and we're due in Foggia in about four hours."

Lane piped up with his two cents, "C'mon Hoff, let's get to base. We four can't make much of a difference, and we might be kicking a hornet's nest."

Hofer brushed off the negativism and cajoled some cooperation. "They haven't seen us, which means we can attack from their six, make a single pass, knock some down, and hightail it out of there. We've got the speed, climb, and range advantage. C'mon it'll be easy."

Hofer succeeded in recruiting Callahan. He broke formation from their course of 220, and headed due west, 270, chasing the unsuspecting Germans.

Callahan followed, "Callahan here, Hofer, I'm on your right wing."

Gillette radioed, "Good luck, guys, see you in Foggia. I hope."

The four German fighters, all 190's, were headed due west with the morning sun at their back. It appeared to be a perfect bounce. But the 190's were faster than anticipated, and after about five minutes, Hofer and Callahan hadn't gained much. Then Callahan spotted some ominous dots in the distance.

"Hofer, tally-ho, bandits, one o'clock high. Looks like more Huns, and they're headed this way."

Hofer looked up and spotted a gaggle of at least two dozen dots, all of which were on a course to join up with the four original targets. This changed the math considerably. Two against four, in a surprise bounce was pretty good. Two against 25 or more was suicide. Even for Hofer.

"Roger, Callahan, nobody's seen us, let's bug out."

Hofer turned to 220, their original course, and he and Callahan set up a shallow dive to keep their silhouette out of the sky, trying to make sure they were masked by ground clutter.

After about three minutes on the new course they realized they were clear of the German planes, but now they had another problem. Flying due west at combat speeds they had used up a lot of fuel, and now had changed course to Foggia. With no idea how far they had flown, and how much they needed to correct, it was time for some dead reckoning; hoping they didn't wind up "dead" from lousy "reckoning."

Hofer radioed Lt. Callahan, "Whadayathink, Callahan? 220?"

"I dunno, Hoff, I think we covered about 30-40 miles chasing the Huns, so we need to fly more south—I think."

"Ok, how about 180?"

"Right, 180. How's your fuel?"

"I've got about four hours. You?"

"About three and half. When we broke, we were about two hours out, so I think we're safe."

They corrected farther south and started watching for landmarks or recognizable land masses. They were basically skirting the Black Sea and hoping to cut across the Adriatic to hit the Italian coast directly east of Rome. Since not all of Italy was in allied hands it was important not to hit the coast north of that latitude, because the Huns still owned that part of the isthmus.

For two hours they droned south. The water all looked the same and the coasts didn't seem to match what they'd been briefed to expect.

Hofer called, "Do you think we ought to turn west and just find Italy?

"Not yet. I think we're still too far north. If we turn west, we're flying into German controlled airspace. I vote for farther south before we turn west."

Another hour passed.

Callahan called, "Hoff, I'm really low on fuel. Where do you think we are?"

"Well, from the shape of things, I think we're way too far south, over the Italian boot, and that's Sicily just ahead. We own Sicily, I think."

Continuing to keep their heads on a swivel, Callahan made out more black dots off their left wing; from the direction he determined Germans from Turkey would approach the Italian mainland.

"Hofer, tallyho, bandits, nine o'clock level."

Hofer looked over, picked up the dots and exclaimed, "Oh, shit, Callahan, I'm sorry. If they attack, you make for land, and I'll hold them off as long as I can."

Having no fuel with which to maneuver, the two pilots watched anxiously as the four dots approached, waiting for the bright winking of gunfire on the cowl and the leading edges of the wings. They would then have split seconds to break and avoid the aiming point of the anticipated fire.

The four bandits get closer and closer, but then, instead of opening fire, they banked gently south, showing their silhouettes, complete with RAF roundels. It was a flight of four Spitfires.

The lead plane called to the Americans, "Tally-ho chaps, Malta patrol here. You Yanks out for a joy ride?"

After yelping in joy, Hofer answered. "Thank God for the RAF. Negative, Malta flight. We're trying to find Foggia, Italy."

"Well, Yank, you missed it by about 200 miles. That's Sicily up ahead."

Callahan broke in, "Malta, I'm bingo fuel, can you help?"

"Roger, Yank. Not to worry. We'll escort bingo to Sicily, and if you have 15 minutes of fuel, we're just north of Malta, where we're based."

Hofer called back, "I've got at least 30 minutes of fuel."

The Brit chuckled, "You Yanks are very lucky. Lots of Huns around here. Dodger, you and Lum escort Bingo to Sicily. Chappie, join up with me on the Yank leader, and we'll escort him to Malta. Everybody ready? Break."

As they split up, Callahan and Hofer wave a friendly goodbye.

Minutes later, Callahan ran out of fuel and crash landed on the beach at Sampieri, Sicily. He was picked up unharmed and taken by the British to Catania, but his plane was a total loss. Since Sicily was owned by the Allies, the wreck could be left for salvage.

A little while later, Hofer landed at Malta, with just a few minutes of fuel left. His good luck charms had worked again.

As he cut his engine on the flight line in Malta, he patted the picture of Virginia. "Thanks, baby."

In Foggia, Gillette and Lane had been on the ground for over two hours, and there had been no word about Hofer and Callahan. Sitting in his office in Foggia, Blakeslee was absent-mindedly wrestling with paperwork when Sgt. Minter stuck his head in the door.

"Colonel, we just got a call from Malta. Lt. Hofer landed there after being escorted by Spitfires. Lt. Callahan crash-landed in Sicily. He's Okay, but the plane's scrap."

Blakeslee sat back, fuming. "Oh, for God's sake. He got lost again?"

CHAPTER TWENTY-EIGHT

The next morning, Hofer flew to Catania to check on Callahan, who was hospitalized with minor injuries, and then went on to Foggia and reported in to Colonel Blakeslee.

Blakeslee was pre-occupied with all the details of trying to operate from a foreign and unfamiliar base, gathering scattered forces, cooperating with the 15th Air Force, and planning their return to Debden.

"Hofer, I really don't have time for you right now. I'll take care of you when we get back to Debden. In the meantime, we have a fighter sweep to Budapest day after tomorrow. Make sure you're ready to go."

Hofer saluted, and escaped, figuring that time was one his side and hoping something would happen to mitigate Blakeslee's ire before they got back home.

But the next morning, Hofer was summoned to Blakeslee's office. Blakeslee was brusque and direct, not even looking up as he issued his command. "Hofer, report to this office this afternoon at 1600 hours. Be on time. It's important. You are dismissed." Blakeslee returned to his paperwork.

Hofer slipped back out. What was a guy to do for six hours? There was nothing to do in Foggia that hadn't already been done in Debden, and Hofer was pretty tired from all the long distance flying and the adventures of getting lost on virtually every leg of this trip. Getting back home, to familiar surroundings, and well-known landmarks, would be a welcome relief to the stress and fatigue he was feeling, so he returned to his bunk and napped, before and after lunch.

At 1600 hours, he knocked on the door to Blakeslee's office.

"Enter."

Blakeslee was on the phone and motioned for him to take a seat. Into the phone he said, "Yes, this is Colonel Blakeslee. (Pause) Yes, he's here. Hold on."

Blakeslee wordlessly handed the phone to Hofer and left the room.

Puzzled, Hofer accepted the phone, and to his astonishment, heard a familiar and beloved voice.

"Ralph, Ralph, can you hear me?"

"Ginny, is that you? What are you doing? Is something wrong? How did you do this?

Over the static, and tinny sound, he listened to her explanation. "No, nothing's wrong. I just needed to hear your voice." There's a long pause. "I pleaded with General Auton. I'm in his office. He agreed to let me have a couple of minutes, so I have to be brief. I just wanted to tell you I'm praying for you. I'm ready for forever to start. I love you, Ralph. All of me loves all of you. Come back to me."

"I love you, too, baby. Today is Saturday. We've a big mission tomorrow and then we're coming home. I'll be back by Tuesday. We can celebrate the Fourth of July together. How does that sound?"

"Great, honey. See you then. Be safe, Okay?

"Right, baby, see you Tuesday, Lord willing and the creek don't rise."

They hung up. Hofer stepped to the door and looked out into the hall. Blakeslee was waiting for Hofer to appear. Grunting, he stepped back in, and motioned for Hofer, who followed and shut the door.

Blakeslee walked around his desk and stood there for a moment looking at Hofer.

"Hofer, I'm at my wit's end. I thought giving you a pass on your birthday might turn you around. You're four days late. You've been running around Southern Europe causing trouble to virtually everyone. I should kick you out of the group, and court martial you, but you're our leading ace. I don't want to stir up the press. What in the hell are you thinking? What are you doing? Why don't you help me instead of driving me bat shit crazy?"

Blakeslee was genuinely surprised at Hofer's reply, since it was not his usual offhand, half-assed excuse.

"Sir, I've seen Jesus."

Blakeslee did a double-take worthy of the Marx Brothers. "What?"

Hofer continued, "It's just an expression, sir. I mean I'm sorry. You're right."

"I'm right?"

"Yes, sir. I'm ashamed of misleading Callahan. I talked him into an unnecessary sortie. His crash was my fault. When Goody was around, I let him run interference for me, and it was fun to see what I could get away with. But the last few days, I realized I'm hurting the people I care about most. This Group."

Blakeslee was a little suspicious, "The Group?"

Hofer rambled on, obviously he had given a lot of thought to what he wanted to say. "I know you think I'm incorrigible, but I spent my 23rd birthday thinking about where I was going, what I wanted, and what I was doing. I didn't like the answers. Then I nearly killed Callahan by being stupid. I'm done being a screwball. I want to be an example, not made into one."

"I'm stunned, Kidd." Blakeslee sat down, still not fully assimilating what Hofer was saying or sure that he was actually saying it. "If anybody else said this, I'd call them a liar. Pretty words are all right, but talk is cheap. When does the *new Kidd Hofer* go into action?"

"Tomorrow, sir. I'm flying with George Stanford as wingman. I promise to take good care of him."

Weighing the words, and intensely studying the man, Blakeslee decided he was sincere. "Okay, Hofer, this is your last chance. Now get out of here. We've got a ramrod to Budapest tomorrow with the 15th Air Force. Seems like they've got a pretty nasty little war going on down here in Southern Europe. We're going to do our best to help. Dismissed."

Stepping out, Hofer was full of resolution. He was in love with a wonderful woman, she was in love with him, he had turned a corner in maturity, and it was time to prove the new Hofer was real. The future was bright with promise.

He had nothing more important to do now but get ready for Budapest. It ought to be easy. He would be back with Ginny in 72 hours, and he would have enough combat time to rotate home.

Home. They could get married. Home of course, being where the heart is, and his heart was forever with Ginny. And Duke. His heart swelled with anticipation and excitement.

The next morning, the 4th, being led by Colonel Blakeslee, joined up with the 52nd and 325th Fighter Groups. Take off was at 0750. They formed up over Lake Lesina, Italy, and headed north on a joint fighter sweep to Budapest, Hungary.

They arrived about 1045, and they were met by 75 to 80 ME 109's. But something was very different. The American fighters, about 100 strong, were accustomed to the Germans being reluctant to fight unless they heavily outnumbered the Allies. But not today. The Huns were very aggressive, pressing attacks at all altitudes and against all odds.

Hofer, as wingman to George Stanford, listened as Colonel Blakeslee made the call, "Tally-ho, Bandits, 12 o'clock high. Get 'em boys." He switched on his guns and began the climb, getting rid of his wing tanks.

Only seconds into the fight, Stanford called to Hofer, "Kidd, I'm losing airspeed. My wing tanks won't drop."

Kidd throttled back and maintained Stanford's slowing pace. The rest of the group was out-climbing them, and gradually pulled away.

"Don't worry, George, I'm with you," Hofer said.

Stanford sounded worried, "Damn, there must be 100 of them. We've flown into a hornet's nest."

Hofer stayed close, hoping Stanford's wing tanks would drop before the Kidd lost his chance for more combat and adding to his score.

But more bad news from Stanford. "Oh, shit, my engine just blew. I'm going down. Go ahead, I'll be Okay."

Hofer radioed back, "Nothing doing, buddy. I've got your six."

As Stanford began to circle down, Hofer maintained close cover, watching to see if any Huns had noticed the crippled fighter. As luck would have it—bad luck—one had.

The lone ME 109 attacked. Hofer turned into him, which caused it to break off before it could get any hits on Stanford, but Hofer wasn't able to get any hits on the ME, which seemed to fly off looking for easier targets.

Hofer watched as Stanford bellied in on the edge of a small dirt road. At least he got down in one piece.

Hofer turned and buzzed Stanford several times, waggling his wings in farewell. He had done all he could do. Stanford waved at Hofer as he went streaking by.

Then Stanford heard the unmistakable sound of another plane. He turned, and a chill ran up his spine. An ME 109, the same one or another, had begun chasing Hofer, apparently unnoticed, and was already in firing position.

Just above Stanford, the Hun opened fire, his guns deafening at the close and low flyby. Stanford was mesmerized, he had never witnessed mortal combat up close and personal, it was very different from outside the cockpit.

Soon, they flew out of sight behind a low rise and there was an explosion. Someone had gone down. Stanford could only wonder who.

Hofer was intent on rejoining the battle; he could only hope Stanford would be okay. As he started heading back to join the main group, tracers from the unseen ME 109 flecked by his cockpit. He could tell he had been hit and started evasive maneuvering to shake the German but also to lead him away so that Stanford, helpless on the ground, wouldn't become a strafing target if things didn't go Hofer's way.

Pulling hard banks and pleading with his engines for speed, he led the 109 so far away he would never rejoin the main group. He continued to take damage and evade, but then he saw his chance. He reefed up and over in a loop few planes, and fewer pilots, could manage at such a low altitude, got on the Messerschmidt's tail, and began peppering the German with .50 cal fire.

The enemy, obviously damaged, pulled away and the two fighters lost each in the landscape. Hofer, shaken but satisfied, climbed to get his bearings, but after several minutes it was no use, he had no idea where he was. His craft was hobbled, and he wasn't even sure if he could make it back to Foggia, but he headed for the coast and stayed low.

His engine was beginning to sound rough, and as he mentally calculated his return route, he realized that he would fly over the cliffs at Mostar, Yugoslavia. Mostar rang a vague bell, from one of the briefings, but he couldn't quite remember what was said.

As he droned on southwest, he knew his kite was nearly finished. He flew the nap-of-the-earth, certain that losing himself in the ground clutter, and relying on the olive drab of the plane he was flying to disguise his passage was his best chance to survive.

As he neared the Dalmatian coast he noticed a pronounced rise. Taking the gentle climb, he was startled when the ground sharply dropped away in a steep cliff, and below him was a German airfield, full of planes. Suddenly, he started taking AA fire from the ground, seemingly from every direction at once. He was trapped, without options. Climbing out would make him a better target, limping along low and slow was suicide. So, he decided to do what he did best and flicked on his gun switches.

His only hope was that the batteries in front of him would shut down as the gunners ducked his fire, and the batteries around him and behind him would miss him because of his speed.

He hit the trigger and started emptying his guns into the flak batteries and the planes in front of him. The roar of his guns filled his ears, the bright flashes of his rounds striking home among the enemy filled his gunsight. He was bleeding his own plane for everything it could give him, to find a target, hurt the Huns, and if he couldn't find any in the sky, the enemy on the ground counted too.

~~~

Back at Debden, just a little before high noon, Duke was asleep in Hofer's favorite chair. Suddenly, the big dog awakened, whined, and sat up. He seemed to be seeing or hearing something. Genuinely agitated he jumped out of chair, circling and pacing. The few men in the ready shack looked at the big dog, and at each other. *What was going on?*

After a few more seconds, Duke began to howl mournfully, a moan of heart-rending grief and distress at something the dog sensed.

As the men listened to the expression of Duke's grief, it cast a pall of gloom over the room. Three times more he circled the chair, howling, crying, and moaning sorrowfully, then he stopped and laid down in front of Hofer's chair, whining. After a few moments, he got up again and retreated into the darkness of the 334th hangar.

~~~

Two days later, on July 4th, having just arrived after her wild drive to Debden, Virginia Irwin entered the hangar. As she hurried across the dark hangar towards Salem Representative the only sound audible was the sharp clicking of her heels on hard concrete, her eyes fixed on the plane.

Reaching the left wingtip, she stopped, peering into the shadows.

"Hey!" she cried, in a choked, dry, squeak, barely able to speak.

After a few agonizing seconds, from out of the darkness came Duke, his ears perked at attention, his deep brown eyes bright with recognition, and joy at hearing the sound of someone he knew and loved.

Trotting silently and quickly to her, the great dog rose up on his hind legs, his muzzle level with Virginia's face. He placed his paws on her trembling and heaving shoulders, and began to softly, and lovingly lick her face.

At the touch of Duke's kisses, Virginia completely broke down, embracing the great animal to her she began sobbing uncontrollably, tears soaking the coat of her canine companion, and saturating her stylish brown gabardine suit.

"Oh," she cried. "Duke. Duke. Duke."

EPILOGUE

Kidd Hofer had been right. The German pilot didn't exist that could shoot him down.

After the war, his grave was eventually discovered in a civilian cemetery in Mostar, Yugoslavia. His badly mangled remains were returned to the United States in 1948, and re-interred in a mass grave at the National Cemetery at Jefferson Barracks, Missouri, just west of St. Louis, the closest national cemetery to his beloved hometown of Salem, Missouri.

The details of his fate went unknown for over half a century, with speculation he had been shot down by German Aces over Budapest, since he was last seen by George Stanford. It wasn't until German records were discovered decades later indicating he had been shot down while engaged in the extraordinarily dangerous mission of strafing an airfield at Mostar that it became clearer what might have happened.

The airfield laid on a straight line between Budapest, and Foggia, so he apparently decided, in a split-second decision, and in his usual devil-may-care attitude, to strafe the airfield while returning from the big fight over Budapest.

But, as Virginia unintentionally predicted, and as the upside-down horseshoe in his nose art had foretold, his luck had run out. So, Kidd was right about not being shot down in a dogfight.

Indications suggest that in a last-ditch effort to give meaning to his last few moments on Earth, the Kidd used his hobbled and, by now, fuel starved aircraft to take out flak emplacements at an enemy airdrome. Kidd joined the unfortunate statistic which reflected that the ratio of American pilots killed by ground fire to those shot down in aerial combat was five to one. The men who chose to do the dirty work close to the ground paid a heavy price for their courage.

The Fourth Fighter Group in World War II was the all-time top scoring fighter group in U. S. Air Force history destroying 1,016 German planes as well as producing eighty-one aces. The 56th Fighter Group came in a close second with 1,006 e/a destroyed.

Kidd's 334th Squadron (QP) was the leading squadron of the 4th, being credited with 395 victories. Kidd Hofer was the leading ace of the 334th, being credited with 31.5 e/a destroyed in only 276 hours of flying in nine months of combat—an average of one victory for every 8.7 hours of flying.

By way of comparison, the all-time leading ace, with 352 victories, Bubi Hartman, of the Luftwaffe, flew combat continually from 1936 to 1945, was shot down 17 times and averaged a victory for approximately every 10 hours of flying.

No pilot in the history of the Eagle Squadron or 4th Fighter Group exceeded Hofer's score. He is the U.S. leading Ace of the leading squadron of the leading fighter group in the European Theatre of Operations in World War II. Several other U.S. pilots had higher scores in the Pacific but given the superiority of the American fighter planes and pilots in the Pacific, over the pilots, and planes of the Japanese, it is this writer's opinion that Kidd Hofer is the greatest fighter pilot ever to fly for America. His name should be on the lips of every American who remembers and reveres the heroes of the greatest generation.

This author was privileged to attend a reunion of the 4th Fighter Group in 2001, and visit at length with Don Blakeslee, James "Goody" Goodson, and Frank Speer about their flying experiences with Kidd. Even after more than half a century, the recollections of these men obviously touched nerves of affection, and nostalgia about the bright, cheery smile and the irrepressible spirit of the Kidd from Missouri and his grand adventure in combat.

Virginia Irwin soldiered through her grief and continued to meet with and write about the men who would contribute to the resolution of the war in Europe, VE day, only ten months later.

Following the Third Army as it pushed across Europe to the front she endured the hardships of war like any soldier, she crossed the channel, and witnessed firsthand its horrors and hazarded the risks.

In April of 1945, along with a fellow reporter, Andrew Tully, she commandeered a jeep, got Sgt. Johnny Wilson to drive, and was among the first war correspondents to enter Berlin as the end of the war was approaching. Just days before the fall of the German command structure and the suicide of its leader, she sneaked into the city without official sanction, connected with some Russian troops, and covered Berlin's last moments under the yoke of the Third Reich.

In her words, "As I write, the Russians' artillery is pounding the heart of the city (Berlin) with a barrage... The Earth shakes."

She was ultimately disciplined for her actions by Eisenhower.

Due to the covert nature of her coverage, the fact that her visit was unsanctioned and possibly because of her gender, it took several days for her report to cut through the red tape and find its audience, but when it did she was hailed as a hero.

After the war, she moved to New York City, and had a distinguished career in journalism as the New York correspondent of the St. Louis Post Dispatch. She eventually moved back to St. Louis in 1960, worked for the paper until they put her to work as an advice to the lovelorn columnist, which prompted her to retire. She moved to rural Missouri to be nearer family and lived a life of quiet tranquility until her death on August 19, 1980. She had married only once, a short union right out of Business College that ended in divorce long before the events in this account. After returning from the war never married again.

Don Blakeslee retired as a Colonel from the Air Force in 1965, moved to Miami, Florida, and lived a quiet, almost reclusive life, rarely making any public appearances, or granting interviews. Only in the last few years of his life did he begin to talk publicly about the war, including his visit to the Fourth Fighter Group reunion in 2001. He gave several interviews during his last few years, and stated unequivocally that as for the Germans, he "hated the sons of bitches, and anything I could do to kill them, I'd do".

He passed away peacefully in Miami on September 3, 2008.

James Goodson was a prisoner of war until May 1945. On active duty from 1941 to 1959, he served with the RAF, the RCAF, the USAAF, and the Air Force Reserve, retiring as a Lt. Colonel.

After the war he stayed in England in the small English town of Sandwich. He had a distinguished business career and wrote several books about the Fourth, and the Air War in Europe. He moved back to Massachusetts in 1993 and died peacefully at his home in Duxbury on May 1, 2014.

Pierce McKennon stayed with the Fourth until the end of the war, had 560 combat hours of flying, got shot down twice, evaded once, was rescued in a famous "piggyback" rescue by a fellow pilot landing in a field in combat conditions, and carrying him to safety, was credited with 21.68 victories and was CO of the 335th Squadron Commander for 8 months.

He originally lost his RCAF wings through court martial for "beating up" an RAF airbase in a Spitfire, but won a second chance and was restored to the rank of Sergeant Pilot before being transferred to the Fourth as a Second Lt. in November 1942.

Staying in the Air Force after the war, he was killed in a flying accident at the controls of a T-6 Texan trainer at Lackland AFB, San Antonio, Texas on June 18, 1947.

Don Gentile was transferred back to the States for a war bond tour after his epic crash in front of the press on April 13, 1944. He wound up with 27.83 victories and retired as a Major in 1946. He returned to active duty in 1947 as a Captain and was killed in a flying accident at Wright-Patterson Field, Ohio, at the controls of a "Shooting Star" F-80 jet on January 28, 1951.

Johnny Godfrey was known in the Fourth as the most "eagle eyed" pilot around. He once called "bogies at 3 o'clock", and it was almost a minute before anyone else saw them. Credited with 30 victories, he was shot down by ground fire and became a POW on August 24, 1944.

After the war, he served briefly as a test pilot at Wright-Patterson Field, Ohio, and then went into the lace manufacturing business in Coventry, Rhode Island. He served one term as a Rhode Island State Senator in 1952.

In October 1956, he was diagnosed with ALS (Lou Gehrig's Disease), and passed away quietly at his home in South Freeport, Maine, on June 12, 1958. His book on the Fourth Fighter Group was finished shortly before his death.

Duane Beeson's "ace race" with Don Gentile ended on April 5, 1944, when he was shot down by ground fire and became a POW. His final total was 22.08 victories.

After the war he stayed in the Army, was promoted to Lt. Colonel, transferred to the regular army, but died at the age of 25 on February 13, 1947, from a brain tumor. In November 1993, the Terminal at Boise International Airport at his hometown of Boise, Idaho, was renamed Duane W. Beeson Air Terminal.

Howard "Deacon" Hively was the closest thing to a "master" that Duke had after Kidd was killed. The two can be seen pictured together several times.

Deacon finished the war as a Major with 14.5 victories, having scored three in a day twice (May 19, 1944, and July 2, 1944).

After the war he retired to West Virginia but spent most of his time visiting with his mates from the Fourth Fighter Group. While visiting a friend in Florida in 1982, he was killed in a boating accident.

When Virginia left for the continent, Duke had to be left behind. And though "good buddies" with "Deacon Hively", Duke retained his independence. He remained the base mascot but was never again the devoted daily companion or the bosom buddy of anyone the way he was with Kidd.

The fate of Duke is unknown.

THE END

Made in the USA
Lexington, KY
06 May 2019